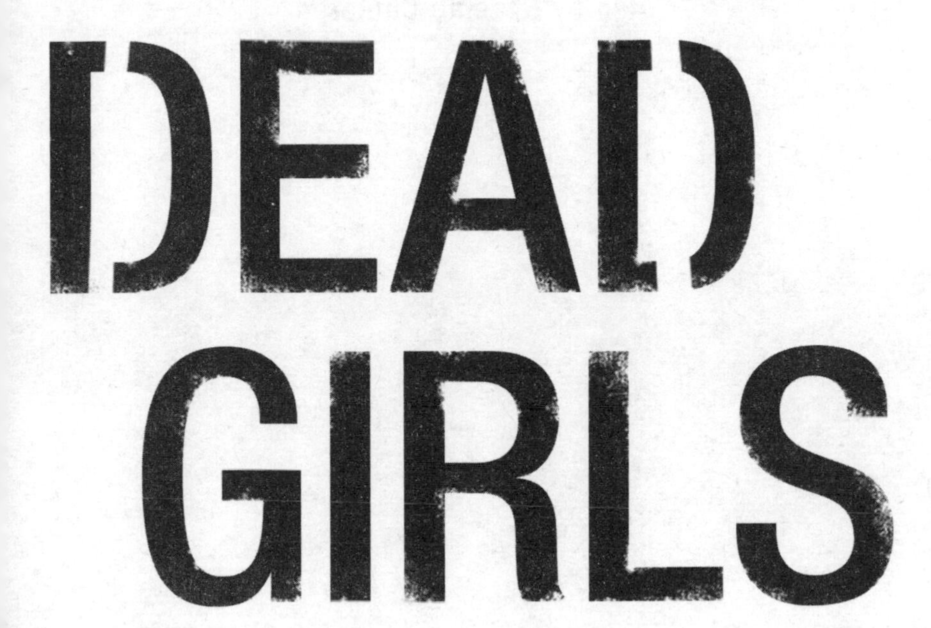
DEAD
GIRLS

Also by Graeme Cameron

Normal

GRAEME CAMERON

Recycling programs
for this product may
not exist in your area.

ISBN-13: 978-0-7783-6898-4

Dead Girls

ParkRowBooks.com
BookClubbish.com

Printed in U.S.A.

For Helen Cadbury, the best and bravest

And

For Derek

DEAD
GIRLS

"Something's wrong."

Detective Sergeant Eli Diaz, formerly of Thetford CID, latterly seconded to the Major Investigation Team at police headquarters, and until today engaged in the search for a number of young women missing from across the county, took a moment to consider the redundancy of his statement.

He was standing at the foot of a metal-framed single bed bolted into the ground through the black rubber floor. The bed was in a steel mesh cage some twenty feet across, the cage in a basement, the basement concealed beneath a garage, the garage nestled beside a stone cottage in a twenty-acre clearing in the forest.

It belonged to a man largely suspected, at least until that moment, of harboring Erica Shaw, formerly a missing young woman, latterly upgraded to the status of fugitive and last seen in front of the garage an hour ago, shooting one person dead and attempting to kill two of Eli's fellow detectives before effecting her escape.

And now one of those detectives, Sergeant Ali Green, formerly of Norwich CID, latterly of the aforementioned Major Investigation Team and currently somewhere up there alone with that man, was not answering her phone.

Diaz snatched up his own phone from the floor where he'd thrown it and made for the door of the cage, throwing an afterthought of a wave at a constable who was about to feel very alone and decidedly uneasy. "Keep trying to call her," he barked.

He took the stairs two at a time, ignoring the splintering pain in his skull from misjudging the height of the false cupboard as he burst through into the garage.

"Green," he snapped, seizing on the first pair of eyes to meet his own—one of the DCs from Norwich Road, he thought. Winters or Winterbourne or something. "Have you seen Ali Green?"

A shrug. A confused shake of the head. A voice from somewhere behind him: "She's with the owner. They were heading to the house."

"Fuck." Less a word than a grunt, choked by panic. Diaz bolted from the garage into chaos and driving rain, shouldering aside the crime scene techs struggling to erect a white tent over the body on the drive, forgetting his breathing, legs out of sync, staggering at full tilt toward the house, nothing like the machine he imagined himself on his morning run, as though the absence of Lycra and trainers and a Fitbit reduced him to a gangly, stumbling foal.

He knew before he got there that he was out of control and wasn't going to stop, that if the door didn't break when he hit it, then this was going to hurt.

It was ajar. He wasn't expecting that. It cannoned back on its hinges, barely slowing his progress, and his feet found a bundle of coats and an overturned hat stand and then he was sliding on his face across the hallway, breath punched out of his lungs, skin peeling from his nose and elbows and knees.

He didn't notice the pain. Fear had him on his feet and pushing off from the wall that had further dented his head and he whirled around from door to door, from kitchen to stairs to living room.

He stopped dead still and held his breath, strained his ears over the roar of the rain and the chatter of radios and uniforms and diesel engines.

Silence.

He gambled on the kitchen, sliding to the edge of the door frame and peering inside. Empty. Chair upturned. A slippery crimson mess on the splintered oak floor. His stomach flipped and he tasted bile in his throat. *Christ, no, what did he do to her?*

Opposite the kitchen, the living room. The door open. A sense of something inside. A sofa. A spray of dark hair. Stillness.

Diaz panted three painful breaths and, with one eye on the top of the stairs, edged to the door, darting his head just far enough inside to get a snapshot of the room.

Empty, except for her.

"Shit," he muttered. His back to the hallway. His ears wide open. "Green?"

No reply.

"Ali?" he snapped, loud enough to startle himself.

Nothing.

He blew out the adrenaline from his lungs. Checked the stairs again. Winced at the pain in his head. Squeezed his fingers into his palms and nodded some kind of vain self-encouragement. Then he said, "It's okay, I'm here," and stepped inside the room.

It was cold. Cold, and still, and quiet. The television was on, but it wasn't regular programming; it was something else, and

Diaz knew what from a single glance. It was a high-definition feed from inside the cage, where the constable he'd just left behind was still poking at his phone, presumably searching for a number he didn't have.

It was dark, too. The curtains were drawn across both of the windows, one to the front and one to the side, and the lamps were off and the fire unlit and everything was shadow—the hulking bookcases overstuffed with books and trinkets and paperwork, the corner tables with their strange disfigurines, the long, low couch and the wingback chairs and the coffee table with the two full mugs and the solitary mobile phone—everything but the TV screen and the dome of light that it cast, unflickering but dancing with particles of dust, and reflected as two tiny pinpricks of silver in Ali Green's eyes.

They were open, but vague, unfocused. Her legs had fallen open and her hands lay at her sides, fingers curled into her upturned palms, and her hair was splayed roughly over the back of the sofa where she'd slumped down in her seat. Her mouth was open and as Diaz knelt, cursing, between her knees, he could see the pool of saliva around her tongue and hear it bubbling in her throat as she took each shallow, unsteady breath.

"Ali," he whispered, suddenly painfully aware of the silence and the need to preserve it, to hear whatever small sound she might make, should it be her last. "Can you hear me?" He placed a hand on her arm and could feel a trembling that he couldn't see, a vibration almost, from deep inside her somewhere, but she didn't respond, didn't so much as blink.

He leaned in closer then, moved to put his lips to her ear, but the blood stopped him. A thin trail, trickling through the neat channel between her ear—such delicate ears, he noted, and pointed sweetly at the top, like pixie ears—and the back of her jaw, and down the side of her neck and onto the collar of her shirt, to bloom inside her jacket.

He painfully swallowed his breath and rocked back on his haunches and pulled out his phone from his pocket and said, "It's okay, it's okay, Ali, you're going to be okay," as calmly as he could, as though he believed it. And he punched in the code to unlock the phone, and keyed in the number to summon help, and he looked up into her eyes and was startled to see that she was looking right back at him in piercing focus, and her lips were moving as though she were trying to speak, and he let the phone drift away from his ear as he nodded and said, "You're okay," and placed a comforting hand on her knee.

"B—" she whispered. "B—"

"It's okay," he said, shaking his head and nodding at the same time and hearing the voice on the other end of the phone and shushing and telling her, "Help's coming. Just relax, you'll be okay. We're going to find him."

And he raised the phone back to his ear, and the voice on the phone said, "Sarge?" and Ali Green said, "Beh—" and a single tear rolled down her cheek, and his breath caught in his throat, and in the second before she closed her eyes, one of the tiny spots of silver turned black.

And all he could think of to say was, "He's behind me, isn't he."

GRAEME CAMERON

DEAD GIRLS

EPISODE 1

CHAPTER 1

Two Months Later

It's funny, isn't it, how your mind can always find a way to surprise you? Take mine, for example. After thirty-four years together, I like to think I know it pretty well. And having spent the whole of my childhood being forcibly drummed into myself, and most of my adult life breaking my back to conform to it, God knows I should. And yet, here I was with an unexpected dilemma.

I could hear my phone ringing over the splashing and thumping coming from the bathroom, and I knew that at six in the morning the call was likely important enough that I should answer it. But I didn't know where I'd left it, and that was a problem.

Normally, like anyone else, I'd crawl out of bed, take a moment to steady myself and for my head to stop spinning, and I'd assume I'd left it in my bag and that my bag was in the lounge, and I'd go find it. And if it wasn't there and had stopped ringing, I'd call it from the house phone and sooner or later I'd track it down and return the call and receive some bad news and then drink a gallon of coffee in the vain hope that it might make me somewhat safe to drive, and I'd get dressed in a hurry and be on my way.

But I couldn't do that, not this morning. For one thing, unlike most mornings, I was completely naked under the duvet, and the one eye I could open was so blurry and achy that I couldn't see any of my clothes. Which, given the mortifying likelihood of bumping into whoever was about to jump out of the shower, meant wrapping myself in a king-size quilt and stumbling around trying to figure out the layout of this house, which, I dimly realized, wasn't mine.

And now the ringing had stopped, and the light shafting through the thin blind was a dagger to my skull, and then the shower was abruptly silent and my heart began to thump against my ribs and all I could think to do was pull the covers over my head and pretend I didn't exist.

I don't know how long I waited. I heard footsteps on the landing, the creaking of stairs, assorted kitchen clangs and clunks and tinkles. My phone again. Damn it. And then the footsteps coming back up the stairs, and the ringing getting louder, and, oh God, it was coming into the room.

"Hmm."

I froze.

"Well I'm sure she was in here a few minutes ago." A woman's voice, faintly familiar. "Where on *earth* could she be?"

Dazed now, utterly confused. The phone still ringing. A clunk above my head—a mug on the table? A weight beside me, the edge of the bed sagging beneath it, pulling me toward it.

"Are you alive under there?"

I took three breaths, and nodded.

"Are you nodding?"

I shook my head, and heard a giggle.

"There's coffee here. And your phone's ringing."

"I know," I croaked. "Thank you."

"I'll just leave it here for you. Are you hungry?"

I wasn't sure. Horror kind of feels like hunger, right? "Probably."

"Bathroom's free," she said, and patted my hip through the duvet. "I'll let you answer that." Then she stood up and was gone.

I unscrewed my eyes and eased the duvet aside. Blinked the blinding light out of them. There was a plain green mug steaming on the bedside table, face cream and biscuits and tissues and a library book shoved aside to make room. And on the floor beside the bed, my bag, jangling incessantly.

I reached down, hissing away a twinge in my back, and dug out my phone. I begged it to stop ringing, but someone was unshakably determined to speak to me. Kevin, as it turned out. I answered. "Kevin." I sighed.

"Ali," said Kevin, "it's Kevin." Which I knew. "Where are you?"

I have no fucking idea. "What do you mean, where am I? I'm in bed. It's fuck-off o'clock in the morning. What do you want?"

"It's 6:18," he said, "the sun's been up for over an hour and you need to be here twenty minutes ago."

From the gentle mooing in the background, I deduced that he was most likely overdramatizing. "I can hear cows." I yawned, and peeked inside the little drawer of the bedside table. It was full of hair ties and old sweets, pastel-colored biros and Blu Tack and various kinds of charger.

"I'm standing in a field."

"Sounds thrilling," I said, "but you've got the wrong Monday. I'm not back until next week." I picked up the library book; *The Good Girl*, it was called. I cringed.

"Not anymore."

"I think you'll find I am." I laughed. Laughing made my forehead throb. My mouth tasted like a badger's arse. "I only saw Occy Health on Friday. I'm still off sick, I'm in bed, I've got another headache, which *you've* just given me, I've got a million and one things to do today, none of which involve farm animals, I'm desperate for a wee and unless the next thing you say to me is 'I'm sorry, Ali, pret—' no, '*Sarge.* I'm sorry, *Sarge*, pretend I never rang, take care of yourself, have a good weekend,' I swear to God I'm going to hunt you down and beat you savagely about the face and neck. In a week." She was using her library card as a bookmark. It said, *Edith Macfarlane* on it. Christ on a bike, I *knew* her.

"I *am* sorry," he sniggered as my heart sank further into my bottom. "DCI says otherwise. I thought you'd had a call already, but I guess I'm not surprised. Whatever, this one's kind of got your name on it." He waited for what seemed like days for me to ask him what he meant, but it was quite obviously nothing I wanted to hear, so I didn't. Also, I was holding my breath in an effort not to wet the bed. Finally, he said, "We've found John Fairey."

And I exhaled.

The bathroom was still warm, the window and the mirror still steamed over from Edith's tenure. The dregs of her bathwater lingered in the bottom of the tub, sending my feet aslither as I cranked open the shower. I braced myself against the tile, gritted my teeth through the cycle of polar-cold and scar-hot until the water settled on a comfortable shade of warm. I scrubbed myself with Edith's soap until the knot of panic began to unravel. Lathered with Edith's shampoo. I rinsed the strands of Edith's hair from my fingers as they attracted to me from Edith's conditioner bottle. I would have used Edith's facial scrub, but there was only a small squeeze left in the tube. Instead, barely five minutes after I got in, I shut off the water and, in spite of it still being damp, dried myself with Edith's towel.

Thankfully, I did have my own clothes, although they were crumpled and smelled of pub and my knickers were a bit the worse for wear. Hearing Edith still downstairs, I eased open the top drawer of her dresser, avoiding my own eye contact in the mirror as I rooted around in the tangle of loosely balled briefs at the back, behind all the neatly folded silky arrangements. I tugged a pair free and shook them out. *Hello Kitty.* Fine, whatever.

Everything else would have to do. My bra was on its third outing, the cropped black denims maybe their sixth. I had a bright yellow off-the-shoulder top that was okay under the arms but reeked of booze and perfume everywhere else, although deodorant and fresh air would sort that probably. And I had at least had the accidental foresight to wear shoes I could run in, inclined as I was to duck my head and sprint straight out the door.

But to where?

I gingerly opened the blind, shielding my eyes with my spare hand and squinting through my fingers at the view. There wasn't much of one—just a row of boxy houses on the other side of the street, driveways lined with German and Swedish cars in various shades of black and gray, including the one directly below the window. Mine is bright red, so it was immediately apparent that it wasn't there. God, where the hell was it? And, more to the point, where the hell was I?

Edith was easier to locate. She was at the breakfast table, and she greeted me with a "Hey" and a smile. Nothing between the lines—just your usual good-morning pleasantry.

She'd clearly been listening out for me; she'd poured me a fresh cup of coffee and a bowl of Rice Krispies and the latter were still popping and cracking, or whatever it is they do. "Made you breakfast."

I sat across from her, silently giving thanks for my complexion; the Middle-Eastern half of me is all on the outside, so I don't burn in the sun and, more importantly, I blush very, very quietly. "Morning," I said, my deliberate effort to keep a steady voice naturally achieving the opposite. "Thanks."

"Sleep well?"

My insides recoiled in horror. Was it a trick question? Could she tell that I had no recollection of the night before? "Like a baby," I said. "You?"

Another neutral smile. "As well as can be expected. Did you find your towel?"

Oh. "Yes," I lied, giving it away by shaking my head at the same time. "Thank you."

I watched her read the *Independent* as I crunched a mouthful of cereal, wishing there was a radio or television to muffle the sound of my munching. Her own efforts seemed so much more refined than mine.

She'd finished dressing—a black tailored five-button jacket with matching skirt to just below the knee. Her legs stretched beneath the table, her ankles—slender, lightly tanned—crossed comfortably beside my own. Chestnut hair lowlighted in black, thrown up into a loose ponytail. Sunlight, splayed and rainbowed by the flowers and antique bottles on the windowsill, playing on the triangles of her neck, settling in the hollow of her collarbone where it peeked from behind her shirt. The swell of her breas—

"You okay?" *See anything you like?*

I looked up, startled. Felt my face flush. "Hmm?"

She folded the paper and tossed it aside, slid her coffee close to her and spooned in sugar from the bowl in the center of the table. "You don't look very well," she said, circling the spoon handle at me as though casting a spell. "You're not going to throw that back up, are you?"

I realized I had a mouthful of lukewarm milk and soggy Rice Krispies, which, somewhere along my train of baffling distraction, I'd somehow forgotten to swallow. I did so now. "I'm fine," I said flatly.

She gave a cynical snort. "Oh, really?" Stirred her coffee. "I've seen you looking fine, and it didn't look like that." Raised it to her lips, blew primly across the surface before taking a sip. "You're not upset with me, are you?"

I dropped my spoon into the half-empty cereal bowl and pushed it away, my appetite lost. "Of course not." Mortified, yes. Confused, bemused and deeply, shamefully embarrassed, but not *upset*.

"Good, because...you know..."

Doesn't mean I want to talk about it. "I know."

"I mean, it's not like..."

"No, I know."

"I mean, I had a great time last night, but—"

I choked on my coffee. "But now I have to go to work." I smiled.

She smiled back, and thought for a moment and then looked at the table and nodded firmly and said, "Yeah. Me, too."

"Only I don't know where my car is."

"Ah," she chuckled. "You left it at the pub, remember?"

No.

"I'll drop you off," she said. "Ready in five?"

I nodded. I didn't know what else to say, really, so I just blurted out, "I borrowed some knickers. Hope you don't mind."

She gave a snort and a sideways look. "No, that's fine." She laughed. "Just...have a good day, okay? Be careful, and don't work too hard."

"Oh, I don't intend to." I laughed. Riding out on a shudder of relief at the rapid change of subject, it was a laugh I would have found disproportionate and vaguely chilling were it directed at me. Fortunately, Edith either didn't notice or at least had the good grace not to raise an eyebrow. "I'm—" trying to think of something to say "—planning on shouting at my boss for dragging me out, and being home in time for *Cash in the Attic.*"

"Sounds like a plan," she agreed, and then giggled to herself. "Hey, you know what'd be even better?"

"What?"

"Tango & Cash in the Attic."

Ha ha.

I knew I'd be fixed by lunchtime. The cold light of day would see my head straight and my priorities in order in no time. Or at least that was what I thought.

As it turned out, the light of day was already as hot as the belly of hell when I stepped from my car onto flame-scorched sand, hung my badge from its lanyard around my neck and entered a world of violence and horror for the likes of which even the most depraved of my many nightmares had left me woefully underprepared.

It was 6:59 a.m. My name is Alisha Green, and this, to the best of my understanding, is the truth about Erica Shaw.

CHAPTER 2

A squirrel darted a stuttering dash along the bough above my head, twitching its velvety gray nose at the edges of the shadows among the leaves and sniffing suspiciously at the encroaching sunlight. In the dense cover high above, a lone wood pigeon flexed its wings and fluttered the sleep from its rumpled feathers. He looked like he'd had a rough night.

I looked worse, if my reflection in the car window was anything to go by. I'd had them both open all the way here, and my undried hair had frizzed up into a bouffant bird's nest. I slipped the hairband from my wrist and bundled the mess into a rough, damp knot at the base of my neck. If it didn't improve me, it might at least give the pigeon second thoughts about moving in.

I propped my foot on the sun-bleached picnic trestle beside the car and bent to tighten my shoelace. A pair of wasps buzzed hungrily around the rubbish bin beside me, keeping a respectful distance from one another as they took turns to dive inside for a bite. A third investigated the sticky rim of a Coke can, idly dropped in the grass not three feet away, the silvered peaks of its crushed carcass shimmering thousands of tiny jewels of light across the fixed-penalty warning notice plastered to the receptacle. No Littering: Maximum Fine £2,500. The futility of mandatory environmental correctness, summed up in a shiny red aluminum nutshell. I picked up the can and disposed of it properly. The wasp didn't flinch.

This, right here, is the kind of peace I crave: the early-morning sun prickling my upturned face; the idle lapping of the river against the pebbles on the bank; the soft *quirrup* of ducklings perpetually distracted from the arduous task of keeping up with mum; the merest whisper of distant traffic, just *there* enough to temper the isolation without intruding on the blissful, cossetting quiet of—

"Oi! Pocahontas! Over here!"

Oh. Right. Kevin.

I took in a lingering lungful of cow shit and pollen.

Geoff Green—no relation—greeted me with an indifferent nod as I slipped between my Alfa and the adjacent patrol car. I'd seen the burly constable around often enough to know his name, but his snakelike eyes and disdainful demeanor had always deterred me from wanting to know much more about him. Whether he perpetually wished he were somewhere else, or simply didn't like the look of me any more than I did him, I couldn't entirely tell. Nor did I particularly care.

Geoff had been left in charge of guarding the inner perimeter. It was clearly a hurried affair, the blue-and-white warning tape sagging between posts speared skew-wiff and at random intervals into the sandy earth as it bisected the picnic site. It also seemed a somewhat extraneous measure, given that the access road was barricaded by patrol cars at its inception half a mile back, the car park entrance was itself taped and guarded and a fourth cordon encircled what seemed to be the object of the collective attention—a burned-out car slumped at the far side of the clearing.

If I'd known him better, I might have accused Geoff of erecting the barrier himself, just to look as though he had something important to do. However, half a dozen years having passed between us without the need for small talk, and with neither of us any more inclined than the other to fix what wasn't broken, I kept my suspicions to myself and simply returned Geoff's sulky nod as I ducked under the tape, which he lifted just high enough to garrote me had I not been half expecting it.

At the other end of the mood swing, and entirely at odds with his tone on the phone, Kevin McManus was a veritable grin on a stick. He picked through a maze of yellow plastic markers and staked-off squares of sand, sterile suit rustling, teeth flashing, arms wide like he thought he was going to get a hug. "You know, for a minute I thought you might blow me out," he crowed, his voice sounding hollow and windswept against the squawk and chatter of radios and crime scene techs and the rattle and hum of a diesel generator.

"Save it," I warned him. "You're at the top of my shit list today."

"Well, aren't we the little ray of sunshine?" In defiance of the mechanics of the human face, and presumably working on the assumption that I was joking, he broadened his smile to within a whisker of obscuring his own vision. "Listen, don't go shooting the messenger, okay? You know I wouldn't kick you out of bed without—"

I choked on my own spit.

"I mean… You know, *drag* you out of—"

"Where is he?"

"Who?"

Oh, Jesus Christ, Kevin. "Anyone you like. Take your time, I've got all day."

"John," he remembered, with none of the exaggerated embarrassment you or I might affect when caught with our wits down. Instead, he ran a hand through his dark, wiry mop and scratched at the short patch over his crown, a remnant of a recent pistol-whipping. "He's, um…in the car," he said. "I think."

"You think?"

"Well, it's…" He glanced over his shoulder at the remains of the car and just sort of sighed.

"What about DC Keith? Any sign?" John Fairey hadn't been alone when he'd seemingly vanished into thin air; there was no trace of the freshly minted detective he'd snagged for a dogsbody, either.

Kevin gave me a shrug and a sympathetic smile. "I'll get you a suit," he said.

"Where's Mal?"

"The what?" Kevin dropped a fetching pair of white rubber boots at my feet and handed me the paper jumpsuit he'd retrieved from the back of the nearby CSI van. He'd tried to flirt with Sandra, the duty pathologist, but she was on the phone and had batted him away with an irritable glare. His smile had faded rapidly.

"Mal," I repeated. "Mal Lowry. He should be here."

Kevin narrowed his eyes and nodded with a look that said *No shit, Sherlock*. "I know," he said. "We've all got *personal problems*, right?"

I didn't know what he meant by that; I just knew it didn't explain where my DCI was. I flattened the suit out on the ground and slipped my feet into the leg holes. "You know what else I can't see?" I pulled it up to my waist and realized I had it back to front.

"What?"

"Any bodies in that car. Where are they?" Did I turn the suit once or twice? It now appeared to be upside down.

"I was getting to that." Kevin eyed the jumpsuit curiously

as I attempted vainly to pass it behind my back without reversing it. "Do you want a hand?"

"Could you?" I don't know how many of these godforsaken things I've had to clamber into over the course of my career, but it's one of those tasks—most of which, come to think of it, seem to involve items of apparel—for which practice will never make perfect. I will never be able to tie an apron behind my back, and I will never be able to get into a front-fastening one-piece paper jumpsuit without the assistance of a third party. Fact of life.

"Don't worry about Lowry," he said, which seemed strange, because I wasn't. "Just enjoy the peace and quiet while it lasts." He turned me around by the shoulders, scrunched the suit up in his hands and squatted behind me, tapping each of my legs in turn as he wanted them lifted and lowered. "'Scuse fingers."

"Keep them below the knee," I laughed. "Geoff's watching."

The constable looked casually away as Kevin yanked the suit up over my hips and said, "I think he's got the hots for you, you know."

I stifled a chuckle. "Well, he all but pulls my hair every time he sees me," I said.

"Boys are always mean to girls they like," he agreed, standing to guide my arms into the appropriate holes and slide the shoulders of the suit up onto my own. "You can manage the zip on your own, right?"

I gave him a withering look and said, "Ha bloody ha. Who called us?" as I fumbled hopelessly with the zip and Kevin pretended not to notice the trembling in my fingers.

"The usual," he said, handing me a full-face particulate mask. "Dog walker. Said his dog wouldn't stop barking at it, so he took a peek. Watches a lot of true-crime shows."

"Him or the dog?"

"Not sure."

"What time?"

"Five thirty-five."

"Where is he?"

"I sent him home. He'll come in this afternoon if we need him to."

"You talked to him yourself?"

"Yep."

"How did he seem?"

"Genuine."

I nodded and snapped the mask over my head and Kevin did the same. "Ogay," I said, waving to Sandra and getting a thumbs-up in return. "Ned dayg a nook."

There was no denying it was my old partner's Mondeo. I'd spent a lot of hours staring pointedly out of the window of that car, or gripping the sides of my seat, or instinctively thumping my right foot onto an imaginary brake pedal. I was in it when he creased the wheel arch against a bollard, and I was standing right where I was now when he kicked the dent into the front wing in anger at some humiliation or other. My seat was gone, just a buckled metal frame remaining. The worn carpet in the footwell was gone, too—in fact, everything was gone; it was just a ravaged shell. But those dents were as good as a fingerprint.

It wasn't blue anymore. It was orange and black and brown, rust and soot and death. It sat sadly on its sills in the sand, one back door hanging limp on twisted hinges. The roof sagged from front to back, the tailgate bent on its frame so that the lid reared up, arched like a mouth shrieking in horror. And in that mouth was what I could only assume were the remains of my two former colleagues.

Bone is bone. It doesn't really look like anything else. I suppose I could have convinced myself it was coral, or pebbles at a push, but I didn't bother to try. It was a gray rubble of bone, fragmented, cemented with splatters of rain-pasted ash. To my untrained eye, it could have been anyone, or anything. Sure, I know all the words; I read the same books you read. *Skull sutures. Pubic symphysis. Phalanges*, which just reminds me of Phoebe from *Friends*. I could even tell you what they mean, and relate the most reliable method of estimating the height of a person from their skeleton, or of determining the gender and racial profile of a skull. But I'm no more than an armchair expert; my opinion isn't worth the calories I'd expend merely forming it, and the jigsaw puzzle in front of me now was far beyond my understanding of how a person could even begin to make sense of it. And so, knowing in my gut that this was the final resting place of Detective Inspector John Fairey and Detective Constable Julian Keith, I resisted the urge to plunge my hand into the ashes, pull out a shard of calcined something-or-other and shout, "Aha," and I walked away from the car.

"Okay, first screamingly obvious things first," I said, once I'd flicked the mask off my face and could breathe again. I pointed at the square of blackened grass beneath my feet—one of a dozen I could see, evidence of a summer of careless barbecuing. "There are burn marks just about everywhere except under the car. Who's out looking for the crime scene?"

Kevin looked from me to the car and back again, and scratched the back of his head. "Not organized that yet," he said, which I had to concede was an accurate if inexhaustive statement. "Been a little bit busy on my own here. I haven't even had a cup of tea yet."

Signed off till Monday. *Not* going to feel guilty for having breakfast. "You've done a good job," I said, although I knew Sandra had probably beaten him here and taken control of the scene herself. "We haven't got the whole car here. The bumpers, the tires, all of the plastic and rubber bits that have melted off. They're not here. We're missing a debris field. Plus there are no drag marks, but there's a trail of mud and oil at least all the way back to the top of the road. See?" I indicated a set of thick, wide-treaded tire tracks printed in clumps of earth and clay, leading to and from the Mondeo and punctuated by a circular swirl on the tarmac at the entrance to the picnic site. "Someone carried it here on a tractor, right? Front loader, teleporter, whatever you want to call it."

Kevin nodded. "Which was thoughtful of them."

"Ha. So who, and why now? It's been two months."

He thought about it for a moment. Scratched his head. "Is there anything significant about the date?"

"Not that I can think of."

I knew where he was going to go before he went there. "Well, if we were in a film, I'd say, 'The perp is sending us a message,' but...we're not, are we?"

"Well, you might be," I conceded, "but whoever dumped this here isn't. We've got a convenient trail of bread crumbs, but it's just muddy tire marks and you can't really engineer those. If they lead all the way to the burn site, it's an accident. Also, never say 'perp' again. You sound like an idiot."

"Agreed."

"It's a pretty thin theory, isn't it?"

"Kind of."

"So what am I going to find when I leave you here to chase around after Sandra and go follow that trail by myself?"

"Oh, come on!"

CHAPTER 3

No, *you* come on. I was tired, hungover, thirsty, more than a little confused, and I wasn't even supposed to be here today or indeed any day this week, and I thought a nice gentle drive in the countryside would do me good. Frankly, I thought it was probably a waste of time; you can only load your tires with so much muck, so the trail was bound to go cold in short order, leaving me free to pop into the nearby village and buy some sugary drinks for myself and maybe even Kevin, if I was feeling more generous by then.

He didn't put up too much of a fight, either. He was obviously enjoying his moment, peacocking around the place as the only—and therefore most senior—detective on the scene. He probably had another hour to enjoy it, so I was happy to let him. And Geoff was clearly happy to let me go, too, because he lifted the tape clean over my head this time.

The trail was laughably easy to follow: clumps of earth and sand and clay, and weeds snatched out from the verge by a vehicle clearly a few inches wider than the single-track road. And leaky, too. Whether it was oil or hydraulic fluid, it shone beautifully in the sunlight, a spot the size of my fist every ten yards or so.

I was in no hurry. I didn't even touch the throttle, just stuck it in second and let the clutch out and allowed the car to roll along at its own leisure. It was that kind of morning. The roadblock slid lazily aside to let me out, and we all exchanged smiles and waves as I idled by. Then I was free, turning right onto the little B-road that led to the village, and immediately I knew my hopes for a jolly to the shops were dashed, because there were muddy tracks and spots of oil on the other side of the road, too, and I only had to follow them for a couple of miles before they arced left onto a wide concrete track and escaped under a three-bar metal gate.

I stopped the car, and sighed, and thought about what I might do next. I knew exactly what I *should* do, but my mouth was dry and tasted evil, and my temples were threatening to throb, and I had no phone signal, anyway, and the village was only a mile farther down the road, so I thought *Fuck it*, and did that instead.

There was, thank God, a newsagent's shop in the village, and it was open, if not altogether welcoming. A portly, ruddy-cheeked old chap in a tweed jacket eyed me from behind the counter in some kind of appraisal or other, his eyes boring into the back of my head as I grabbed three cans of coldish Coke from a chiller that was probably older than me. I forced myself not to meet his eye, instead scanning dusty shelves packed with canned goods and decade-old toys, looking for something I might want to eat at this time of the morning and happily finding a box of Nurofen that was, surprisingly, in date. That would do, although I grabbed a handful of Twixes and a mint Magnum for good measure and finally gave the guy a smile as I dumped the lot on the counter. "Morning," I said.

He gave me a tight nod and a casual, "How are you today, Officer?" as he rang up the till.

My neck prickled and my breath caught in my throat and I instinctively flashed a look over my shoulder at the empty shop. Was his face familiar? Should it be? Was *mine*? "I'm sorry?"

He paused for a beat, then hit a button on the till with a sound like crashing thunder. The total flickered green on the little pop-up display. "How are you?" he repeated.

I held his stare for a moment, perhaps a moment too long. His left eyelid began to twitch. "I'm good," I said. "Thank you. Sorry, have we met?"

He narrowed his eyes, flickered an inscrutable thought and said, "I don't think so, miss, no. That's six eighty-five."

What does "six eighty-five" mean? Mind racing, panic setting in. This was not expected. "Six eight—" I noticed the till then: £6.85, all squared off and glowing green. Right. "Right." I nodded, shaking the blankness out of my head and fumbling for my purse. Only then did I realize that I was still wearing the lanyard around my neck, which of course made me bark a startled laugh that must have made me look even more special than I already did. *"Right,"* I reiterated, holding the badge up meekly as I handed the guy a tenner. "God, I thought you'd recognized me from somewhere. Sorry, I'm not awake yet." I smiled in an effort to pretend I wasn't suddenly entirely on edge.

He relaxed visibly, even if he didn't return my grin. "Best part of the day," he said, handing me my change.

I took the opening. "It is peaceful," I said. "I'll give you that. I don't suppose you have the need to call my lot out too often, do you?"

He regarded me curiously, a blue twinkle flashing across his bloodshot eyes. I'm sure he knew as well as I did that I already knew the answer to that. He humored me, though. "Not really," he agreed. "We don't have a lot of differences we can't take care of between us. They say strange things pass through here at night, but the streetlights go out at eleven so I don't see none of 'em."

I hid the shiver that ran down my spine, and asked him, "What about in the daytime?"

He just shrugged. He wasn't going to tell me anything, but he might at least be able to save me some time, so I pressed on. "Maybe you can help me," I said, undeterred by his blank expression. "About a mile back that way, on the right-hand side, there's a concrete track with a gate across it. Can you tell me where that goes?"

He gave it a moment's thought. Probably figured it was nothing I couldn't look up on a map, anyway. "The old airfield," he said.

"It's not an airfield anymore?"

"Not since the war. Bomber base."

"So what is it now?"

"Wheat and barley now."

"Can you tell me who owns it?"

"That'll be Giles."

I waited for him to crack a smile, but his poker face was strong. "And Giles is a farmer?"

"That's right."

"Farmer Giles."

He nodded slowly. "I never heard it like that before," he said. "That's funny," though he still didn't smile.

I quit while I was ahead.

Farmer Giles timed his arrival perfectly. I knew full well that the creepy shopkeeper would phone him the second I was out the door, so I saved myself some hard work and just sat in the entrance to the old airfield until he turned up, which he did, in a brand-new Range Rover, just as I was nibbling the last of the chocolate from my ice cream stick.

"Giles, is it?" I said, stepping from the car as he did the same. "Thanks for getting here so quickly. I'm Detective Sergeant Green. I was wondering if you might be able to help me out with something."

"Giles Wynne-Parker." He extended his hand to shake mine. "What can I do for you?" Cut-glass accent. Neatly cropped hair, graying at the edges. Strong, dimpled chin.

I flicked the Magnum stick away to shake his hand. He watched it fly with a raised eyebrow. "Oops," I said. "There's probably a law against that." I paused, just long enough for his face to register that his jig was up. "Your tractor could do with a service," I suggested, indicating the trail of oil on the ground.

Giles sighed and nodded at his strangely unmuddied Buckler boots. "I know," he conceded with a resigned smile. "It's hydraulic fluid. I've got a leaking piston."

"I'd get that seen to before you leave any more anonymous donations," I said, ducking my head to peer up into his eyes. "But thanks for giving us our car back—we've been wondering where it went."

He snapped his head up at that, and the eyes that met mine now were a little wider than they had been a moment ago. "Your car?"

"Oh," I laughed, "yeah, it's a police car. That's not really the worst of it, though."

"Oh, bloody hell," he said. "How much trouble am I in?"

I chewed over that for a moment, let a few scary thoughts roll through his head, just for the sake of it. Finally, I said, "Let's not worry about that. I mean, yes, you've been a bit of a plank, honestly, and you did dump it right next to the sign *telling* you not to dump anything, which, you know, we could easily take as you sticking two fingers up at us, and on a personal level, I'm not actually supposed to be at work today, so I kind of wish you'd waited until Monday, but right now, what I really need more than anything is for you to take me to wherever you moved it from, because there are a few bits still missing, and it's also potentially a murder scene."

The color drained from his face faster than piss from a flushed toilet. "Murder?"

"Why did it take you two months, Giles?"

"Two months?"

"That's how long we've been looking."

"I..." He shook his head, eyes wide, nervous. "We were away. Florida. We've only been back a fortnight, and I don't really use this gate. The main one's at the other end of the runway. There's nothing over here. I only came because some of the chickens got out. I..."

"Why didn't you call us?"

"Wh—" He puffed out a sigh and shook his head. "Honestly?"

I waited for him to tell me that we wouldn't have bothered coming, that the council wouldn't have been interested in removing a burned-out car from a private field. And he'd have had a fair point, but he didn't go there; he just shrugged and said, "I don't know."

"Okay," I said. "Relax. Don't worry about it. Just how about you show me the spot, okay?"

He took a moment to breathe, and then nodded and said, "Sure. Okay." Then he took a heavy bunch of keys from his pocket and unhooked the gate and opened it a crack and said, "You won't need your car. It's right over here."

It was barely inside the gate, on a barren patch of clay off to the right of the track, shielded from the road by a grassy bank and from the rest of the farm by a clump of trees and overgrown bramble bushes. A twenty-foot black square, dotted with lumps of twisted, melted *stuff,* identifiable only by guesswork and its relative placement—a bumper here, a tire there.

The ground was hard, but two months ago it hadn't been; there were wheel tracks leading to the burn site, until this morning cast into the earth but now crumbled and flattened by Giles's tractor, its hefty tires overlaying them with a patchwork of deep chevrons. I tutted at him quietly, although it made no real difference; this was quite evidently the crime scene, however much he'd trampled on it.

And more than that, Giles had approached and retreated from the spot in a straight line, and hadn't strayed around the edges of the square, and this, I realized as I surveyed the scene, might be very good news indeed. I turned to him as he stood awkwardly beside the Range Rover, picking at the skin around his thumbnail, and pointed at his car and asked him, "Giles, did you drive that over here at any point?"

He took a few steps toward me and shook his head. "No, I don't think so. Why?"

I indicated the patch of ground between the scorch marks and the road. "You didn't pull up alongside the car to have a look?"

"No, definitely not."

I nodded thanks, and looked back to where a second set of churned-up tracks splintered off from the rest and curved around the burn site at the foot of the roadside bank, coming to an abrupt end a few yards beyond where the car had sat. As they straightened, they became clearer, and where they ended they were very clear indeed.

They were perfectly preserved, the tread pattern pressed into soft clay and then baked in the persistent sun, this heatwave of which the Great British Public had grown weary within a matter of days, but for which I now offered up a silent prayer of thanks.

"So you're telling me," I called, "that there's no reason you know of for anything to have been parked here?" He shook his head. I nodded mine, and took out my phone. Still no signal. I stood, gritted my teeth through a twinge in my hip and joined him beside his car. "Next question," I said. "Have you got a phone on you that works? I need to make a call."

I surveyed the scene as he mumbled and fumbled in his jacket. I didn't know the circumstances. I didn't know whether John and Julian had died here, and if so, whether they'd come of their own free will. But common sense told me this would be a strange place to arrange a meeting, especially with the kind of man who'd shared their final farewell.

Because yes, as much as I didn't know the order of events, I sure as hell knew who was responsible.

Sort of.

CHAPTER 4

I can't remember his name, or what he looks like. However many times they tell me, or show me his picture, it's always the same: within minutes, I've forgotten.

I've all but given up trying. His picture is only an e-fit, anyway, and no one really knows his name; he went by so many that in the end they just picked one and stuck with it, even though they knew he'd stolen it from a baby's grave. I tend to just call him That Man. That man who hurt me. That man who took away my memories, my hopes, my future. That man who all but killed me with his bare hands.

It's not just the forgetting. There's the falling down, too. Some days I can't walk very well, because the nerves to my right leg are fused, or snagged, or...something. I've got it all written down. In any case, I might be in the street, or in the supermarket—never anywhere soft like the garden or a bouncy castle—and oh! There it goes, folding under me like the bolt just fell out. It happened in the car once, and I couldn't get to the brake and had to swerve into a hedge to avoid a cyclist. I didn't tell anyone in case they stopped me from driving, but I'm scared sometimes.

Often, I feel like I'm not entirely inside myself, like I've fallen out of my body and haven't quite slotted back in right. It's like there's a satellite delay between my body and my senses, like having a fever but, most days, without the cold sweats and the nausea. It's surreal and a bit frightening, and when it happens it's often accompanied by a little shock, like when something makes you jump. I used to pay good money to feel like that of an evening. I miss having the choice.

But it's not every day. Some days I can walk and grip and find things funny. And there are a lot of things I can remember, too. Most days I can think of my own name, which comes up more often than you'd guess if you've never had to write it on your hand in biro.

I can remember liking broccoli, which makes me gag on sight now.

I can remember my wedding day, looking at my ridiculous cake of a dress in the mirror and wondering how I'd ever let him talk me into it. I can remember holding my decree absolute in my hands and trembling under the sudden weight of my freedom.

I can remember sunshine and walks in the park, watching other people's children hurtle down the slide and boing around on those spring-mounted wooden horses, and wishing not to be among the throng of parents standing by with pride or impatience or overprotective anxiety or idle indifference, but to dare to come back when they'd all gone home and play on the rides myself.

I can remember our family Keycamp holiday in France, a hundred degrees, me at eight chaining Calippos in my mini-bikini, my sister, Reena, at thirteen head-to-toe in black and wincing through cups of bitter coffee, trying to impress the pool boy with the 750 Suzuki. I can remember him offering her a ride to the beach on the pillion seat, and Dad's face turning from brown to purple at the very idea. I can remember the sirens blaring past the caravan site when he roared off on it alone and died under a farm truck.

I can remember my first day at school, screaming for my mum while the other kids stared at me blankly, and I can remember my last day, laughing off my A-level results and wondering how I was going to break the news at home.

I can remember all of my first days as a police officer: my first day of training, my first as a probationer on the beat, my first dead body, my first arrest of a blushing teenage shoplifter who didn't run, struggle or even argue but just sat sadly in the back of the car, crying over the trouble he was in. I can remember my first day as a detective, my first incident room, my first postmortem. And, clearest of all, I can remember the first time I knew I was going to die.

It was 10:25, Tuesday morning, nine weeks ago. Twenty-six degrees C and pouring with rain. I was standing in the car park behind the constabulary's headquarters, watching it bounce off the tarmac and soak through the canvas of my shoes. I was wearing a twenty-year-old pac-a-mac from The Gap, which in the heat was keeping me as wet inside my clothes as out. I was confused.

I'd read the DNA results four times and I didn't understand. The victim, Mark Boon, was a twenty-five-year-old convicted sex offender. He was one week dead, his neck snapped, his face slashed with a knife as an afterthought. His apartment, a grim, barely furnished sweatbox on a council estate north of the city, had been a mine of bodily secretions, hair, fibers, fingerprints. But none of it made sense.

His bed had been made up on the sofa, the stains all his. Though he ostensibly lived alone, the bathroom had been littered with women's clothing and beauty products, and the one bedroom had reeked of perfume.

There had been three distinct DNA profiles in that room. One, naturally, had belonged to Mark Boon, and its makeup had been fairly repulsive: specks of blood on the skirting board, traces of vomit on the carpet, fossilized tissues under the bed.

The second had belonged to Erica Shaw, twenty years old, missing from home for three months by then but known to be very much alive. I'd seen her with my own eyes, two days before Boon's murder, in That Man's home—that man who, at the time, despite circumstantial evidence linking him to a disappearance, I suspected of being little more than an arrogant prick.

Erica seemed to have been sleeping in the bed—hair and other traces on the sheet and pillow, and her underwear strewn about the place. There was no indication that she'd shared the bed with Mark or with anyone else, or, crucially, that she'd touched anything but her own belongings. And that's where it began to baffle me.

The third profile had been that of Erica's best friend. Sarah Abbott had vanished on the same morning as Erica, and by all accounts she hadn't been seen or heard from since. But there'd been a thong with her DNA on it stuffed behind the bed, and a hairbrush in the bathroom wrapped in strands of her hair. And yet there'd been only one batch of her prints in the entire flat, on a pack of cigarettes and a lighter with her initials engraved on the side. And for however long they'd sat in the center of the chipped old fake-pine coffee table, nobody else had laid a finger on them.

"It's horseshit," I said, to no one in particular.

"What's that?"

Kevin had emerged from the building, having done whatever it is he spends so long in the toilet doing, and he was standing behind me, just far enough away not to give me any of the benefit of his umbrella.

"What are we supposed to believe?" I asked him. "That Erica's been shacked up with a rapist for three months, and now she's killed him, and what? That she's on the run with Sarah? Or that Sarah *was* with them, but Boon did something to her? And that's why he's dead? She did it in self-defense? In which case, where is she? I don't get it. Why now?"

Kevin gave me the side-eye and said, very slowly, "Well, that's what we're meant to find out, isn't it? That's what detectives are for."

I ignored his sarcasm, for now, because actually it was Kevin who was being a bit thick. "You're missing my point," I told him. "It's bollocks. Sarah Abbott hasn't been living in that flat, for a start. A few strands of hair and a packet of fags is hardly proof of residence. They could have come from anywhere. She *might* have been there at one time, but if that's the case, where else has she been? She's been nowhere. So if Boon killed her, he did it back in February. In which case, why was Erica still around? We know Boon wasn't keeping her hostage. So did she plan Sarah's murder with him, or just choose to carry on living there like nothing had happened? And in either case, why were those cigarettes still on the table?"

He thought for a long moment, and then shrugged out a "Dunno."

"Can we talk about this in the car? I'm getting soaked."

A glimmer of mischief flashed across Kevin's face, but he followed me into the Focus, anyway.

"Think about the one other place we know she's been," I said. "Which, coincidentally, happens to also be the home of someone I questioned myself because we suspected *him* of being a killer. Is this making any sense to you?"

"Not really. It all seems a bit..." He shrugged again.

"Far-fetched?"

Nod.

"Exactly. It's horseshit."

"So what do we *actually* think?"

Well, that was the question, wasn't it? "Christ knows, but someone's been playing us for idiots. We've been told a story that makes no logical sense, and the only part of it that's demonstrably true is that Erica is still alive, or was a week ago, and the only reason we know that is because I saw her."

I didn't bloody *realize* I'd seen her until after the fact; she wasn't even my case then, and by the time I'd notified the Major Investigation Team, and we'd secured a search warrant, and Mal Lowry and Eli Diaz and John Fairey and I had piled into a couple of cars and sped out to the forest in the south of the county and searched every square inch of that house and questioned That Man, whom we knew at the time as Thomas Reed, all knowledge was plausibly denied and the trail had run cold.

"So," Kevin said, stifling a yawn. "Now what?"

"Simple," I said. "We start again, at the last place Erica was seen alive."

"Reed's place?"

I nodded. "Happy with that?"

"Makes sense to me," he said. "Can we stop and get a McDonald's on the way?"

"If you're pay—" I was interrupted by a startling thump on the window. Kevin jumped in his seat. I gave Eli Diaz a smirk as I slid the glass down a crack. "You made one of us jump," I said.

Diaz laughed. "Sorry, Kevin. Ali, you haven't seen John Fairey this morning, have you? He was meant to be taking the new guy out canvassing toms last night and they didn't check back in. Their phones are off and apparently no one's heard from them since lunchtime. Any ideas?"

Knowing John, they were probably locked in a pub somewhere, but my blood ran cold of its own accord. "Can you not track his car?"

"What do *you* think?"

I glanced over at Kevin. There was no way of telling whether he was thinking what I was thinking, but he looked distinctly uncomfortable. "This is all about Erica, isn't it?"

"You read the report," Diaz reminded me. "It doesn't add up, does it?"

"That's exactly what I was about to ring Lowry about," I said, which was only a white lie. "I want to head down to the Reed place and reinterview him. Maybe we can stir something up."

He nodded. "Great minds think alike," he said. "We'll be ready in twenty minutes."

Fine with me. "I'll meet you there," I said. "Kevin needs feeding."

Diaz patted the roof of the car and tried to get back in through the fire escape he'd emerged from. It was shut. He swore to himself and hurried off around the corner of the building, out of sight. Kevin laughed.

"Grab my bag from the back," I said once we were a few miles from the house. "My notebook's in there—it's got Reed's number in it."

Kevin wiped his greasy fingers on a paper napkin and retrieved the book. "Dial it?"

"Yes, please. Let's rattle this guy's cage. Use mine, it's on the hands-free."

He held my phone up for me to tap in the unlock code, and then keyed in the number. It went half a ring before That Man's voice barked out of the speaker, startling both of us.

"I'm here! Where are you?"

I had a brief moment of doubt then. He couldn't have known we were coming, could he? "H-hi," I stuttered, trying to sound unfazed. "It's… Are you okay?"

"Who is this?" he said. That voice. I remember that voice—deep, like a river of dark chocolate. Like leaning over an abyss. I wasn't who he was expecting to hear from, but that knowledge didn't settle me one bit.

"Sorry," I said. "It's Ali Green. Have I caught you at a bad time?" I sensed Kevin shifting to attention in his seat, and glanced at him, mirroring his raised eyebrow.

"Sergeant Green," That Man said. "No. Perfect timing. I'm having a shitty day anyway. You can't ruin it this time."

I feigned laughter. "That's not my intention," I said. "I was hoping I'd catch you, though."

"You don't say," he replied. Indifferent. Smug, almost.

Kevin chuckled beside me, and I shot him a look. Then I went for broke. "I'm on my way there," I said. "There are a few things I need to talk to you about." Silence on the other end. "And before you say it, they're actually not all about you."

There was a long pause before he said, "I don't understand." There was a definite crack in his voice then, barely detectable, but there. Something wasn't right.

"Neither do I, believe me. The sky's probably about to fall down, but I've been over and over it in my head, and it's hugely irritating, but we might actually need each other's help." We were ten minutes away. "I'll be there in about twenty minutes. Okay?"

Another interminable silence. Then, "Actually, I was just about to go out."

"You'll wait," I said, perhaps a little more firmly than I intended, but it seemed to do the trick because his tone lifted instantly.

"Oh, yeah, of course," he said, and faked his own laugh. "I just meant I've got to fix something around the back, that's all, so if I'm not around when you get here, just come in and make yourself at home."

Kevin's face twisted in exaggerated incredulity, and he mouthed *what the fuck* at me as I tried to keep a straight face. "I've got a better idea," I said. "I'm going to stop and get a cup of coffee and a muffin. Let's say I'll be there in an hour, how's that?"

"That would be better," he said. I was sure he knew it was a lie, but that suited me just fine. Whatever happened next would happen through a jumble of double-and triple-guessing. "Can you tell me what this is ab—" He stopped so suddenly I wondered for a moment if we hadn't been cut off, but the speaker was clear enough that I could still hear him breathing. Fast, shuddering breaths. Either he was playing with himself or he was nervous as hell.

"Are you alone, Mr. Reed?" I said.

"Yes."

"And you're sure you're okay?"

"I'm fine," he said hoarsely, forcing the words, sounding for all the world like he'd just seen a ghost. "Sorry, I'm just getting dressed and I strangled myself."

"Right." I was already pressing the throttle to the floor. "In that case I'll let you go before you come to any more harm. But to answer your question, we urgently need to discuss Erica Shaw."

"Oh God," he said. "Ms. Green, I've already told you everything I know about that girl. I really don't know how else I can help you."

"It's just routine," I told him. "Crossing the *i*'s and dotting the *t*'s. I'll see you in an hour."

"Okay," he said. "One hour." And then he was gone before I could say goodbye.

Kevin opened his mouth to speak.

"I'm going as fast as I can," I said.

Whatever I'd been expecting to find when we arrived, I was completely unprepared for what happened. I'd radioed for urgent backup; I'd called Diaz, and he was on his way with the DCI and an armed response unit. I knew I should have waited, hunch or no hunch. But I didn't.

I stopped for nothing but the heavy iron gate across the track that led half a mile through the woods to That Man's house. Kevin was out of the car before it stopped rolling, and then the gate was open, and I was already moving again when he scrambled back in. My temples were pounding, my eyes as focused as a hawk's. Kevin was silent beside me, a little pale, gripping the grab-handle above his head.

When we reached the far side of those trees, the car sliding sideways out onto the wide gravel driveway in front of the house, the shooting had already started. And it was Erica Shaw behind the trigger.

I don't remember much of what happened after that. I remember staring down the barrel of a revolver. I remember being on my back on the ground, Erica's nails pressed hard into my cheek. I remember the rain hitting the gravel, and bouncing back red with a young woman's blood. I remember That Man, weak but in full control, deciding Erica's fate with nothing more than a look. And I remember Eli Diaz's face staring up at me from the pool of blood in my lap, his body sliding away, slumping across my feet, detached.

The blood. I remember all of the blood.

CHAPTER 5

DCI Malcolm Lowry was missing. No one was saying it, but everyone was thinking it. Losing Eli had triggered the breakdown we'd all known was coming since his wife had filed for divorce a month before. He'd been in the hospital with chest pains within hours, signed off by the end of the day, and by the end of the next he was holed up in a static caravan on the Welsh coast, ignoring all offers of counseling and pleas to go back to the hospital. After a week he'd stopped returning anyone's calls, and within a fortnight he'd fallen off the grid altogether.

I learned this from Jennifer Riley as I stood openmouthed in the shambles of an incident room trying to figure out exactly who was in charge. Jenny and I came up through training together; she was always a couple of steps ahead of me, always seemed more suited to the touchier, feelier side of the job. And now, true to that, she was hugging me tightly, telling me how glad she was that I was back, how much she'd missed me, and how was I, and how sorry she was, both as my friend and now also apparently as my acting DCI, that she'd thrown me straight into the deep end without offering any briefing or preparation or indeed any kind of communication as to what the hell was going on. "I'm sorry," she said again, plucking one of her long copper hairs from the side of my face. "I know it's my arse. To be honest, everything's my arse right now. I've only been active on this for a week. Look at the state of the place. This whole thing's been a fuckup from the start. No offense."

I scanned the room, the rogues' gallery of whiteboards lined up along the wall beneath the windows, each plastered haphazardly with photographs, names, dates, but nothing, as far as I could see, of any real substance.

On one, the sorry, bedraggled mugshots of Kerry Farrow and Samantha Halloran, two working girls at the bottom of their profession and the top of their narcotic dependency, and both missing within weeks of each other. Fairey and I, at the height of our differences, had been working on Kerry's disappearance when I was seconded to the search for Erica Shaw.

Erica's face, full and pouting and framed by a long, dark mass of tight curls, shared a board with her best friend Sarah Abbott and former schoolmate Caroline Grey—both of them tall, slender, high-cheekboned and blonde and missing from within a couple of miles and less than a week of one another—and Rachel Murray, who wasn't missing at all when she died. Below them, a column of faces: girls of a similar age, with glowing hair and sparkling eyes and perfect white teeth beaming from school photos and portfolio shots. Beside each, a town: Reading. Bristol. Portsmouth. Guildford. Bradford. Chelmsford. A lot of *Fords*, I noted, shuddering at the photo of the white Transit van beside the e-fit of That Man on the third board.

Nothing in that face I recognized, or in the half-dozen views below it of the inside of the metal cage I now knew to be secreted under his garage. But there was no doubt in anyone's mind that whoever and wherever he was, he was behind those girls' disappearances.

On the fourth board, Mark Boon. A fright of pumpkin orange hair and an impetuous sneer. And below, with a gashed cheek and bloodshot eyes, the same face staring up from the floor, dark and unseeing atop a body that faced resolutely down.

And finally, blown up from their personnel files, Fairey's and Keith's ID photos, the only note below their names a giant black question mark in an emphatically drawn circle.

"Do you want to talk me through it?" I said.

Jenny nodded. "I'll get us a coffee first, though, yeah?"

"Tell me what you saw this morning," she said, sipping from a mug that read Despite the Look on My Face, You're Still Talking.

My mug had disappeared from the kitchen, so she'd given me one that said I'm Not Dead Yet, which made me laugh, but not in a good way. "It's John's car," I said. "Whether the remains are his and Julian's, I have no idea. It's a bootful of calcined bone, shards of it, bits and pieces. Whether it's two bodies' worth, or whether it'll even be possible to piece it all back together, God only knows. Either way, it's obviously a deliberate act, I'd say fueled by a *lot* of accelerant. I don't know what temperature you need to melt steel and cremate bodies, that's not my field, but it was a hell of a fire. Twisted the whole frame of the car. And, you know, what or whoever burned up in there, they *were* in the boot. So there's that."

Jenny nodded quietly, her eyes dark, her thoughts her own. I sipped my coffee. It needed more sugar and less milk, though I was sure I'd watched her make it the same way she always had.

"Also, we've got tire tracks," I said, swiping open my phone and loading the photo to show her. "At the burn site. Landowner says they're nothing to do with him, but they're clear, clear enough to get a brand and size at least. Sandra's got Jim processing them. May give us something."

"What's your instinct?"

"I don't know." My instinct was still in intensive care, is what it felt like. "How is it that we weren't able to track John and Julian?" I asked her.

"We were," she said. "There was no tracker in the car, but we pinpointed the phone signals as soon as we knew they were missing. They were at that house the day before you..." Her eyes flicked away for the briefest moment. The slightest hitch in her breath. "Before what happened. But the last signals came from right here, at five in the afternoon. We knew that before it all went down, I think."

We might have done. "I don't remember," I said, and left it at that.

"No," she nodded. "Well, that's yet another thing that muddies the waters. They were out there, but as far as we know they came back. Just...nobody ever saw them again."

I didn't know what that meant, or why it only cemented the connection in my head, but it did. I studied the e-fit again. It was utterly generic. Just a nothing face. Two eyes, two ears, a nose, a mouth. A chin. Some hair. "How," I said, "can we not have a better picture than that? It could be anyone."

Jenny nodded and put her coffee down on the table between us, a spark of triumph returning to her eyes—a question she could answer. She flipped open her laptop, tapped in her password, opened a folder and spun the machine around so we could both see it. "We've got a driving license," she said, opening a scanned image of a photo card. "The two vehicles we recovered are registered to this guy. You know the name: Thomas Reed. Look familiar?"

I laughed. The man had a full beard and shoulder-length hair, his dark eyes all but hidden behind two great draped curtains of it. "Jesus Christ," I said, cheaply.

"I know, right?" She clicked through to an image of a passport in the same name, with the same photo. "If I was religious I'd call it a miracle, because this Thomas Reed doesn't exist. Or not anymore. He died of whooping cough in 1980. Unlike—" next image, a second driving license, same photo "—James Faulkner, who drowned at the age of three." Click. Another passport. "James owns the house and the sixty acres around it."

"What about bank accounts?"

"We haven't found those yet. And neither of these characters is paying any kind of income tax. HMRC have nothing registered at the address. But also, he was holding keys to at least eight other properties."

"So, what, he rents out properties? He's a landlord, maybe?"

She shrugged. "Right now, there's no money trail at all. No mortgage, no car payments, no credit cards… If we had him actually buying something, then *maybe*, but short of tracing the serial numbers on everything in that house, and then hoping he didn't pay in cash…"

I gave her a look that I hoped said *It might yet come to that.*

"I know," she said, and gulped down the rest of her coffee.

"What about DNA?"

"Oh, yeah, we've got fucking tons of the stuff. Just nothing to match it to. There's no Breckland Butcher in the database, unfortunately."

"No what?"

"That's what the papers have been calling him."

Ugh. "Well, they can piss off."

"Yes, I told them that."

"So." I scanned the boards a second time. "Aside from Erica, how many of *them* can we place there?"

"One," she said. "Kerry Farrow."

My stomach flipped. "Kerry," I repeated. I'd been there, looked That Man in the eye as he swore he'd never laid eyes on her, as he smugly pointed out the errors in our evidence, even as he correctly predicted that a body we'd found didn't belong to her. "Where? In the…that cage?"

She nodded again and then cocked her head at the photos of the cage, I guessed as much to avoid my eye as anything else. "Yeah, and only in the cage," she said. "Unlike Erica, who'd been all over the place. The cage, and every room in the house, including sleeping in the master bedroom."

I heard a voice in my head then, although it was indistinct, genderless, and I couldn't for the life of me place it. *I'm not going back in a cage*, it shrieked.

Jenny saw me shudder and said, "You okay?"

I wasn't. Trying to think felt like staring into a black hole. I'd already forgotten the names she'd just given me, and the rest, whatever she said before the part about the DNA, was little more than a faint echo. "Kerry," I said, for no reason other than to try to hold my focus. "Kerry was at the house."

"It's not your fault," she said, but I didn't know what she meant, and had I done so, I probably wouldn't have believed her anyway. I needed to press on.

"No trace of Samantha?"

"None. Nothing in the van, either. All we harvested from that was bleach."

I thought back to the first time I'd met That Man. I'd been there, right in the back of that Transit. It had smelled of sweat and peroxide. There'd been a box—a large one, large enough to hide in, and filled with thick gray woolen blankets. "Was there anything in the back when you recovered it?" I wondered aloud.

"No, I think it was empty. Why?"

"If there's a box of blankets in the inventory, they need swabbing."

She made a note.

"Is there any connection between Samantha and Kerry," I asked, "besides their job?"

"Not that we've established yet. But what we have got is footage that puts Reed, or whatever we're calling him, close to where Kerry was last seen, and we've got her DNA in a dungeon under his property. That's a done deal, Ali. Anything we find on Samantha is a bonus at this point."

"A bonus?"

Jenny raised a defensive hand and said, "I know. I know what you're about to say. But right now, we've got nothing on Samantha, and the only way we're likely to *get* anything is if we find Reed and he talks to us, because no other fucker is."

I tried to take stock, to dismiss the feeling that it all made less sense now than it had when I'd walked in. What had Jenny said about Erica? That her DNA was all over That Man's house? It didn't fit with what I thought I knew about her, but what was that, really? That she was an innocent victim, an abductee? I couldn't know that, could I? She'd come out of that house shooting, but at what? At whom? "Jenny," I said, almost afraid to ask the question that was playing on my mind. "You're not entertaining the idea that Erica and that man could be collaborating, are you?"

Jenny looked at me like I'd completely lost the plot. "I don't know what the hell I think," she said. "But frankly, I hope they are on the run together, because we've got about as much chance of tracking him down on his own as we have of catching Jack the Ripper. The man's a ghost. We don't know who we're looking for. He could be anywhere, or nowhere, and everyone who's seen his face is either dead, missing or in this room."

And I couldn't remember it. "And Kevin," I reminded her. "Kevin's seen it."

She dropped her eyes to the desk and heaved a deep sigh. "Yes, well, Kevin took a blow to the head too, didn't he."

"So what you're saying," I said, the dread tingle of hopelessness trickling through my veins, "is that we're absolutely nowhere?"

Jenny, expressionless, sipped her coffee. "We've got four missing women we think are connected," she said. "We've got one gunshot victim, two presumably dead detectives, a basement, a van, a shitload of keys and a man who doesn't exist. So yeah, to all intents and purposes, we've got fuck all. We're nowhere. Square one."

I looked back to the board, to a photograph of a collection of door keys arranged in a neat square on a table, all but one or two attached to hand-numbered yellow tags. "Christ," I thought aloud. "You said at least eight potential properties?"

Jenny nodded, sniffed, frowned. "I know," she said. "Meaning at least eight potential cages, and no way of tracking them down."

We shuddered in unison, and shared a moment's silence. And then I was confused again, and feeling like I'd missed something. "Wait," I said. "Did we lose the witness as well?"

She looked at me blankly for a second, and raised an eyebrow and shook her head and shrugged. "What witness?"

"The witness John interviewed. Who was with him on the night Kerry disappeared. It was the first thing he told us when we questioned him."

A flash of panic passed across Jenny's face, though she tried to hide it. She took a slow breath, and leaned forward across the desk, her brow furrowed deeply. "Ali," she said. "What are you on about?"

I felt heat spread through me, shame and panic and frustration all tangled together as I tried to remember. "John," I repeated. "He talked to a woman. Anna? Annie? A witness. An alibi, I guess. Didn't you know?"

Jenny shook her head. "When was this?"

"I wasn't with him," I said. "It was after that first interview, though. Look it up. It's in the file, right?"

"No," she said. "No, it isn't. There's no mention of any of it. What are you... Ali. Look at me."

I met her eye. It was emerald green, bright with adrenaline. I felt sleepy all of a sudden, and my leg hurt.

"Ali," she said. "What witness?"

CHAPTER 6

Annie was drunk, just like yesterday, but just like yesterday, she wasn't going to let that stop her. There was daylight left, hours of it, but it wasn't enough. Between them, the plodding train, the circuitous bus and the overstretched minicab company would ensure that darkness was waiting when she got home.

It had beaten her before, the sunset, two weeks ago, when she'd been late coming off shift. The village got dark too quickly—too many trees, not enough streetlamps. No noise pollution out there, away from the city. Just shadow, and sky. She'd pulled up a few houses from home, main beams illuminating the road, the fence line, the hidden places between the hedgerows, and there she'd sat for a quarter of an hour until she was certain nothing was waiting for her. Or at least nothing that walked upright. Afterward, she'd swung the car across the road and lit up the front of the house, aiming the lights through the windows, searching for silhouettes. By the time she'd made it inside and turned on all the house lights, her head had been throbbing from the tension in her shoulders. She hadn't slept all night.

It wasn't going to happen today; she was confident of that as she stumbled against her fossil of a Renault and dropped her keys on the ground. She laughed hoarsely to herself and tried to focus on them steadily enough to pick them up; took a deep drag on her cigarette before bending adeptly at the waist and scooping them up on the end of her finger. "See?" she said aloud, for the sake of the imagined company that comforted her when she was alone. "I'm not even actually drunk."

She carefully turned the keys over in her palm and selected the one for the car door. It slipped to an oblique angle between her fingers and she couldn't quite slide it into the lock. The more she twisted her wrist to compensate, the more it rotated until the shaft was resting on the back of her hand. "Oh, for the..." She sighed, and dropped them again.

The hairs went up on the back of her neck then. She didn't remember a lot, not lately, but the memory of all those films was clear in her head: panicking women with big '80s hair, fumbling their car keys to the ground as the killer bore down on them. Her pulse quickened in her throat, squeezing out her breaths. Her body chilled and prickled to high alert. Her mind raced. There was someone behind her.

Annie spun around with a bark that first made her jump, and then, as she encountered no one, embarrassed her. She caught her breath as the adrenaline sparked out of her, and then she shook her head and said, "For fuck's sake, Annie," and bent to scoop up the keys again.

She got one into the lock this time, but it was the wrong one, so she tried again, more successfully this time, albeit at the expense of a few more paint chips as she stabbed all around the door handle.

Finally the door was open, and she took another look over her shoulder before she tossed her bag inside and her cigarette to the ground and tumbled into the car.

Her eyes were heavy now, but she couldn't worry about that. She slammed the door and found the ignition key and somehow rattled the car to life. "Fine," she said. "Everything's fine." Then she looked up at the rearview mirror, and everything was not fine.

It had been knocked askew, so that it afforded a view of the worn and bobbled headlining. She reached up instinctively to adjust it, and then froze. She'd seen this film, too, and so she knew without a doubt as the fear slithered up her spine that the last thing she'd see as she twisted the mirror into place was a pair of eyes staring at her from the backseat.

She closed her own eyes, all but oblivious to the spinning of her head. "Please," she said. "Please don't."

Out of town, the traffic was light, but she didn't want the traffic to be light because there was a police car behind her and nothing in front, no flow to keep up with, and the road was twisty with a fifty-mile-per-hour speed limit, which seemed generous considering the blindness of some of the bends, but she didn't want to appear to be driving *too* slowly. And concentrating on her speed and constantly checking her mirror for signs of interest was tightening her grip on the wheel, making her turns sharp and sudden and her straights a series of imprecise corrections. Every time she tried to relax her grip and focus on the road far ahead instead of right under the nose of the car, her speed crept either up or down, depending on which was more wrong.

She'd turned the radio off to concentrate, and what felt like a sizable swerve had resulted from that, so now she was afraid to adjust the heater, which was inexplicably on, and so was simultaneously burning up on the inside and shivering under a cold sweat on the outside.

Annie was probably going to be sick.

Finally, having endured this torture for what seemed like hours but in reality, she knew, was only five and a half miles, she witnessed a ray of glorious sunshine slice through the clouds of her panic: the little Gulf station she drove past every day but at which she'd never had cause to stop, save for that one time the garage next door had put an old convertible BMW up for sale on their cracked concrete forecourt. What a heap *that* had turned out to be.

Annie mirrored, signaled and maneuvered all at the same time and without slowing, so that she crossed the corner of that forecourt at forty-nine miles an hour before standing on the brakes and bringing the Renault up at a neat twenty-degree angle, ten feet past the pumps. She didn't look over, just swiveled her eyes as far as they could go to watch the patrol car cruise past, braking as it did so, which gave her a fright, although the driver wasn't watching her. She held on to the door handle nonetheless, ready to spring out of the car and attempt to vanish into thin air if it turned around.

It didn't.

Annie gave it a full minute before she stepped out of the car, met the eye of the station attendant peering curiously out at her from the window and strolled with what in her head was a kind of whimsical purpose into the store. She knew, though, as she stepped into the air-conditioned chill and felt her forehead light up with icy beads of sweat, that the attendant could see every one of her nerves jangling, and so, not trusting her voice any better than the rest of her, she didn't try to speak. She just gave him a polite nod and a crooked smile and bought herself a Cornetto and a packet of crisps.

Some time later—she couldn't say how long, but her foot ached from feathering the accelerator and her eyes from bobbing on the ends of their stalks—she made it home. Or at least, she made it to the side of the road in front of her house. Home was another matter. The closer she came, the farther she felt from the sanctity of that locked door. Like that famous shot in *Jaws*, where Chief Brody's face zooms into tight focus as the background shrinks away, blurry and sickly and terrifying. A "trombone shot," they call it. Or a "dolly zoom," because that's how it's done—dolly in, zoom out. Dolly in, zoom out. *Dolly in, zoom out. Breathe in, breathe out. Breathe in, breathe out. Calm the FUCK down, Annie.*

Annie breathed, and gripped the wheel, and listened to the tick of the cooling engine, and tried to laugh at the thought of changing her name to Dolly Zoom. Maybe it could be her stripper name, she thought, if things got any worse at work.

Eventually, her heart and her breathing slowed to something like a workable rate, and she rolled down the window and lit a cigarette, and smoked it right down to the filter as she stared in turn at each of the windows of the house. And then she stared a little bit longer, until she was satisfied that it was just a house, *her* house, empty, familiar, safe.

Ha. *Safe. Yeah, right.*

Annie reached up and twisted the rearview mirror around to look at herself. She sighed at her smudged mascara, the worry lines etched black around tired, bloodshot eyes that had lost all of their sparkle, all of the intelligence that had set her apart from the pretty but vacuous girls at school, for better or worse. She thought, briefly, about digging some wipes out of her bag and cleaning the paint off her face then and there, but, deciding that while she was sober enough to notice, she was still too drunk to bother, she left it. Instead, she slapped the mirror roughly back into place, grabbed her bag, took a deep, steadying breath, and threw open the car door.

★★★

It was only twenty yards to the house. She had the key out ready, gripped tightly between her thumb and forefinger and angled so that, hopefully, it would slip smoothly into the lock without her dropping it. Deep down, out here in the crisp afternoon light, she knew no one was going to sneak up behind her. She just didn't think she could take another shot of adrenaline—that pure, irrational it's-behind-you fear that would inevitably accompany a floorward fumble of the keys. And so it was, the jagged little shaft click-clicking happily into the lock, the lock turning smoothly within the door, the door falling ajar, Annie swatting it open with the palm of her hand and stepping inside and throwing it shut behind her without the merest glance over her shoulder. Whatever was out there was staying out.

The relief, however, didn't come.

The house was cold, downstairs at least; the hedges and the blossom-laden trees shaded the south-facing windows. Upstairs, where the slope of the roof cut through the bedroom ceiling, it would be sweltering, particularly in that spot below the skylight so beloved of next door's cat. But the cat hadn't been around in a while, and the heat hurt Annie's head when the drink started to wear off, so she dropped her bag beside the sofa and just stood for a while in the cool gloom, rubbing the goose bumps on her arms and trying to figure out what felt different. For a minute, or maybe three or four, she managed to distract herself from the unease in her belly by cataloging the contents of the room: the lamps with their cracked-mirror finish, seemingly absorbing rather than reflecting the smoke-tinted magnolia of the walls; the television on its ill-fitting mahogany-look flat-pack unit, its screen partly obscured by the stack of unwatched films; the cabinet full of Wade Whimsies, fastidiously collected in childhood but now little more than a twee reminder of an alien past. The ashtray that seemed to fill and empty itself of its own accord. The sofa that wouldn't stay plumped up between her leaving for work and staggering home. The faint, sweet aroma that was sometimes there and sometimes not, and impossible to place when it was. The ticking of the clock. The ticking. The ticking. The ticking of the clock...

Annie stared at the second hand as it did what a second hand does, at the precise speed a second hand does it. And she was sure, she was *sure* she hadn't replaced the battery in that clock. However much she'd drunk, however many minutes or hours ago she'd drunk it, she was sure that clock shouldn't be running. And she was sure, without daring to drag her eyes to her watch, that as much as it shouldn't have been showing the correct time, it very much was.

But there had to be an explanation, right? After all, she couldn't remember *everything* she did after a drink or six. Most of the time she flat-out didn't want to, but in this case she was willing to make an exception. So she stared at the clock and chewed her nail and racked her fuzzy brain and conceded that she *had* been under a lot of stress lately. That was why she'd been drinking so much, wasn't it? The stress? It wasn't a need, an addiction, even a habit. It was just stress. And stress can do all kinds of things to a person's brain, her perception, her memory. And, even to Annie, that made a damn sight more sense than someone—than anyone—than *that man*—coming into her home and changing the battery in her clock. Didn't it?

"Twat," she said, out loud, to herself, because however she may or may not try to convince herself otherwise, she knew that there was nobody else in the house, and nor had there been. Whatever odd thing she was feeling, it definitely wasn't that. And the sound of her own voice echoing around the room calmed Annie, and momentarily she dropped her arms and tore her eyes from the second hand of the clock and thought about making a cup of tea. And so she went to the narrow little kitchen that led off the lounge, and she filled the kettle and switched it on. And then she saw the mug upside down on the draining board, the one with the chip in the rim that had cut her knuckle the last time she'd washed it. The one her mother used to use when she'd come to stay for the weekend. The one she couldn't throw away. The one she'd put back in the cupboard and never, ever used again. Upside down, on the draining board, a dozen tiny spots of water tracing a drying path to the sink.

Annie took a breath and waited for her heart to start beating. And when it finally did, she slumped to the floor in the corner of the kitchen, and shuffled back into the crook of the wall, and drew her knees up to her chest, and listened to the kettle boil, and cried and cried and cried.

EPISODE 2

CHAPTER 7

"Michelin Agilis," Kevin said.

"Who?"

"*Adj*-i-lis. Ad-*jeel*-is."

"What?"

"It's a van tire. Two-one-five mil. Standard fit on a Transit." Which was the answer I was both hoping for and dreading. And so it was that I drained my fifth coffee of the afternoon, and tried in vain to rub some of the pain from my temples, and left the finger-thin file open on my desk and walked quietly with Kevin over to the impound garage.

It was chilly inside, and harshly lit by fluorescent strips that were like daggers to my eyes, so I put my sunglasses on and tolerated the *CSI* jokes between Kevin and the pale but craggily handsome chap who signed us in, whose name I'm going to say was Paul, though I might be wrong.

Paul directed us to a bay more or less in the center of the warehouse, so I ducked out of the line of mirth and set off at a purposeful stride, leaving Kevin halfway through a joke about me auditioning for a *Hangover* sequel. That he assumed

I was still hungover at five in the afternoon, I mused to myself, was the reason he was still a constable.

The place was laid out with a certain kind of haphazard logic. The vehicles that came in under their own power—the uninsured and ill-gotten ones—were lined up on the far shore of a sea of jagged wrecks, crushed and burned and prized apart. In time, Fairey's Mondeo would be slotted among them by an indifferent forklift driver, just another tombstone, all in a day's work. But for now, there was only one thing in here that bothered me.

There was no dramatic reveal; the Transit was the largest thing in the warehouse, looming above and beyond its devastated neighbors, and I could see it soon as I walked in. It was parked with its back to me, the tall white double doors ajar, like an invitation. I'd accepted once before, and noted with indifference the ratchet straps, the ceiling hooks, the hose-down floor liner, the white vinyl covering the walls. It had looked to me, back then, like any other van, albeit a sparkling clean one. Now, it looked like such a glaring cliché that I wondered if I hadn't simply subconsciously dismissed it for being too ludicrously obvious.

Or maybe it was all about context. Here, in this place, under these lights, knowing what I knew now, every step I took toward it made me shiver a little bit harder.

It was certainly no longer sparkling. It was caked up to its door handles in dried-on mud, some of which had cracked and fallen away to form a dusty brown ring on the garage floor. The mirrors were missing, the front tires flat and the length of each side was streaked with dirt and crushed weeds and metal-deep scratches ingrained with splinters and bark. And at the front, it was no longer a van so much as it was the mold for a tree trunk.

It had hit just left of center, the front fascia punched inward in a ragged semicircle to the base of the shattered windscreen, the door on that side creased and limp on its hinges, the buckled wheel jammed back into its arch. The bonnet was folded in half and pitched in the middle, the white paint cracked away, exposing glistening sharp edges like knife blades. I stared them down for a moment, trying to feel some—any—kind of emotion, but none stirred in me. It was just metal.

Inside was different. The driver's door still worked; I unlatched it and it swung stiffly back on its hinges until it caught against the displaced front wing. And here the carnage continued: the dashboard shunted back on the passenger side, pinning the seat against the bulkhead.

It was the undamaged driver's seat that held my stare, though—the seat from which Erica Shaw had fled the scene of the van's demise in the woods and somehow spirited herself away from the marksmen, the dog handler, the damn helicopter for heaven's sake—the seat in which That Man had presumably stalked and watched and waited to himself spirit away Kerry, and Samantha, and God only knew who else.

For a split second I thought that I could smell him in there, beneath the oil and the mud, but I knew it was just an illusion. He had no smell, to my mind. Just the smell of that house—of frying meat, and citrusy bleach, and the blood in my nostrils.

"She was lucky."

I jumped half out of my skin at Kevin's words. I hadn't heard him sneak up on me; in fact, I might even have forgotten he was there. "Stop fucking doing that," I snapped.

"Sorry," he said. "Didn't mean to," which I knew was a lie.

I let him squeeze into my personal space to get a look inside the van. I didn't care about his elbow digging into my ribs; I was too preoccupied with the thought of That Man's sweat soaked into the seat, my brain like a black light in one of those germ commercials, luminescing the oil from his fingers on the steering wheel, the gear lever, the stalks and the switches, the sun visor and the door handle, the parking brake and th—

"I just meant," he said, "she could have been badly hurt."

I snapped back into myself. Shook the shudder from my spine. "We don't know that she wasn't," I said, and then let the moment's silence between us fill in the rest.

"We'd know, though, right? If she'd been treated anywhere?"

I shrugged at his optimism. He knew as well as I did that it was a lottery, that whatever name she gave at a casualty desk would only lead us on a wild-goose chase.

I couldn't know what Kevin was thinking, of course, but in my mind, his words had triggered a vision, or perhaps a memory; I wasn't sure which. I saw Erica, a gun in her hand—not a replica, not an air gun or a starter pistol, but a functioning firearm, which I'd seen her discharge, seen the spray of blood from That Man's arm, seen her turn it on me, the barrel a black, hungry tunnel, all-consuming, with no light at its end. I saw her above me as I lay on the ground, my hand around her throat, hers clawed and desperate, nails breaking the skin of my cheek. I saw That Man pull her away, and I saw her look down at me and aim the gun again, not at my face this time but a little away, somewhere to the side of me, her eyes frightened and hurt and filled with a knowledge she was too young, too naive, too *human* to have to bear. She spoke, though I couldn't make sense of the words. They were just a jumble—too many for an apology, too few for an explanation. I couldn't remember, and it hurt to try.

And then I saw her climb into the van and turn the key and drive away, over the field and into the forest, although I may have been imagining that part, just as I was imagining her now, falling from this smoking, gushing wreck, clutching herself tightly, her legs folding beneath her. I saw her force herself to her feet, clawing at the van for a hold to pull herself up, a sheen of blood sliding like a visor down over her forehead, over her eyes. I heard her cry out, saw her swipe at her face with her sleeve. I saw her double over and sway and throw up between her feet. And then the sound of engines, and the bark of a dog, and the rattle and hum of rotor blades, and I saw her running, hunched and unsteady, willing her legs to work. I saw her plunge into the river, sobbing in lungfuls of air, thrashing her way through the water until she could crawl, thigh-deep in mud, onto the opposite bank. I felt the adrenaline coursing through her, the urgent noise of her pursuers filling her ears, and I shouted at her to *Run, Erica, as fast as you can, just run, sweetheart, and don't look back!*

"Ali? You alright mate?"

I realized my leg was shaking and my eyes stung like hell, and then I saw the worried look on Kevin's face and away they went, spilling fat tears down my cheeks before I could stop them. I pretended not to notice. "I'm fine," I said. "Why, what's up?"

I could see he didn't know what to say. His hands fidgeted awkwardly at his sides and his mouth flapped open and shut, and for a moment I thought he was going to try to hug me again. If I'm honest, and a little bit cruel, I quite enjoyed watching him flounder, though had he actually tried to hug me, I probably would have let him. But he didn't, which was equally fine, and so I forced a bemused expression and said, "Are *you* alright?"

"I..."

Come on, McManus, you can do it.

"Yeah," he shrugged. "Just..." He glanced over his shoulder, pointedly. "You know, that was a bit loud." He nodded backward in the direction of the office door and, beyond it, Paul.

My heart sank, though I made the best attempt I could at keeping the horror from my face. How much had I said out loud? And why did I not know the answer to that?

As frustrating as the holes in my memory were, my brain noted that moment as the first in which I was truly afraid of it. And now it was my turn to not know what to say, although however freaked out and confused I was all of a sudden, I was damned if I was going to show it, or stand there and say nothing at all, so I shook my head and brazened it out and said, "I didn't hear anything."

"You were shouting ab—"

"I didn't hear anything," I repeated, fixing him with an unblinking stare that probably made me look like a fucking lunatic, on top of sounding like one. "You're mistaken."

He was blank for a moment, silent, but sure enough it sunk in eventually. He furrowed his brow and nodded down at his feet, bald crown flashing in the harsh light, and then he said, "Right then," and looked at me and nodded again, to himself, I figured, and turned neatly on his heels and added, "Well, if you're sure you're okay, we should probably be getting on."

With his back to me, I felt my confidence return, displacing the trembling in my hands and the jiggling of my right knee, so I pressed the point home. "I'm fine," I said. "I hope we're agreed on that."

"Roger that," he replied, "all received," and started walking.

"Oh, and Kevin?"

I could see that he tried not to stop, his leg swinging forward and dangling there midstep, trying to decide of its own accord whether to stay or go before retracting to the vertical and giving him back his balance. He looked back at me, his face suddenly lined with sadness and fatigue. "Sarge?"

"The tires match."

CHAPTER 8

I knew I'd hurt Kevin by shutting him down. I should have talked to him there and then—I knew that, too. He'd been there that day, huddled into a ball, bleeding, when I fought Erica and lost, and when I dropped the ball with That Man and nearly paid for it with my life. I knew he felt responsible, blamed himself for his incapacitation, his inability to "protect" me. I'd heard him at my bedside while I pretended to sleep, confessing all to Lowry and being told not to be so bloody stupid. I'd heard my sister telling him she was certain he'd done everything he could. I'd even heard him being comforted by Eva Diaz. In fact, when I thought about it, I couldn't say with any degree of certainty that he'd ever left my side.

It wasn't his fault, of course; it was *our* fault. We simply didn't know what we were blundering into. We just charged in, thinking we were oh-so-clever, and found out the hard way that we weren't. Not clever, not infallible, not invincible. Just a couple of—

"Clueless twats." Kevin threw his phone at his desk, and then made a desperate lunge to catch it before it connected, which resulted in him spilling his coffee and kicking the bin over as he juggled it to safety.

"No joy?" I spun my swivel chair again, lifting my feet and watching the office whirl around me: desk Kevin clock door desks cooler window Peter door mug Kevin clock thing man window poster door Kevin thing for clipping papers together. I like spinning. It didn't make me feel any more or less dizzy. My head still hurt.

"Is anyone's network working?" Jenny Riley at her office door, a frazzled look on her face, the hair on one side of her head ruffled and twisted and standing on end.

A male voice choir from four corners of the room: "No."

"Has anyone called IT?"

"They're running an update." Kevin waved his phone at her, as if to cite his source. "Said it should have been on the briefing list."

"For fuck's sake," she sighed, and shrank back into her office. Then she reappeared and said, "Did you get anywhere with those tires?"

"Well, they match the van," I said.

She beckoned the two of us into her office and sat down behind the landfill site that was her desk, gesturing for us to do the same. "But?"

"But nothing. We were about to try to figure out possible routes from the house to the crime scene, and see if there's any ANPR that might have picked it up." In case you don't know, that stands for Automatic Number Plate Recognition. They read the registration numbers of passing vehicles, and if we're looking for you for any reason they'll flag you up in real time. We have them in our patrol cars, but they're also fixed in strategic locations around the county. Get me drunk and I'll tell you a couple of good places to avoid.

Just kidding, I'd never do that.

"Can't hurt to try," Jenny said after a moment's thought. "Although I know we ran a countywide search for John's car as soon as we knew he was missing, and we didn't get a single hit. Are either of you trained on ViPER?"

I can't remember what that stands for, but she was talking about the software we use to access the ANPR database. I shook my head.

"Ali is," Kevin said, helpfully.

"I'm really not," I assured him. "I mean, I did the course, but it was one day, like, five years ago or someth—"

"That's fine," Jenny said, waving away my excuse, "someone can do it in the morning. I think we can safely assume it's the same van until then, so don't get too hung up on it. What else have you got?"

"Well." I picked up a sheaf of paper that Kevin had just kicked off the edge of the desk as he crossed his legs. "I'm thinking the same applies for petrol stations. As in, it's a safe bet that the fire was started with a lot of petrol or diesel, but none of the reports list any kind of storage tank on the man's property and we didn't see any evidence of it any time we visited, so it stands to reason he had to buy it somewhere. Probably after he killed them, because whatever went down, and whatever they were all doing on that airfield, it doesn't seem to have been planned before that afternoon."

"Unless he had a store somewhere else," she pointed out. "We don't know about any other properties, remember, and nor do we have any other bodies. Who's to say he didn't burn all of them?"

I let that roll around for a moment, just as I had when the thought had occurred to me ten minutes earlier. "I don't know," I said, honestly. "I'm not sure he did, and I don't know why...just a hunch, which—I know what you're going to say, but I think this was something different. He had two coppers and a police car to get rid of, and…" There was a memory trying to push through. A knife? Like the sharp edges of the wrecked van, lethal, glimmering. And that smell, ever present, in his house—the smell of frying meat.

"Okay," she said, and I realized I'd drifted off midsentence and that Kevin was looking at me sideways and trying to hide his dark expression. "So what are you suggesting?"

"Sorry. I was just thinking that if we can get him on CCTV buying a lot of petrol in cans, then a) we'll have that, and b) we'll have a picture of him on CCTV, which is better than anything we've currently got for actually finding the cu—"

"That's a lot of hours of footage," Kevin cut in, "assuming it even exists." Which took me aback somewhat, and raised one of Jenny's eyebrows in a subtle way I remembered from years gone by. I'd only ever seen it aimed at men, funnily enough.

"It is," I agreed, "and it isn't. We know when John and Julian were last *definitely* alive, and we know we're looking for a big white van you can see from half a mile away, across a fairly small number of stations, starting with the closest one to the burn site. He's not going to have driven miles out of his way to buy fuel, especially if it was unplanned. And if we can get an ANPR hit, we'll have a precise route and time, so the window's only going to be a matter of an hour or so anyway."

Kevin sniffed and gave a little shrug, which I chose to ignore for the time being.

Jenny nodded. "Alright," she said. "Draw up a list of locations tomorrow. If we don't get a hit on the vehicle, just work along a straight route between his home and the airfield and I'll try and palm it off. I've drafted some extra bodies in to lighten the load a bit—start going back over witness statements, reinterviewing, whatever. Donkey work. Clear some of the backlog. I'll find someone to trawl through anything we can get. But look, as far as John and Julian are concerned,

I think we can agree it's pretty clear what happened and who did it, so I don't want you to get too bogged down in tedious bollocks that anyone can do. We've wasted enough man-hours, so there's no sense in the two of you sitting around watching telly. We need a positive ID on the remains, and if we can find some CCTV then great, it's another rivet in the Reed case. But in the meantime, I'm going to ask you to focus on the main lines of inquiry, starting with Erica's friend, the Abbott girl."

I glanced at Kevin, expecting him to meet my eye with a look that said *Did she just call two dead coppers a rivet?* He didn't; he just nodded slowly at her and said nothing, and so then I felt guilty for thinking she'd be that cold.

I was considering how to respond when she said, "Look, Ali, I know what you're thinking. It's tough. You and John didn't see eye to eye, just like he and I didn't. And I feel guilty in a lot of ways, because I've never been shy about saying what I thought of him, and being dead doesn't make him any less of a dickhead, but he was a copper, and not a particularly bad one at the end of the day, just a twatty one, and more to the point he was our colleague, and a human being with a wife and a baby, and none of us wanted this to happen. He didn't deserve to die, however fucking irritating he was, but at the same time, we can only resolve it if we find out who Reed is, and the only way we're going to do that is by getting to the bottom of all this other shit." She swept a hand across the pile of disordered crap in front of her, her face falling as though she was seeing the magnitude of the mess for the first time. "So," she sighed. "That's what we're going to do. Right?"

I wished I could share her optimism, however forced it was. But I nodded anyway, and said okay, and we all took a moment to stare at the desk in silence before Jenny ran her hands roughly through her hair and said, "This is shit. Let's go home."

★★★

Kevin was still silent as we gathered our things and threw them haphazardly into our respective bags, and as I discreetly wrote the words *petrol stations* on the inside of my wrist with a biro, below the smudged and faded reminder I'd penned there earlier: *Jen act ng SIO.*

He waited until we were outside the building before he turned to me sharply and said, "Ali, can I as—"

I walked right into him and my bag slid off my shoulder, plopping onto the tarmac and spilling its contents into the car park.

"Fucksake, sorry," he flustered, swooping down to gather my things and shove them roughly back in.

"What's the matter, Kevin?" I said.

He straightened, then stooped back down a little to try to meet my eye, so that he looked even more uncomfortable than I could already tell he was. "Can I ask you a question?"

I nodded. "Questions are free."

He was fiddling with his fingers again, his eyes jittering between my own and a point somewhere on my forehead. "I don't want to be out of order or anything," he said, "but are you *actually* alright?"

I could feel my face burning, and a knot forming in my belly, but apart from that and all of the other things, I felt pretty okay, and I told him so.

"Only..." He hesitated, possibly in the hope that I'd shut him down and save him saying something I might make him regret, but I just waited him out until he found his voice. When it came back, there was a hard edge to it. "Ali, you keep zoning out," he said. "And earlier you gave me a can of Coke, and half an hour later you told me you'd got me a can of Coke but you couldn't find it. I'm worried about you, mate. I don't know whether you should be—"

"Occupational Health signed me off," I said, looking for a tone that conveyed my unwillingness to have this conversation. "I'm cleared to work."

"Oh, come on," he groaned. "We both know that's bollocks. Tell me honestly, how many times have you been in there before and just told them whatever they wanted to hear? You came to work with a broken hand once, remember? You couldn't even lift your mug."

I did remember. I'd been standing on an office chair, trying to retrieve a paper plane that had wedged itself under the edge of a ceiling tile. The X-ray showed two fractured bones in the back of my hand, but I told Tim Hopgood it was just a bruise and he let me come back the next day. It was a bit stupid, to be fair. Hurt like all buggery. And now I had a choice to make. I could back down, admit to Kevin what he could already see. I could laugh and tell him I was just finding my feet, I'd had a headache all day, something something hangover, ha ha ha. Or I could shift my weight onto my good leg, stand tall, get in his face. Counterattack. *How's* your *head, Kevin? How's that little dent in your skull? You're not making a lot of sense, Kevin. Your memory's playing tricks on you again, isn't it? Why do you keep calling me Helen, Kevin? You're looking a little bit peaky. Why don't you sit down for a minute?*

I can be as much of a bitch as I need to be, trust me. But, "I'm tired," I said, choosing to address his worried face rather than the aggression in his voice. "We both are. It's been a long day."

I bore the weight of his stare for a moment longer, until he sighed and turned and nodded at the setting sun. "Fine," he muttered. "Better get some rest, eh?" Then he gave me a thin-lipped smile and walked to his car.

I watched him back out of his space and drive away without another glance in my direction; waited until he was out of the gate before I let out an unsteady breath, shook the heat from my face, and tried to remember what I'd done with my car keys.

When I got home, there was a car. Just a black Audi like a million others, but it slowed to a crawl as I pulled up onto the driveway, and idled at the curb a house and a half away while I locked the car and fiddled with my house keys. I tried to take in as much as I could without staring, but beyond covertly digging out my notepad and scribbling down the registration number, there wasn't a lot to deduce. It needled me, though. Whether it was down to familiarity or just plain old cop-brain, there was something about that Audi.

I slipped the little rubber car-shaped fob from my key ring, where it serves as a reminder that I've locked the house while I'm out, and hung it on the nail beside the door, then slipped inside with only the slightest glance over my shoulder.

I kicked off my shoes and dumped my bag on the living room floor. Picked up the junk mail from the mat and tossed it straight into the recycle bin. Filled the kettle and switched it on. Peered through the net curtains to see if the Audi was still there, which it was. Fished a clean mug from the dishwasher and spooned in a heap of instant coffee. Dribbled in the last of the milk with a sigh and idly stirred it into a paste while I waited for the water to boil. Then I jumped out of my skin at the first of three slow knocks on the front door.

I stood stock-still for a moment, letting my pulse and my thoughts race and the kettle bubble and click off, and brown milk drip from the spoon in my hand onto the floor. At some point I came to my senses; decided I was simply spooked by the day's events and that I was in no more sinister demand than I had been yesterday. I'd probably just ordered something on the internet, or...

Three more knocks, closer together this time, and quieter, not louder—fading in confidence.

Finally, shaking the last ringing alarm bell from my head, I dropped the spoon back into the mug and went to the door.

"Don't tell me you didn't mean it," Edith said, wincing at the surprise I clearly couldn't keep from my face, and at the bottle of Prosecco in her hand. "Oh God, that's awkward."

I could only guess at what she might be referring to, but whether I'd meant it or otherwise, I was glad she'd turned up, because I suddenly and urgently needed a drink.

CHAPTER 9

Annie was trying not to panic, and the vodka was helping with that to an extent, but equally, it wasn't much helping her to figure out what to do.

She wasn't an idiot; she knew deep down that the e-fit on the television, the one from all those posters, was the man she knew as James, however laughably generic it was. She knew it was the man she'd met flat on her back on the path beside the river, her jeans unbuttoned, the late Mark Boon struggling to tug the waistband past her hips. She knew it was the man to whom she'd felt indebted enough to answer his call for help. The man about whose movements Detective Sergeant Fairey had so awkwardly and sensitively questioned her without recording a single word she'd said. The man who'd taken care of her when she was sick. The man she'd slept beside, willing him in vain to touch her. The man with whom she'd felt safe enough to give him the key to her house. The man who'd made her feel, for once in her life, something more than plain old Annie Average.

She'd told the truth about that man, more or less, when Fairey had come to ask. And yet the evidence at that house in the woods told a different story, one she couldn't reconcile even now, as she sat staring at footage of a burned-out car and the anchor's words echoed through her head: *The bodies have not yet been formally identified, but the families of the missing officers have been informed.*

Annie shuddered in her seat and gripped her glass so tightly that she thought it might break. Her cigarette had burned itself out in the ashtray. Her head swam. He'd been alright, John Fairey. Understanding. Gentle. He hadn't judged her, at least not openly. And, it seemed, for whatever reason, he'd kept her name to himself.

But this: this changed things, didn't it? For every night that changed nothing—every night she'd come home expecting to find a killer hiding in the shadows, expecting to have her silence brutally, terminally guaranteed—this one night turned all of that on its head. This...this mug, which now stared back at her from the coffee table in her unlit lounge, where that man had once rested some other mug—the one with the pink bands around it, she thought. She'd sat in this chair and hidden her blushes as he'd casually flirted from the sofa opposite, his face as clear in her mind as if it were still right there, right below that framed photograph of her mother as a skinny child, scowling her disapproval from before the dawn of color just as she undoubtedly would be now from beyond the grave.

Annie presumed to know enough to be sure that he'd cleaned *this* mug beyond any forensic usefulness. But it was real enough, and that meant *he* was real, and that ever-present tingle among the hairs on the back of her neck was real, too. The nagging feeling that he was close by, that he was watching. He wasn't just a figment of her imagination. That man was here.

When the incident room number had finally disappeared from the screen, and the pictures of John Fairey and Julian Keith and the footage of their burned-out car had been replaced by scenes of Sheriff's deputies combing the scene of a mass shooting somewhere in Middle America, Annie silenced the television and deep-throated her vodka and watched her glass jitter and spin and settle where she'd all but thrown it onto the table. She dug her hand down the side of the seat cushion and pulled out her phone; listened to the voicemail instructing her to report to head office at 9:00 a.m. tomorrow. She'd listened to it four times already, but no amount of replays changed the instruction or its meaning.

She'd had meetings at head office before. She'd bowed her head before her boss and promised to attend those *other* meetings, the ones with steps and sponsors and *admitting you have a problem*. She'd even gone to a couple, though mostly she just *said* she'd gone. This time, though, she knew it would be a different kind of "meeting." The kind where she just quietly nodded, acknowledged that she'd been given every chance to change, and made an appointment to go collect the contents of her desk.

And so Annie knew what to do. At her lowest ebb, with no job left to lose, with no way to feed herself or to pay her mortgage, and with a killer circling at the periphery of her vision, stalking, threatening, reminding her that she'd never be free of her complicity, she had two choices: curl up and die, or tell CID everything she knew. And Annie was too young to die.

She had two packets of cigarettes, four pints of milk, three quarters of a bottle of vodka and a wedge jammed tight under the front door. For the next twelve hours, Annie was going absolutely nowhere.

But tomorrow morning, at ten o'clock, she'd pay a visit to Acting DCI Jennifer Riley of the Major Investigation Team, and draw her a proper picture, and let the chips fall where they may.

CHAPTER 10

I lay awake but silent and still, listening to the clock and watching the flutter of Edith's eyelashes as she dreamed. The room was hot, her liquid-smooth skin glistening in the rising sunlight shafting through the blind. I wanted to touch it, but I didn't dare wake her.

Eventually, she stirred a little and reached for me, laying her arm across my waist and nudging her feet between mine. Still I didn't touch her.

When she finally opened her eyes and smiled and said, "Hey," and hooked my hair behind my ear, I longed to do the same, but I couldn't.

Even as she dozed contentedly and idly stroked my body; even as a comet-tail of goose bumps chased her fingertips over the ridge of my hip, all I could do was watch her face, taking in every tiny detail, from the single freckle on the right side of her chin, to the three healed piercings above her intricate pink crystal flower earring, to the sprinkling of gray roots in her hair. If I stared long enough, I thought—if just one of those things stuck, even if it was just the loose eyebrow hair threatening to fall ticklishly onto the bridge of her nose, then at least I'd have made one new happy memory.

Then the phone was ringing, and I sighed the sigh of a lost moment as Edith opened her deep brown eyes again, and rolled them, and laughed.

It was Jenny on the phone, and she got straight to the point. "We've found Mal Lowry," she said.

Her tone told the pit of my stomach that it wasn't good news, but I tried to remain optimistic for as many more seconds as I could. "Cool," I chirped, tickling the bottom of Edith's foot with my big toe. "How is he? Alright? How's Wales?"

She was silent for a moment, just as I knew she would be. Then, "It didn't work out for him."

I didn't know what doom-laden answer I'd been expecting, but it wasn't that. "Right," I said.

"Fishing boat picked him up on Sunday," she said, "about five miles out from Three Cliffs Bay. He's probably been floating around in circles since the last time we heard from him."

I didn't know what that meant, or how to process it. Deep down, I suspected I didn't *want* to know. "We're sure it's him?" I tried.

Edith had narrowed her eyes by now and was watching me with grave concern. She mouthed *You okay?* and went back to chewing her lip when I didn't know how to respond.

"Dentals check out," Jenny said, her voice level, professional. I wondered if mine sounded the same. "Tattoos check, or what's left of them. It's definitely him."

I let the sadness in then. I couldn't pretend Lowry was a great friend; I knew him as a colleague, and we'd been in the pub at the same time once or twice, but I'd only worked closely with him for a couple of weeks. I didn't know his wife's name, or his children's, or whether he even had any. Maybe he'd been a cat person. Maybe he had a boyfriend. I had literally no idea, I now realized as I lay there in my bed, looking through Edith to the picture forming in my head, of a bloated and greenish corpse, its fingers and face nibbled off by whatever monsters lurk in the cold, gray shallows of the North Atlantic. And yet I could feel on my face what Edith could plainly see as she tenderly touched my arm and gave me a reassuring smile. "Cause of death?" I muttered.

"Not yet. He's, um..." She hesitated, and I knew it was because she was trying to be delicate, but I couldn't find the words just then to tell her it wasn't necessary. It's just her way, after all. Touchy feely. "You know, propellers and whatnot."

"You mean he's cut up?" I said. Edith wrinkled her nose and snatched her hand away, and then immediately looked remorseful and gave it back. I took it in mine and squeezed her fingers and smiled.

"I don't know what this means," Jenny said.

"Me neither," I replied, though deep down, I realized, I knew exactly.

I'd copied the notes from my arm onto a Post-it before washing both them and the scent of Edith's perfume off in the shower. Now, I sat staring blankly at my laptop background, a view across Rome from the roof of the Altare della Patria, my sister and me huddled together, giggling like schoolgirls from the corner of the frame.

We'd walked and walked and walked that weekend; we must have clambered up and down a thousand steps, to the Pincio, the Palatino, the top of the Colosseum. As with all the best holidays, we'd come home needing a holiday.

It had taken me two weeks to finish sorting through my photos. Changing my wallpaper was the last thing I'd done the night before I got hurt. It had seemed so important at the time.

Anyway. Petrol stations. A maximum of seven of them, according to Google, along or around the one realistic route from That Man's house to the place where he'd killed Fairey and Keith. Which I was assuming he had, right there on the edge of that airfield, where...where what? Where he'd known they'd be? Or where he'd arranged to meet them?

Those two possibilities had, at first thought, very different connotations. If it were the former, then they'd obtained some intelligence about that place that related directly to him, and he'd known about it. Perhaps even been the one to give it to them.

But if he *had* given it to them, then it couldn't have been about himself, could it? Because he'd driven there himself; he hadn't been under arrest. And *surely* he wasn't arrogant enough to set fire to two policemen in the very place he'd buried Sarah Abbott?

But if the intelligence was about something else—if he'd offered to show them, to lead them to a big score of some kind—then what? What could possibly have enticed John Fairey into a clandestine meeting that was more important than trapping a serial killer?

(Lowry. Dead.)

It simply didn't make sense, and the more I tried to think it through, the more muddled it seemed to become, so I just copied and pasted the addresses of the petrol stations and printed them off, and then, as an afterthought, wrote *Airfield—GPR?* meaning ground penetrating radar, in green biro across the top of the page, just in case anyone thought it was worth bothering to scan there for a dump site. Which, given its failure to turn anything up at his house, I expected they probably wouldn't.

Edith brought me a cup of coffee and a croissant with butter and jam, placed them gently on the table beside my computer and swept my hair to one side and kissed the back of my neck. I didn't really like it, not right then, though I knew she wasn't being anything other than nice to me. "Are you going to be okay if I go?" she whispered.

I nodded. The words were all in my head: *I'll be okay. Thank you for being kind. I have to leave in a minute anyway. Have a lovely day at work. I'll talk to you soon.* I couldn't seem to say them, though. I didn't want to be nice, or to make her feel good; I felt empty, numb, nothing. I just wanted to be alone.

She squeezed my shoulder, and I felt a surge of anxiety that held me rigid until she'd quietly let herself out. I sat and listened to the thunk of her car door, the starter motor, the first blip of the throttle, the low hum as she drove away. Then I closed the lid of the laptop, took a bite of croissant and a mouthful of coffee, let out the fart I'd been holding in since Edith had come downstairs, and had a little bit of a cry.

I found Jenny in her office, staring blankly at her computer monitor with much the same dazed expression I assumed was on my own face. She didn't look up when I knocked and let myself in, closed the door behind me and sat in one of the chairs in front of her desk. She didn't say anything, either—just sat with her hands in her lap, breathing steadily, her pulse slow in her temple, until after a minute or two she shifted in her seat, gave a dry sniff and swiveled the monitor around to face me.

She gave me a minute to take in what I was looking at before sliding the mouse across the desk and sitting back in her chair and winding her hands into her hair.

It was… Well. I guessed it was a photograph of Mal Lowry,

although, as Jenny had warned me on the phone, I wouldn't ever have recognized him.

The image Jenny had turned to me was a full-length shot from above, the body laid out on its back on a stainless steel mortuary table, a harshly lit greenish-gray horror of fine detail against the shiny bright white tiles on the floor.

Lowry's face, like the rest of his body, was grotesquely bloated and devoid of extremities. His nose, eyes and lips were missing, perhaps once lividly but now just colorless ragged holes in his otherwise tightly skinned flesh. He had no fingers, and no toes on his left foot; I can't speak for the right one, because his leg was gone at the knee. And between his thighs, there was nothing; or rather, there was a hole, bordered with loose flaps of black skin, that stretched upward almost to his waist, and I don't know how deep.

I'd seen these things before, of course. People go into the water all the time; some of them come out after a couple of days, some after a couple of months. Some, inevitably, never come out, though it's impossible to know how many. But Lowry's was different. The cuts were different. The cuts were brutal.

One slashed across the tops of his thighs, exposing his left femur where the fish and the crabs had nibbled at the edges. The next ran diagonally across his chest, and, clicking through the series of close-up photos, I could see the sharp ends of sheared ribs, stripped of flesh. And the fourth had neatly sliced off the top of his head, maybe three inches above his eyebrows.

I remembered Edith's eyebrows, and her gray roots, and felt, in spite of myself, a spark of relief that they were still there in my head, and indeed on hers. I allowed myself to enjoy it, just for a second, before I clicked back through to the third cut.

The third cut was different. The others were bold, wide,

sweeping—strikes from something large and heavy and fast. A propeller, or two, or even three. But the third cut wasn't. The third cut was narrow and precise, made by something smaller and scalpel-sharp.

A propeller to the neck would surely have knocked Lowry's head clean off, but it was still there, attached at the spine if almost nowhere else. In the second photo of the set, it was tilted back to show the edges of the wound, and they were too clean, too clinical. I didn't need to be a trained pathologist to know what that meant.

I returned the mouse to Jenny's side of the desk, and rotated the monitor back to where she could see it. After a long moment of silence, she spoke.

"What do you see?" she said simply.

I was very clear on what I saw, and fairly certain about what it implied for my own safety, among others'. But I didn't want to think too hard about that, lest it color my judgment, so I just stuck to what we had in front of us.

"This wasn't any boat accident," I said, and felt a second wave of relief when she nodded. "Someone cut his throat."

She carried on nodding for a full minute, eyes narrowed in concentration, thumbnail wedged between her teeth. Then, when she was happy that she'd straightened out the wisdom in her head, she looked me dead in the eyes and gave me the full benefit of her many years of insight and expertise. "Fucking shitting cunting fuck," she said.

I agreed, then went and made us a nice cup of coffee.

"I want you protected," she said. "I'm not letting this happen to anyone it hasn't already happened to, least of all you. If this is what he's doing—if he's taking out anyone who's seen his face—then I want you chained to your desk where I can see you, and I want you escorted home every day, and I want surveillance on your house every night until we catch the fucker."

"You can't afford it," I laughed.

"I don't care. I'll cancel the support staff if I have to."

"And then it'll take ten times longer. Look, Jen, I know you're worried, but I'm not going to be made a prisoner by that man. If you lock me up for weeks and months, then a) I'm going to go out of my mind, and b) you'll run out of budget before you find him, then you'll have to call off the secret service, and then I'll be a sitting duck anyway, only a stir-crazy doolally one who can't remember how to take care of herself. Seriously, don't even think about it. I'd rather be out there tied to a post than stuck in here breathing Steve's BO all day, and I'm sure Kevin would, too, although I noticed you didn't say anything about protecting *him*."

Jenny sighed and shook her head and gave a weary half laugh. "Ali," she began, but I interrupted.

"And to be honest," I said, "I think our priority should be to identify the witness, assuming he hasn't already got to her. Me and Kevin are still walking around, and Mal died on the other side of the country, so is it safe to assume he's not hanging around stalking us?"

"I don't know. Look, Ali, I don't want to sound like a dick, but this witness..." She bit her tongue and winced, not by accident, I thought, but I just sat upright and nodded, forcing her to press on. She sighed. "Ali, no one knows what you're talking about. There's no record of any witness. I'm not—"

"Me, neither, but I didn't just make it up, so it can't hurt to get a fresh appeal out for her to come forward, can it? I'll check missing persons for anyone with the same name," whatever it was—I had it written down but I couldn't access the memory of it just then. I didn't have my notebook with me, either, so I reached over and grabbed a pen and tore the blank sheet from the top of Jenny's legal pad and wrote *Witness missing* on it. Then I thought I'd probably find a way to misinterpret that later, so I amended it to say *Witness: missing persons. Check this.* That should do it.

Jenny was watching me with an eyebrow raised, so I threw back the pen and nodded decisively and said, "Sorry."

"You alright?"

"I'm good," I lied. "What's next?"

She narrowed her eyes at me, perhaps puzzled by what I had to admit sounded a little too indifferent to what we'd just been looking at. No, it wasn't that. She was thinking. She'd forgotten what she was going to say. "I've forgotten what I was going to say," she said. "What did we talk about last night?"

"Petrol stations," I replied, surprising myself. Then I remembered I'd made that list. "I've got a list in my bag. You were going to get someone to look at traffic cameras."

"Yes. Shit." She snatched up her desk phone and stabbed at one of the buttons. "Hi, it's Jenny," she said. "Is the support team out of briefing yet?" She opened her top desk drawer and pulled out a packet of Maltesers, teased it open and popped two into her mouth before holding it out to me across the desk. I wasn't really in the mood but I took a couple anyway. "Okay, you've got an analyst apparently. Or someone who knows how to use ViPER. Do you think you could get him to come and find me?" She seemed to like to suck the chocolate off her Maltesers. I just crunch mine like a normal person. "Thanks, hun." Ooh, I hate it when people say *hun*. She dropped the handset back onto its cradle. It bounced off onto the desk. "Take some more, I don't really like them."

"Why have you got them, then?"

"Machine was out of Crunchies."

"Fair play."

"No Prawn Cocktail, either."

"That's shit."

"I'll make us another coffee in a minute."

"Okay."

"I don't know what the fuck I'm doing."

"I know."

"Cheers."

"I can't remember what day it is."

"Tuesday."

"Oh."

Sniff.

"Can you put a forensic suit on by yourself?"

"Yeah, why?"

"Just wondered."

"Wh—"

There was a gentle knock at the door. We both looked at it. "That was quick," she said, and, louder, "Come in." The door remained firmly shut. I couldn't see anyone through the window. "Fucksake," she sighed. "Go let him in."

I got up and went to the door. Turned the handle and pulled it open. Looked up into the face of a man who wasn't there, and breathed in a lungful of Poison with a faint note of liquor.

There was a woman outside, of average height and average build, with an average face and average dark hair, and she smiled nervously and said, "Hi. I'm Annie Fisher. Did someone order an analyst?"

CHAPTER 11

Erica Shaw looked as happy as a pig in shit behind the wheel of That Man's Transit, three hundred yards from a BP service station on the A11, head thrown back, mouth twisted open, apparently in full song. It was a startling—and startlingly clear—photograph.

"This changes things," Jenny said quietly.

Annie Fisher, who hadn't taken her hand off the picture since she'd printed it off and followed me into Jenny's office and slapped it on her desk, stared silently at it with a haunted kind of focus that I found mildly unsettling, though having only met her an hour previously, I didn't make anything of it. I just assumed she was proud of the efficiency of her work.

"Why does it change things?" Kevin asked, kicking the door closed behind him and setting down the mugs of tea and coffee hooked around his fingers and the pocketful of chocolate I'd sent him to fetch from the vending machine.

Jenny gave him a withering look and pointed at the photograph and said, "Look at it."

He did. He shrugged.

"Kevin," I said. "Really? Do you need me to explain this to you like we're in an American TV show?"

Annie broke out of her trance then and looked between the three of us as we looked between one another. She was waiting for someone to laugh, I think, but no one did. "Um..." She took a deep breath. "I missed the last episode, too. Sorry."

Jenny afforded her a smile, and Kevin's shoulders dropped a little, though not entirely. "I wasn't expecting to see evidence that Erica Shaw was working with Reed," she said simply.

Those words didn't sit easily with me. I'd seen Erica in That Man's house, yes. And, ostensibly, we had evidence that she'd been in Mark Boon's flat, too, though I didn't believe that any more now than I had when I'd first read it. The most compelling proof, to me, was the terror in Erica's eyes when she'd told me she wasn't going back in a cage, a second before she'd tried to shoot me in the face. Which detail, admittedly, weakened my argument somewhat, if not my conviction. I opened my mouth to express all this, but Kevin got in first.

"Ali," he said, "she shot someone right in front of us. She shot *Reed* in front of us, for Christ's sak—"

I stopped him with an aggressively pointed finger. "Exactly," I said. "Exactly that. She shot *him*. You know what that tells me? It tells me that whatever she might have done, she did it under his control. It was an escape, Kevin." *I'm not going back in a cage.* "Her DNA was all over that cage. I don't buy Erica as the Bonnie to That Man's Clyde. I just don't."

"What about Mark Boon?" Jenny cut in. "Her DNA's all over his place, too."

"No," I said, "it isn't. It was in a couple of obvious places, but missing from a whole load of them. Nothing on the fridge, the door handles, the toilet... It's rubbish."

Jenny nodded. "I know what you're saying, but we can't just ignore the known fact that she wasn't *in* a cage for the whole time she was missing. You saw her with your own eyes, and now, this." She slid the photograph out from under Annie's splayed fingers and spun it around to face me.

Annie snatched back the impulse to chase it across the desk and stood up straight with a crack from her spine.

I took a deep breath, and, a lot more calmly than I felt, said, "It's called coercive control."

Jenny and Kevin narrowed their eyes in unison, but said nothing. I could feel a volatile bundle of anxiety working its way up my back. I knew I was going to either shout or cry. Why couldn't they see it? Why *wouldn't* they see it?

Annie could clearly feel the tension. She reached out and took the mug closest to her. "Is this one mine?" she asked.

Kevin glanced at her tersely and nodded.

"Thanks," she said, and sipped her coffee.

I wanted to punch Kevin, but instead I pulled my mug close and unwrapped a KitKat. Snapped off a finger. Bit off both ends. Dipped it like a straw and sucked a mouthful of hot coffee through it. Jenny watched me, bemused. "Try it," I said.

She shook her head. "I don't eat Nestlé products."

"Try it with a Crunchie."

"Penguins are best," Kevin said, but I ignored him.

"Just a thought," Annie said, "but Ali, you mentioned coercive control..."

I mirrored her earnest expression and nodded, suddenly hopeful that *someone* knew what I was getting at.

"Well..." she hesitated.

"Go on," I said, and slid the whole melted KitKat finger into my mouth.

She smiled and nodded and said, "Well, obviously I don't really know what I'm talking about, but is there a chance you've got it the wrong way around?"

I was fighting my gag reflex and trying to turn the finger in my mouth so I could bite it in half. I let Jenny ask her what she meant.

"I mean," she continued, "what if Erica wasn't working with him, but actually *he* was working with *her*?"

Jenny sat back in her chair and looked a question at Kevin. Kevin fired it straight at me as I tried to swallow some wafer. All I could do was shake my head.

"The thing is," Annie said, warming to her theme, "you told me you needed that picture because all you had relating to Fairey and Keith was the presence of that van at the crime scene. And from what you're saying, there's more evidence that proves Erica was walking around free all the time she was missing than that she wasn't. So what have you actually got on this Reed character? What can you prove *he* did? You've got, what, some CCTV of his van close to where one of those girls went missing?" She leaned in and spun the photo to face me. "But it doesn't tell you who was *driving it*, does it?"

Well, despite the shiver running through me, I could answer that one. "He attacked me," I said. "And he cut Eli Diaz's throat so deep he almost decapitated him. *That's* what we've got on him."

Annie considered that for a few moments while I silently willed her to get onside, though I knew deep down she wasn't going to. I'd sat beside her as she'd cross-referenced maps and input location data into the ViPER system. She'd hit a string of incorrect keys and had to back out again, copied the wrong set of coordinates and caused an error. To be honest I'd had little confidence in her ability to find anything, even if there were anything to be found.

"I'm sorry," she'd said. "I wasn't expecting to be doing this today. It's been a while."

"They sprung it on you, huh?" I'd laughed, trying to make her feel more at ease.

"Well, sort of. I got my emails mixed up, thought I was here for something else. Guv insists he left me voicemails, but I don't know where. Not on my phone at any rate. So, yeah, surprise secondment. Change of plan." She'd stopped short of expressing her displeasure at the situation, but I'd known it was burning bright.

"Same old story," I'd said. "I came in here one morning and the first thing my old DCI said was, 'You're not working with Fairey anymore.' Guess that was no bad thing, though, considering."

We'd shared a moment's silence then, while we'd waited for ViPER to do whatever it is that ViPER does. And then it had thrown up a spreadsheet of results from the list of plates Annie had entered for the locations she'd selected. Or *result*, to be more precise. One result, with a pin-sharp image attached.

I'd sucked in my breath and held it there until I saw stars, desperately trying to make sense of it, scrabbling for the words I was going to use to mitigate it in front of Jenny.

Annie, on the other hand, had visibly relaxed, and had looked a strange kind of satisfied when she'd set off for the printer.

Now, she quietly conceded my point and retreated into deep thought.

"Open mind," Jenny said. "That's what we all need to have on this. Right now, from where I'm sitting, it's clear that Erica was at least complicit in what happened to John and Julian, which obviously raises questions about what else she's been complicit in, and to what extent. We know that she assaulted both Kevin and you, Ali, and potentially would have killed you if it weren't for Reed's intervention. That in itself raises questions, given what we think happened immediately afterward, so the firs—"

"Wait," I said. "Wait wait wait. What do you mean, 'what we think happened'?"

"Okay," she said, as Kevin uttered a little dry cough beside me. "What we *know* is that there was one other person besides you in the room when Eli was killed. What we *think* is that that person was Reed."

I stopped breathing again. She couldn't be, could she? She couldn't be suggesting that anyone other than That Man was responsible for what happened to Eli and me? Surely?

I sensed three pairs of eyes swivel toward Erica's face in the photograph on the desk, and had to swallow the scream that rose in my throat. "You're fucking joking, aren't you?" I said.

"Ali," Kevin began, "Jen's just talking about what we can prove and what we can't—"

I was out of the room before he finished his sentence.

Annie found me in the car park, halfway through my third cigarette. She lit one of her own and stood beside me silently for a moment, not smoking it, just letting it burn. Eventually, she flicked an inch of ash onto the floor and took another inch in one long drag and stubbed it out with her heel and said, "I'm sorry if I pissed you off."

I shrugged and shook my head. "This investigation is a joke anyway," I said. "Some days I feel like I'm the only one here trying to catch a serial killer."

"*Suspected* serial killer," she said.

I gave her a death stare as I finished my cigarette. She held it, but I could see the nervousness in her eyes. I didn't shout, but I did have a question. "Why are you so keen for him to be innocent?"

"What do you mean?" She shook another cigarette out of her packet and slipped it between her lips; offered me one, which I took.

"I mean I can't figure you out," I said, and let her light me up. "What's your angle? You've been in the incident room. You've been briefed on the case. What do you see when you look at all this? What's it all about, to you?"

"I..."

"Because to me, this is about at least four women in this county alone who are still missing, and it's about the man who abducted and murdered them. The same man who nearly killed me. But I saw your face in that meeting. You're ready to pin everything on a twenty-year-old girl who was kept in a cage for three months. Why?"

Annie blew smoke out of the corner of her mouth and shook her head. "I was just saying what I saw," she said. "I didn't mean anything by it. The evidence is what it is, that's all."

I ignored her, because frankly I was angry with everyone and everything and it wouldn't have mattered what she'd said at that point. "I'll tell you why," I spat, and she flinched noticeably but I told her anyway. "Because the fucking media take a man like this and they paint him as some kind of dark fucking folk hero, all sexy and mysterious, and they give him a cool-sounding name that everyone'll remember for years after they've forgotten the names of all the poor girls he raped and tortured and cut into pieces, because you know what? Nobody likes a rapist or a murderer, do they, but everyone loves a serial killer. Everyone wants the handsome, charming psycho to get away with it in the end, and if he doesn't, well, they'll just write him love letters in prison, or write a fucking book about him. And meanwhile, where's Sarah Abbott? Where's Kerry Farrow? Sam Halloran? Caroline Grey? Where are they, Annie? Who the fuck cares about them?"

I don't know what I expected her to say, so when she took a long drag on her cigarette and threw it on the ground and said, "You don't know anything about me," it didn't really take me aback.

I just squeezed my throbbing temples and blew out the hot, furious breath from my lungs and said, "Right. Well, all you need to know about me is that I'm going to prove That Man is a killer, with or without anyone's help."

"I believe you," she said, which was more than I could say to myself. I'd seen the same evidence she had, after all. "But I also believe Erica Shaw isn't as innocent as you want her to be."

Ouch.

"DI Riley said to tell you she's calling a press conference naming her as a suspect. She wants to talk to you in her office."

I waited for my heart to finish sinking, then stopped Annie as she turned to walk away. "You're right," I said. "I don't know anything about you. I'm sorry for shouting."

"It's alright," she shrugged. "It's bloody frustrating to believe something so strongly and have no one want to listen to you. Just...don't assume things about me. Please."

I nodded.

"To be honest," she said, "I reckon Riley's a bit of a wet blanket and I think she'd struggle to catch a cold. But then I don't know anything about her, either."

I met her wink with a smile, and said, "Annie, I know I don't really deserve it, but could you do me a favor?"

"Put the kettle on?"

"Ha, no," I said, although I'd have loved one. "Just...if she asks, could you tell her you didn't see me?"

Annie got a twinkle in her eye right then. That was when I knew I was going to like her—when she twinkled and smirked and slipped back in through the fire escape. It was also when I knew she was going to be trouble.

CHAPTER 12

I had five missed calls from Jenny by the time I got to Erica's house, and two voicemails, which I had no intention of listening to. As much as I could have used some information, I didn't need the questions or arguments that would come with it. Instead, I followed the sat nav to the address I'd pulled via my laptop in the car park, and checked my scribbled notes on the doorstep.

Van/Fairey. Press conference. Erica guilty?

The door opened as I rang the bell, and I was met by a face I recognized from a photograph in a newspaper, or from some other press conference on TV, or perhaps from the dark eyes I'd studied in school photos, and glimpsed in That Man's hallway, and that had bored into my own in the desperate fight before Erica's flight.

"Mrs. Shaw?" I knew she'd long been remarried, but I wanted to see how she'd react to her daughter's name. She frowned and shifted on her slippered feet, subtly but noticeably enough, broadening her shoulders and filling a little more of the door frame. Interesting.

"Formerly," she said.

I held out my ID, mostly to show her I wasn't a reporter. "I'm Detective Sergeant Green," I told her, discreetly checking I was right about that as I folded my wallet. "I've got some news about Erica that I'd like to share with you, if I may."

I expected to see a flicker of fear on her face, some sign that she assumed the worst of a lone female officer solemnly bearing news of a missing daughter. But there was none. She simply stared into me for a long moment, watching me toss my gaze over her shoulder a few times to signal my wish to talk inside, before finally sighing and narrowing herself and stepping aside to let me through the door. "You'd better come in, then," she said, quite aggressively loud in my ear as I squeezed past.

She gestured me through to a living room that had at one time been generously spacious, back in the days before every inch of wall that wasn't obscured by an oversize leather couch was hung with shelf upon shelf of brass ornaments. Brass kettles and brass figurines. Horse brasses and brass horses. Brass plates and brass…fish? It was so far from my own taste that I can't even think of a tasteful way to describe it. Quite honestly, it was brassy as fuck.

"Can I get you anything? Tea? Coffee? Sorry, I've forgotten your name already."

Sunglasses. "Coffee would be great," I smiled. "My name's Ali."

She held out her hand, all but covered by the sleeve of her jumper in spite of the heat, and I shook it. Her grip was weak and slippery. "I'm Carla, by the way. How do you have it?"

I knew that, of course, because I'd looked it up earlier and read it back to myself on the doorstep, but it only now occurred to me to wonder if her own mother, or perhaps her sister if she had one, was named Paula, or Edwina, or…well,

I couldn't think of another one, but, "White, no sugar," because maybe that was how I had my coffee now, I wasn't sure.

She was gone for five minutes, during which time I sat on the squeaky couch and stared at brass things and tried to think of more girls' names that were just boys' names with an *a* on the end. I remembered one, and then eventually I came up with Philippa, by which time I'd forgotten the first one again and Carla was back with the coffee.

"So," she said, perching delicately beside me on the edge of her seat. "You said you had some news."

She quite obviously knew I wasn't there to tell her that her daughter was dead. I wondered how as I blew across the top of my coffee and nodded, took a sip and had an instant craving for doughnuts. I'd probably have to stop at McDonald's on the way back. "Is your husband home, Carla?" I asked.

She looked a little startled at the question, but she kept her voice in check as she answered: "No, he's at work. Which is for the best, I think, considering how you lot treated him when Erica—" She paused and took a breath, offered a polite smile. "He's still a bit sore about being suspected of...you know."

I watched her rub a spot on her forearm with the faintest trace of a wince. "Of course," I agreed, and wrote *Abusive husband* in my notebook at an awkward angle so that she couldn't see it. "Erica has a sister, too, doesn't she?"

She bowed her head in a half nod. "Charlotte," she said, and nothing else, which I took to mean she wanted to say more. I wrote that down, too. Also, bang went my theory, although... Charlie?

"And Charlotte's working as well, or...?"

"So she says."

"You don't think so?"

"I just know she doesn't like spending time here."

"Why not?"

"I don't know. It's not… This hasn't been the happiest home lately, you know?"

"Sure," I agreed. "When did you last see her?"

"Yesterday morning. She slept here last night, but she crept in after I was asleep and left again before I got up."

"And when did you last speak to Erica?"

She started to say something that began with "Sh—" then caught herself without an answer and so just flapped her mouth at me, just for a second, just long enough for me to know for sure that she was going to lie.

"She hasn't been in touch," she said finally.

"Since when?"

"At all. Look, Miss… Ali, what's this about?" Flustered. Flushed. Pants on fire.

I gave it to her straight. "Some new evidence has come to light," I said. "My boss is going to hold a press conference, probably this afternoon, where she's more than likely going to offer a reward for information leading to Erica's arrest on suspicion of the murder of two of my colleagues."

I drank some more coffee while I let that sink in. I wished I'd asked for sugar.

"Now," I said, watching Carla's jaw clench and unclench and the vein throb in her temple. "To be honest, I don't think she did it, either, but I'm in the minority. And to be fair, the evidence looks compelling, and I do have to wonder whether I'm just trying to convince myself she's innocent for some bizarre and unfathomable reason, because she did technically point a gun at my head and pull the trigger at one point. So what I'm saying is, I need your help, Carla. And by help, I mean don't bullshit me."

A spark of recognition. "You're the one," she said. "The one who got hurt."

"I just want to help her out of the mess she's in," I replied.

She closed her eyes, and then covered her face with her hands, and when she took them away and opened her eyes again they were brimming with tears. "I don't know where she is," she whispered.

"That's not what I'm asking," I said. "I'm asking when you last heard from her, and secondary to that, how you get in touch with her."

She started to shake then, and sob, and repeat herself over and over: "I don't know where she is. I swear I haven't heard from her. I don't know where she is. Please believe me. I haven't heard from her." And so that's how I came to hold Erica's mother for a full half an hour while she soaked my shoulder in snot and tears and my sugarless coffee got cold and, once again, I came perilously close to wetting myself.

I could hear Carla loading the dishwasher downstairs when I came out of the bathroom, so of course I checked out Erica's bedroom. There was, though, nothing remotely remarkable or even unexpected about it. It was just a room, with a plain old made-up bed, and a plain old bookcase full of plain old kids' books and pulp paperback adventure stories, and a plain old dresser displaying a small collection of swimming trophies—aha, I was right!—and a plain old wardrobe, and a thin layer of dust on every surface.

So I left. Carla wasn't going to tell me anything, including where to find Charlotte, so there was no sense in me sticking around. I thanked her for the coffee, and gave her my card, which she earnestly promised to use if she heard anything, and asked her the quickest way to get to Sarah Abbott's house so that I didn't have to go online and pull the address.

And so here I was, standing in the overgrown driveway of the Abbott family home—the last place Sarah was seen alive.

The place for which Erica had set out on the morning they both disappeared.

Nobody was home. I leaned on the bell for a while, but no one came, no dog barked, nothing happened. I peered in through the front window into a living room lined with framed photographs and certificates and greetings cards with curled edges, but devoid of any signs of life, except for the thick cobwebs hanging at both far corners of the ceiling.

I turned and surveyed the street, which was as lifeless as the Abbott house. Nobody walking dogs, or hosing down cars, or scrubbing barbecues. Just a drab smattering of newly built houses, uniform in their deliberate differences and looking about as lived-in as the show home at the end of the road. This was truly a place where dreams came to die.

The thought made me shudder, and as I turned back to face the house, I realized that those words felt true. That gnawing twinge at the bottom of my back? That was the knowledge that Sarah Abbott had died in this house.

There was a wooden gate to the side, which led around to the garden. It wasn't locked, so I let myself in and edged past a border of thistles to get a look at the kitchen window. It was a tip inside; the draining board was piled high with dishes that, in my estimation, probably weren't salvageable. The windowsill was covered in empty plastic bottles and dead flies. On the calendar on the wall, it was still snowing.

Wherever the Abbots were, they hadn't been here in a long time.

I picked my way around to the rear of the house. The garden was a no-go; it was thigh-high with weeds and nettles, and there was no back gate—just a high brick wall, probably a foot taller than me, with what looked like woodland beyond. I thought about trying to beat a path around the edge of the plot and hoiking myself up for a look, but I figured it would be easier to just drive round, so I lit a cigarette instead and stared at the pattern in the frosted toilet window.

I quickly deduced that the pattern was random. But what most definitely was not random was the series of notches in the wooden frame below the window latch. They were marks from a screwdriver, or perhaps a small pry bar, used to jimmy the window open from the outside.

I took out my phone and snapped a photo, then curled my fingers around a corner of the window and gave it a tug. It didn't open, but it moved far enough against the latch to be able to get a tool to it.

I slipped back around to the kitchen window and cupped my hands around my eyes to pick out the motion sensor at the corner of the ceiling, draped in silk with what looked like a dead spider hanging from it.

I couldn't see one in the living room, but I guessed it would make sense for it to be above the window. There was, however, an alarm box secured to the wall above the front door—white, to match the paint.

I made a note of the company name on the front of the box—*Abbott alarm activations?*—and stepped back through the gate to get another look at those gouges in the window frame. By then, my cigarette had burned down between my lips and was making my throat sore, so I tossed it to the ground and crushed it underfoot.

I spotted something then: a sliver of a particular shade of yellow that fired a flash of recognition and stopped me in my tracks. It wasn't quite a memory—more of a feeling, the way sounds and smells and colors can sometimes whisk you away to some other time and place. In this case, the incident room at police headquarters.

I crouched down on my haunches and peered under the plastic ledge below the kitchen door, and let a wave of curiously thrilling dread wash over me as I realized what I was looking at.

It was a plastic tag, about two inches in length, rectangular, narrowing to a blunt point at one end, where a small hole was punched through the plastic. The tip had sheared off, opening out the hole and separating it from the split ring I could only presume had once been attached. And on the flank of the tab was a window, behind which was a slip of once-white paper, wrinkled and discolored by damp.

On the paper, I could just make out the faint outline of a handwritten number. *18*, it said.

I banged my head on the door handle as I shot to my feet. Somehow, I managed to get my phone out of my pocket, and return Jenny's seventh call, and not let her get a word in before I said, "I'm at Sarah Abbott's house and you need to get a CSI team back out here right fucking now."

Then I hung up, because I figured I'd get away with it, and because I couldn't quite articulate that the collection of keys we'd recovered from That Man didn't fit rental properties or remote cabins with cages underneath them, or anything else he might own. They weren't his keys at all.

They were trophies.

MEANWHILE...

Carla turned the dishwasher on, and then she filled the kettle and switched that on, too, and she got a fresh mug from the cupboard, and wiped a smudge from the rim with a tea towel, and poured in a finger of full-fat milk, and added a pyramid tea bag from the box on the counter, and shoveled in two heaped teaspoons of sugar.

She knew, of course, that her daughter was innocent of the crimes of which she'd just heard her accused. That was, after all, her duty as a parent, wasn't it? It was immaterial whether she'd committed them or not.

There was, however, a fly in that particular ointment, and he'd be home in a few hours.

Erica and her stepfather had never seen eye to eye. She didn't like his temper, which, objectively, as she stood here alone with her thoughts, Carla had to concede was fair. As much as she told herself otherwise, as much as he made things up to them afterward, as sorry as he always was—and he was always sorry, she truly believed that—he could get a little bit stressed at times.

And Carla knew that wasn't her fault. She did know that, now, here, without his snarling face an inch from hers, without his hands twisting her flesh into a patchwork of blood blisters, without his pale, beer-sweaty body pummeling hers as she lay silently, biting her lip to stop herself from crying out in pain lest it upset him even more. She *knew* it wasn't her fault.

But then, she was still here, wasn't she? And she still said sorry every time she put too much salt on his chips, or missed a crease when she ironed his shirt, or made eye contact with a stranger in the street.

She still got in the car with him, still sat quietly beside him, listening to his ragged, furious breath as he drove her home to show her who her husband was, to make her picture that stranger in her head while he pinched her and bit her and fucked her on the floor. And she still held him afterward, when he cried and told her how sorry he was, and how much he loved her, and how much pressure he was under. She still said, "I know, baby. It's okay. I know." So really, in spite of what she knew to be right and proper and true, who *did* she have to blame?

Who did she have to blame when he hit Erica?

Who did she have to blame when Erica walked in to see him biting a chunk out of her mother's arm?

Who did she have to blame, really, when Erica stabbed him in the backside with the kitchen scissors and ended up in court?

Who would she have to blame this time, when he found out there was a reward to be had and set about beating the truth out of her?

The kettle boiled. Carla poured the water and squeezed the tea bag to the color of a digestive, and stirred it for fifteen stirs and threw the spoon into the sink.

She carried the mug by the rim, the way she'd read she

ought for the best chance not to spill it. Out of the kitchen, into the hall, up the stairs, carefully, one at a time. Onto the landing. She opened the door to Erica's room, and set the mug down on the dresser beside Erica's medals. She breathed in the stale dust, and opened the window to let in some fresh air.

Then she sat on the end of Erica's bed, with tears spilling again from her eyes, and she blinked up at the hatch in the ceiling just outside the door, and she said, "Erica, honey, you can come down now. The coast is clear."

EPISODE 3

CHAPTER 13

"I don't care if you did it. You know that. I mean..." Carla scraped her free hand, the one that wasn't clasping her daughter's like her life depended on it, through her hair, and swiped the tears roughly from her cheeks. "I mean, of course I care, but what I'm saying is, I love you no matter what, and I'll always support you. You're my little girl, you'll always be my little girl, and whatever's happened, whatever you've done, whatever that...whatever he made you do, I'm going to help you get through it, okay? You understand? Whatever happens, it's all okay. You know that, right, sweetie? You know I'm here and I'll help you?"

Erica studied her mother as she trembled and sobbed and sniffed beside her on the hot, uncomfortable leather sofa, and knew as well as Carla did that her promises, while sincere, were hollow. But she nodded, and said, "I know, Mum." Which lack of a denial caused Carla to curl in on herself and sob even harder.

"Oh G-God," she stuttered. "My little..." And that was all she could manage. She was too winded to speak, and too small and broken to reach out and stroke Erica's poor, lost face, so she just cried for the happy, bouncy little girl who got ice cream everywhere but in her mouth, and giggled when a butterfly landed on her knee, and spent hours on end trying to teach herself to tie a shoelace while singing all the songs from *The Little Mermaid*.

Erica watched her calmly, squeezing her fingers and not knowing what to do or say any more than her mother did. She tried to feel something—anything, her brain frantically flicking through its catalog of emotional responses to try to find one that fit, and coming up empty. That was when she knew—really knew—that she was on her own. That she was the only one she could rely on to fix things. That she was no longer the child she could see Carla mourning right in front of her.

And with that realization came a dilemma. Because Erica had walked into her mother's house with a plan—a plan to set her free, to make her safe, to rid her of the tyranny of her monster of a husband once and for all. But as she sat here now, watching the tears wash the concealer from the bruise on Carla's cheekbone, she saw her plan for the childish fantasy it really was.

The rational, grown-up part of her brain knew there was a right way to do it—an official way that was going to require research and phone calls and outside help. But not only was that not going to happen before five o'clock, it was also going to get her caught. And if she got caught, she was never going to make things right for herself, or for Sarah, or Kerry, or those policemen, or Rachel, or anyone else.

Erica screwed her eyes tight against the incoming wave of pressure in her head, and let go of her mother's hand, and reached out blindly to pull her close to her.

"I'm not a murderer, Mum," she whispered, but she had her fingers crossed tight behind Carla's back.

* * *

At 3:15 p.m., while Sandra Gaidamaviciene was securing the Abbott house and Annie Fisher was swigging vodka from a hip flask in the stairwell at police headquarters, Erica's stepfather was looking down Chloe Kimble's blouse as she slipped her ring-binder and pencil case and smooth-spined copy of *Hobson's Choice* into her rucksack.

It wasn't that he had any particular interest in what was down there; it was more that Chloe's plunging neckline was the only class note Jack Carnahan had left for him when he'd agreed to cover his first-year GCSE English class.

He'd long known Carnahan was a little on the pervy side; in fact, he'd reported more than one off-color remark to the department heads in this, his first year of faculty, but evidently they were unconcerned as long as he was keeping his hands to himself. *No need to rock the boat, Richard. We keep our eyes open, don't you worry.*

But he did worry. There was definitely something not quite right about Jack Carnahan, so as the rest of the class filed wearily out of the room, he guided Chloe to one side—without touching her, of course—and suggested that she might want to think about doing up a couple more buttons during school hours.

Five-foot, nine-inch Chloe craned her neck to look up at the gangly, beardy nerd with his shirt tucked into his supermarket jeans and just laughed and fluttered her lashes. "No one else seems bothered, sir."

That round went to Chloe. She'd smelled blood, so tomorrow, of course, there'd be recriminations. Some of the more feral students would no doubt insinuate that he was a bumder, because he didn't want to look at a fifteen-year-old's breasts. But that was just part of the job, and he'd certainly been called worse in his time. He'd smile and soak it up, and teach his lessons well, and like every other day, he wouldn't show them even the slightest sign that they were getting to him. He'd bottle it up, just as he was now, and he'd keep the cork in until he was well away from here, well away from anyone who could do him any real harm.

At ease, thus, with his lot for now, Richard was relatively upbeat as he roughly packed his briefcase and headed for the staff room. He'd already plowed through the better part of his marking while he was babysitting Carnahan's class, so, factoring in gossip and waiting for the kettle to boil, he figured he'd be out of there by half past four, with a whole free evening ahead of him.

The first sign that might not be the case was the sudden solemn silence when he walked into the room. He was used to it in a couple of the pubs in town, the ones where everyone seemed to know and have an opinion about everyone else's business, but not here. Not that he'd been naive enough to believe that rumors didn't make it as far as the staff room; rather, given the apathy afforded to those surrounding Jack Carnahan, he simply assumed that no one cared.

That was his first thought as Tim and Peter and Alison frowned and looked away awkwardly—that somehow, some piece of tittle-tattle had found its way back to them. That everything had changed. That soon enough he'd be sitting in front of the school principal, negotiating a quiet parting of ways by mutual agreement. A glowing reference in return for his own discretion. A new job at a new school, two or three towns from home. He'd done it before; he could do it again.

But it wasn't that. It was something else. Something was wrong. He saw it in the sad smile from Theresa, the school secretary; in the nervous twitch of sympathy in her eyes as she struggled to look at him.

Richard dropped his briefcase at his feet in the doorway and tried to read the detail on Theresa's lined, doom-laden face, but to no avail.

"Richard," she said softly, quietly, a voice that reached out and placed a comforting hand on his arm.

"What is it? What's happened?" Fear rose in him fast, from the pit of his stomach up past his heart and into his throat, and he forced himself to spit out his logical conclusion before it reached his tongue. "My wife? Has something happened to Carla?"

"Oh, heavens, no." She was by his side then, figurative hand replaced with a literal one and an iPad shuffled into his field of view, browser open to the BBC homepage, Erica Shaw's passport photo staring sullenly at him from the screen. "Richard," she said, "it's your stepdaughter. She's all over the news."

Carla threw her phone onto the kitchen counter and took the stairs two at a time. "You need to get going," she panted, pain searing the ribs on her left side with every breath. "Richard's going to be home any minute."

Erica stood in the center of her bedroom, watching the garden that backed onto theirs. The cheerful American was out on the patio, playing with his toddler daughter in an inflatable paddling pool. He'd spoken to her a couple of times, but not about anything of substance and she'd never asked his name. His wife was in the air force, that was all she knew. "I don't care," she said.

"Erica, please. I don't know how he'll be if he finds you here, not now, not until he's calmed down and I've talked to him."

"I've got nowhere to go. I can't live in a bloody car." Erica could see the fear building in her mother's eyes as they flitted to her watch and back. "Mum, I'm not scared of Richard."

Carla laughed, a hollow, ridiculous whinny that made Erica's teeth stand on edge. "Well, you should be," she said. "You're not safe here. I've put the spare key to Dad's caravan in your bag, and some more money for food and petrol, butane, whatever you need. No one'll find you. Stay there, just until we get this mess sorted out, right?"

"You want me to go *camping*?"

"Erica, sweetheart." Her breaths were coming short and sharp now, the fear and pain spreading a toothy grimace across her face. "He can't find you here. You know what he's like. He—"

"So come with me."

"Erica, I can't c—"

"I'll make sure he won't find us."

"Of course he'll find us. He *always* finds me."

"No, Mum." Erica fixed her with a hard stare. "I'll *make sure* he doesn't."

More tears, pooling in the corners of Carla's eyes, trembling with the rest of her but not quite managing to fall. "Please," she said. "Erica, that's not the sort of thing I want to hear from my daughter when she's trying to convince me she's not a murderer."

Erica's breath caught in her throat, she guessed to keep her heart from leaping out of it. She studied Carla's face for some sign of regret; gave her a second or two to backpedal. She didn't, though. "Convince you?" she said finally.

"Erica—"

"*Convince* you!"

"Please, Erica—" Carla threw her arms across her face as her daughter advanced on her, the switch in her mind flipped in a heartbeat—blank, locked, dark, all of its focus on withstanding the blows that she knew were coming. That she knew she deserved.

"Christ on a fucking bike," Erica sighed as she brushed past her on her way to the stairs. "I've seen it all now."

She was halfway down when she saw the shadow fall across the frosted glass in the door and heard the key ratchet into the lock. She froze in place, sensing her mother on the top step, calculating the distance to the bottom versus the time it would take the door to swing open. By the time she realized it was too late, it was too late. Her exits were blocked. Carla behind her, a wall to her left, an awkward fall onto the TV cabinet to her right.

The only advantage she had left was height, and as the door opened, she coiled herself like a rattlesnake and prepared to use it.

CHAPTER 14

"Ali, it's Jen. I don't know where you are. Can you call me, please?"

"Ali, if you're in the building somewhere, can you get back to my office? I need a word, and then I need you to go and talk to Carla Cockburn before I release a statement. Uhh... okay."

"For fuck's sake, Ali, you'd better not be pulling some stupid shit on me right now. This isn't any time to be going rogue. Will you please just bloody ring me back."

"Ali, it's me again. I'm getting worried now. Seriously, don't fuck about. If you're getting this, you need to ring me and let me know you're alright."

Starting to panic. Where are you? Let me know you're alive x

"Do you know how close I was to putting a BOLO out on you?"

"Jen, I was out of touch for an hour and a half."

"Yeah, and you could have been out of the county in the back of a van by then. Are you out of your fucking mind?"

It was a fair question. If I'm honest, at that point I wasn't even sure I knew the answer. "Alright," I said, trying not to let it sound like *Shut up*. "You're right. I'm sorry, I didn't think."

"Well, I don't buy that, but whether you thought about it or not, you disappeared on duty, so now I know you did so of your own volition, you can consider this a bollocking."

"Understood."

"Right. Now bring me up to speed. What's going on with the Abbotts?"

Well, that was the question. I rested against the bonnet of my car and looked over at Sandra, who was similarly recumbent against the CSI van, eating a wilted sandwich. "I don't know what to tell you. None of the neighbors have seen them in weeks," I said. "Or months, depending on who you ask. The place looks pretty much abandoned so I know I shouldn't jump to any conclusions about a break-in, but from what I can see through the windows, nothing obvious has been disturbed, downstairs at least. And more to the point, the house is alarmed, so if it's wired through to us, and it hasn't been activated, then that might suggest it was broken into while someone was home. And if that's the case—if it was broken into while Sarah was home alone, and if the keys really are trophies—then the key tag fits with our guy having taken her from the house and then gone back later, either to clean up, or for some other reason, like maybe gathering DNA to plant in Boon's flat." I let that sit for a couple of seconds, half expecting her to counter with *Or maybe Erica did*, but she just *hmmm*ed, so, "Sandra's lifted a handful of prints but I'm not hopeful about that. My gut says we'll find what we're looking for inside, so the sooner we get a warrant to go in there, the better."

"Yeah, I'm working on that. In the meantime, Kevin's trying to contact family. Passport check is ongoing. I'll send someone to relieve you at the house, there's no point you standing around there waiting. Your priority right now is finding Erica."

"Any response to the appeal yet?"

"I've got—" I could hear her clicking her fingers, trying to remember "—Annie and a couple of floaters answering the phones. Just the usual crackpots so far, nothing to get excited about. Where are we with Carla Cockburn?"

That was the second time she'd said that name. Who the hell was Carla Cockburn? I scraped my nail across the bottom of my phone and said, "Sorry, you broke up then."

"Can you hear me now?"

"Yeah."

"Where did you get to with her mum?"

Oh, yeah, *Carla.* "Says she hasn't heard from her."

"Do we believe her?"

"No, she's bullshitting."

"What about her husband?"

"He wasn't there."

"When's he due back? He's a teacher, right?" (Fucked if I know.) "Get back around there. Rile him up, he hates it when we question him. I'll get local uniform to assist in case you need to bring them both in, so sit tight for, what, half an hour? That'll give Kevin time to get there. By the time you're done with the Cockburns, you should be able to get into the Abbott house and see what's what."

It was going to be a long evening. My heart dropped, and a wave of anxiety broke over me, bringing down the emergency shutters on my cooperative mood. "Not Kevin," I said before I could stop myself.

A sigh broke the long silence at the other end of the phone. "What's going on between you two?" she asked.

"What do you mean?" Stalling for time.

"You've been giving each other dirty looks since yesterday. What's the story?"

I braced myself. "What's he said?"

"Nothing, I haven't asked him, but you've clearly pissed each other off. If there's some kind of personal issue here, you need to nip it in the bud right now."

"It's not that," I said, although I didn't know what to tell her it *was* without actually telling the truth. And if she knew that Kevin had seen what was going on in my head and immediately ceased to trust me, I'd be off the team in a heartbeat. "It's just..." Oh God, was I really about to throw him under the bus? It was like kicking a puppy; it wasn't his fault there was shit on the rug. "I..."

I don't know whether Jen sensed that I was about to drop Kevin in it, or whether she just got bored of waiting, but she interrupted me with, "You know what, it's actually fine. Kevin's got a lot of case knowledge that I could use right here at the moment." Dammit, I wish I'd thought of that one. "What do you need?"

I could answer that. "A fresh pair of eyes," I said. "And preferably someone who hasn't met Erica or whatever-his-name-is or been hit over the head by either of them. I'm tired and emotional, so I need someone calm and analytical."

I almost thought I could hear her narrow her eyes as she wondered what the hell I was up to. It was definitely there in her voice when she asked, "Youuuu...want me to send the analyst?"

I didn't bother telling her that I thought there was something not quite right about the analyst, or that I wasn't sure whether that made me want to keep a close eye on her or just feel comfortable having her around. I just said, "Yes, good idea. Send Annie. I think she could be a big help."

It was an hour before Annie arrived, by which time I'd been to the supermarket, which was air-conditioned, and bought ice creams for myself and Sandra, and a *Kerrang!* she'd asked for, and also some carrot sticks because all I'd eaten all day was sugar.

We were relaxing on the overgrown front lawn in the blistering late-afternoon sun, Sandra teasing me by running through a list of the year's greatest rock acts to see how many I'd heard of. She told me about a Japanese pop-metal band who sang a song about chocolate, which for some reason she thought might appeal to me. I felt a tiny bit insulted, but I knew I shouldn't and so pretended not to. Then Annie pulled up in a white 5-Series BMW with tinted back windows, and stood at the curb tugging at her shirt collar and blowing her fringe around.

"You got promoted fast," I said. "That's the DCI's car."

She looked at it with a shrug and joined us on the grass. "I guess it's DI Riley's now," she said. "There weren't any pool cars left. It's nice, but it took me ten minutes to work out how to start it."

"I guess you couldn't turn the heater off, either," I noted, watching a bead of sweat roll over her slick brow and drop into her breast pocket. "Sandra, this is Annie Fisher. Annie's our new analyst." (Our Annielyst?) They gave each other one of those awkward circular waves, the ones children give the first time they meet, when they're forced to play together because their respective parents want some alone time. "She knows how the computers work," I laughed, patting the grass beside me. "Sorry, I just realized… Annie Analyst."

Annie smirked and sat down. I got that subtle whiff of booze again. Booze and peppermint. "So what are we doing?" she asked.

Sandra held up her magazine. "Music lesson," she said, the lolly stick between her teeth accentuating her elongated Slavic vowels. "Alisha doesn't know nothing about anything. She think Foo Fighters is a cartoon and *Powerpuff Girls* is a band. Annie, you like rock, yes?"

Annie shifted uncomfortably and shrugged and scratched the base of her ponytail. "I don't know," she laughed. "I've got a lot of guilty pleasures, mostly."

Sandra affected a frown and shook her head, fine jet-black hair whipping about her face. "No such thing," she said. "Pleasure is pleasure. Never feel bad for liking what you like."

I thought of Edith. A twinge darted through my belly.

"Unless, you know, is illegal or whatever," she added.

"Wait a minute," I said. "I told you I liked a Céline Dion song once, and you wouldn't look at me for a week."

Sandra sighed and rolled her eyes. "I don't say you can't like it," she said. "I just was sick of hearing you singing it. It sound like an angry cat."

I looked at Annie, who was staring at her feet and smiling the game smile of a newly included outsider, not yet grasping the rules of the group, just keeping her head down, not drawing attention to herself. I imagined she was working pretty hard to keep that smile going. It's not easy being the new girl, especially when the personal questions start flying. "Not being funny, Sandra," I said, "but—"

"What else is new?"

Oh, ha ha. "Right, that's it," I said. "We're not friends anymore. Annie, you've got two minutes to start the car. We're going to go annoy Erica's stepdad."

"Finally," Sandra smirked. "Someone else gets a turn."

★ ★ ★

I didn't fill Annie in on Richard Cockburn's disdain for the police, or on the rumors surrounding his attitude to women in general. "Remember," I told her. "Be the fresh pair of eyes you are. Listen. If anything sounds like it doesn't make sense, speak up. Press it. Interrupt. Stress him out. Okay?"

"I can do that," she nodded. Her eyes were a little glassy, I thought. Maybe she was tired. She seemed alert enough, though, and I wasn't sure I could smell spirits anymore. The few words she'd spoken on the short drive to Carla's had been lucid and clear. She'd had no problem operating the BMW, either, although once she'd mastered the right combination of feet on pedals and tilts of the electronic selector and actually got the thing in gear, it more or less drove itself.

That aside, there was only one other car in Carla's driveway, which I felt had also been the case earlier. Maybe we'd come back too early. That would be awkward. At any rate, I gave a thumbs-up to the two uniforms waiting in their patrol car three houses down, which they returned, and then leaned on the doorbell and nodded to Annie to thump on the door.

Inside, I could hear urgent footsteps on the stairs, and see Carla's fragmented silhouette descending through the frosted glass in the door. Annie took a step back.

"Where the h—" Carla stopped dead, the door swinging out of her hand and crashing against the corner table behind it.

Her hair looked like the birds had been at it. Two buttons were missing from her blouse. She had an angry red lump on the side of her forehead, and her nostrils were blocked with clotting blood.

CHAPTER 15

"I swear to God, I don't know anything!"

"Alright Carla, just calm down and tell me what happened. Did your husband do this to you?"

"No. No, no, it was an accident."

"What was? What did he do?"

"He didn't. I had an accident, it's nothing."

"Where is he now?"

"I don't know. He went out."

"Before or after you had the accident?"

"After. Look, I know what you're thinking, but it wasn't Richard, okay? He didn't do anything."

"It wasn't Richard?"

"No."

"So who was it?"

Carla just shook her head, her face crimson, her eyes squeezed tight. The living room was not as I'd left it; a lamp had been knocked off the table in the corner, and a couple of bits of brass tat had capsized on one of the shelves.

"DS Green?" Annie held up a phone she'd retrieved from the floor just inside the kitchen, its screen shattered and dark. "Carla, is that yours?"

She opened her eyes and glanced at the phone. Shook her head again. "No, his."

"Was that an accident, too?" I suggested.

No answer.

"Did he know we'd been here?"

A nod.

"Was he angry?"

"I..."

I waited. I heard Annie put the phone down on the worktop and pad through to loiter at the bottom of the stairs. "Mrs. Cockburn, sorry, long drive. Is there a bathroom upstairs?"

Carla cast an exasperated glance over my shoulder. Hesitated.

"He's been aggressive before, hasn't he?" I said.

"What?" She looked between me and Annie, and shook her head and nodded and waved a dismissive hand and said, "Look—Sorry, yes love, help yourself. Miss Green, I don't know—"

"Where is she, Carla? Where's Erica? I know you know. Stop lying to me now and you won't have to lie to me at the police station all night."

Her eyes flickered to the stairs, and darted back to mine just as fast. She clamped her jaw shut and carried on shaking her head.

"She's upstairs?"

"No!"

"Jesus Christ." I shot up off the sofa and bolted for the stairs, shouting for Annie.

"Back bedroom," came the reply.

I bounced off the wall at the top of the stairs and staggered onto the landing, where Annie was standing quite at ease in the doorway to Erica's room. "Is she here?" I gasped, a molten shard of pain searing through my thigh.

"No," she said. "But look."

I squeezed around her to see where she was pointing. On Erica's dresser, which a few hours earlier had held only trophies, there now stood a pair of mugs. One white and empty, one blue with a finger of tea in the bottom and a faint lipstick mark on the rim.

"Carla Cockburn," I said, "I'm arresting you on suspicion of assisting an offender. You don't have to say anything, but it may harm your defense if you fail to mention when questioned anything you later rely on in court. Do you understand?" By the time I'd finished saying it, she was sobbing. "Carla, listen to me. I'm having you taken into custody. A doctor's going to look at your face when you get there. If you know where Richard and Erica are, then you might as well tell me now and save us both some time."

A pause. Tears streaming. "They're not together. He knows you were going to Sarah's. I think he might have gone to find you."

"To find me?"

She nodded.

"What, to punch me, too? Why was he looking for me, Carla?"

"Because..."

"Say it."

"I can't."

"Did Erica hit you?"

Her breath hitched and she choked on whatever was trickling down the back of her throat. I let her cough it out.

"She hit you by accident? Was she trying to defend you?"

She shut down again. "I can't help you," she said. "You

can't make me help you. My daughter's a lot of things but she's *not* a murderer!"

"Annie, can you get the guys from outside in here, please."

"Yep." She handed me a framed photograph from beside the television: Carla and two people I hadn't met—a teenage girl and a tall man with thinning hair and wire-rimmed glasses who looked like a geography teacher. Erica, I noted, was conspicuously absent.

"Richard's not going to back you up on this, is he, Carla? His phone's broken, so he's gone to tell me in person that she was here, hasn't he?"

She looked at the picture in my hands and just sobbed. I wasn't going to get another word out of her.

"Fine," I said. And then I felt like shit, because I knew damn well I hadn't spoken to her right. I let myself soften and shrink, sat back down beside her and took her shaking hand in mine. "Hey," I said, as unthreateningly as I could that she could still hear me over her own misery. I forced her to meet my eyes, and gave her my best impression of a tender smile, and said, "I'm going to help you, Carla. I'm going to make sure you're safe from harm. But you need to trust me, and you need to help me, too. Okay?"

I all but heard her heart break inside her chest. We both knew she was never going to trust me.

"I c-can't," she cried. "She's my daughter. You know I can't help you."

And that was the truest thing she'd ever say to me.

"Sandra, is anyone there with you?"

Sandra hesitated a second at the other end of the phone, then said, "No. Why?"

"Have you been there since I left?"

"Pretty much."

"You haven't been there the whole time?"

"I'm not a bloody elephant, you know. I need to pee sometimes."

"Yeah, I—" Christ, I was really having tone problems today. "Sorry, no, I didn't mean it like that."

"I know," she chuckled. "I'm teasing. What's up?"

I was starting to feel tired now, and my head was getting fuzzy. I was going to start struggling to make sense of anything in little to no time. "I might be expecting a visitor, that's all. Richard Cockburn, Erica Shaw's stepfather. He's driving a..." I checked the notes Annie had scribbled in my book from the PNC inquiry she'd just called in. "A gray Volvo." I read out the registration number. "I'll text you a picture of him. If he turns up, can you ring me straight back?"

There was another moment of silence, and then she said, "Hang on a minute. I've seen this Volvo, I think." I listened to her phone rustle against her clothes, the door of the van slam, the clump of her Doc Martens on the driveway. "You there?"

"I'm here."

She repeated the registration back to me. "That's what you said?"

I rechecked my notes, and nodded. Then I remembered to say, "Yep," because she was on the phone and couldn't see me. For fuck's sake.

"Yeah, that car is right over there," she said, presumably pointing, and probably feeling just as stupid about it as I had. "He's inside, I think. You want talk to him?"

"Sure, put him on."

"Okay, please hold."

Boots on tarmac again. A passing car. Sandra, humming to herself. Birds, chirping. I heard her knock on the window, and gasp, and say, "Jesus Chr—" and then her phone clattered to the ground and all I could hear was panic.

I flung myself into the BMW and punched the starter, and flicked it into Drive, and shouted, "Call for backup!" And then Annie, who was sitting sidesaddle in the passenger seat on the phone to the office, reflexively pulled in her legs and let out a yelp as I mashed the accelerator into the carpet.

The Volvo was parked at the curb, one house away from the Abbotts'. I swung in diagonally behind it and was out of the car before it had stopped rocking, sweeping the street first of all for Sandra, who stood shakily from inside the CSI van and raised her phone-free hand, and then for anyone else. Nothing was moving, but I could hear sirens on the main road, heading for the estate.

"You okay?" I called.

Sandra nodded and barked something into her phone and hung up. "Inside the car," she said.

Right. I guessed this wasn't going to be pretty. "Annie," I said, my heart thumping with adrenaline and dread. "Get DI Riley on the line and keep her there." Which wasn't really necessary, but if Sandra was spooked, then I wanted Annie out of the way and focused on a task, rather than staggering around throwing up her liquid lunch all over a crime scene.

I took a breath. Listened to the sirens draw closer. Watched a tabby cat stroll casually across the road from the next house along and hop up onto the rim of an overfilled wheelie bin in the driveway opposite. It tucked its nose under the propped-up lid and had a good sniff, then assumed some kind of liquid form and poured itself in between the bags of rubbish and disappeared. I sniffed the hot air, thinking I might melt, too. The air smelled wrong. Bad. Dark.

I threw another glance back at Sandra, who just stood there beside the van and gave me a sad smile. And then I pressed my nails into my palms and clicked my heels together and walked to the driver's door of the Volvo.

The first thing I saw was blood. Lots and lots of blood. It streaked the windscreen and dripped onto the dashboard, like a can of it had been shaken up and opened. The tan-colored steering wheel was coated in a filmy residue, vivid red in patches, transparent in others where the blood had slid off and soaked into the driver's trousers.

The driver himself was sitting quite upright, his formal shoes still on the pedals, both hands lying palms-up at his sides. He was wearing his seat belt, for all the good it had done.

Richard Cockburn's throat had been cut, and cut deep.

"I saw the car arrive," Sandra said, close behind me now. "I didn't think anything of it. I heard the door slam but I didn't watch. I was there in the van and I didn't see a thing. I'm sorry I freaked out. I didn't expect it. I banged on the window and his fucking head fell off."

Which wasn't far from accurate. Whatever had sliced through his neck had only stopped when it had hit bone, and so that was all that connected his head to the rest of him. It had lolled onto his shoulder, leaving a clean cross-section but for a rough patch at the back where the weight of it falling had torn some flesh.

It was too familiar. The blood. All of the blood. The open, sloshing wound: vivid red muscle and yellow fat and dark, severed vessels, overflowing. It was the last thing I'd seen before I'd passed out on That Man's couch, and it was the last thing I'd seen every night and the first thing I'd seen every morning since. I'd seen it in those photographs on Jenny Riley's computer, from a mortuary table in Swansea. And now it was here, right in front of Sarah Abbott's house, an insult to add to the injury.

And more than that, it gave me a serious problem. Because I knew which way the fingers would point; Erica was Public Enemy Number One, a fugitive, wanted for the murder of at least two of my friends and colleagues. And even if she hadn't been the one wielding the knife, her troubled history with Richard was compelling.

I had my first real wobble right then. Because what if Annie had been right, back in Jen's office what now seemed like days ago? What if I'd got it all out of shape? What if everyone else was right and I was wrong? What if Erica was the one in the driving seat?

I let the thought trickle into the dark corners of my mind as I watched four patrol cars blast into the street, blue lights spinning furiously, sirens wailing. And then I dragged my hand across my face and wiped that shit clean like an Etch-a-Sketch, because whatever the truth about Erica, I had a much bigger problem to worry about.

I knew who'd made that cut, and it sure as hell wasn't Erica Shaw.

CHAPTER 16

Erica Shaw, as it turned out, *was* at that moment in the driving seat, of her late Nana's old Mercedes, heading northeast on the A11 at a steady seventy miles per hour. Within twenty minutes of Sandra's discovery, she was negotiating the beginnings of rush-hour traffic on the Norwich ring road, and forty minutes after that, having pit-stopped at a Tesco for fuel and a few basics, she was leaving the A149 at the top of its lazy inland loop and guiding the big old tank between hedgerows and farm gates, following the sat nav on her phone to the last place on Earth she wanted to go.

It had been a dozen years since she'd last made this trip, in the back of her dad's Éspace, watching *Toy Story 2* for the umpteenth time with Marie from school, and she recognized none of it—not the tunnels of trees, or the remote shack incongruously advertising windows and doors on a faded and splintered hand-painted sign, or the dilapidated old barn with the collapsed roof, or the pretty houses with roadside stalls selling speckled eggs and wildflowers and freshly cut asparagus.

Indeed, she only knew she'd arrived when, on the stroke

of six o'clock, the signs stopped pointing the way to Cart Gap and the road ran out.

In her mind, those summers were endless and epic and impossibly hot, hotter even than it was now as she stood with her back to the falling sun, gazing down the long, steep lifeboat ramp, the one landmark she thought maybe she did remember. The taste of their memory in her mouth, though, was a bitter one.

Her last trip had marked the end of the last summer she'd spent with her father before…what happened. Before people started talking in hushed tones around her, before her friends stopped coming over, before her father disappeared for three days and came back an alcoholic and, ultimately, before that Wednesday afternoon in December, the day before school broke up for the Christmas holiday.

That Wednesday had been a regular day, or at least what had come to pass for a regular day. Whispers behind her back. Huddles of girls she'd thought were her friends, parting in front of her, forcing her to walk between them, her face burning in the heat of their stares. Kids she didn't even know pushing in front of her in the lunch queue. Worst of all, the pitying looks of her teachers as, in every lesson, she sat beside an empty seat.

Marie was the only one who'd talked to her. She wondered now whether it was through guilt or shame or apology, or whether Marie was simply as baffled as she was. Because for all of their passive cruelty, the most hurtful thing those kids ever did was to never tell her what she'd done.

She'd pieced it together by now, of course. As an adult, reminiscing over brunch on a beautiful spring morning, she'd remembered it all as clearly as she could see it now, standing here at the top of the ramp. The five of them—Mum, Dad, her, Charlotte and Marie—traipsing down to the beach, arms weighed down with blankets and clothes and canvas windbreaks and coolbags full of bland sandwiches and packets of Wotsits and cartons of Um Bongo.

They'd walk for what seemed like miles along the beach, trying not to kick sand in anyone's face until they ran out of faces in which to kick it. Miles from the car. Miles from the toilet. If anyone needed a wee, they'd have to squat in a cave. Otherwise, she and Marie would paddle in the sea and skim pebbles and build intricate castles with separate rooms for their action figures, and then patiently build them again when Charlotte knocked them down with her spade, and Dad would wind Mum up while she was trying to read.

At midday, Dad would call lunch, and they'd all sit on the blanket together and eat their sandwiches, which would live up to their name no matter how careful they were. And afterward, Dad would announce that he was going to the ice cream van on the clifftop.

"Erica," he'd say. "I think you want a Cornetto."

She'd roll her eyes and sigh. "No, Dad, you know I want a Feast, like every time you ask."

"I do," Mum would say, and he'd give her two thumbs-up and put on his flip-flops and trample sand all over the blanket as he considered the three girls like it was the first time they'd been through this production.

"Marie. Come on, you can help me carry."

And off they'd go, in the opposite direction from the car, leaving Erica to help her mother put away the lunch things and clean the food off Charlotte's face, and twenty minutes later they'd reappear bearing ice creams, and Marie would always look a little bit scared.

Erica had never wondered until that spring morning how it had always taken them twenty minutes, and yet the ice cream was never melted when they got back. Or why, if the van was close enough for the ice cream not to melt, her dad didn't just park near it.

In any case, if what happened was anything to do with Marie, no one had ever uttered a word about it to Erica. If they ever did, she'd entertain the thought, but she wasn't going to hold her breath. Marie's family had moved to New Zealand, Carla was a master of keeping secrets, and Erica was too late to save her father by the time she found him in the garage, hanging from the rafters.

The lifeboat scrambled just before seven o'clock. It came down the ramp backward on a trailer attached to a blue tractor; a leviathan of a machine, articulated in the middle like an insect, rolling on ridged tires that were taller than Erica. Its grunting diesel engine belched foul breath through a pair of snorkels extended above the raised cab as it followed the boat and trailer into the sea, the volunteer crew wading in beside it to board and launch the vessel.

Erica sat in the shadow of the cliff, watching as the few remaining beachgoers began to drift away from the small crowd that had assembled to watch the action. The tide was coming in and a chill had cut through the air, setting her shivering. The spectators were still in sunlight, just, and dressed for it, save for one or two who'd draped towels over their shoulders. Children ran between their parents' legs, chasing each other in circles, stumbling through abandoned sandcastles and falling in holes.

After twenty minutes or so, the boat returned exactly as it had departed, with no drama and with only its crew on board. The tractor, left napping on the sand, barked into life in a pall of black smoke, and a shoreman urged the crowd to take a few paces back as it began to slide the trailer back into the water.

Within moments, both tractor and trailer were all but submerged, the lifeboat captain skillfully maneuvering the craft to align it with its berth before giving it an armful of throttle. It surged backward between the caged sides of the trailer, and two crewmen from the stern clambered overboard, one steadying the boat as the other attached the winch hook.

Erica watched rapt as the crew secured the lifeboat and themselves within the trailer, and the tractor driver swiveled around in his chair and gunned the engine.

Nothing happened. There was smoke, and noise, but no movement. He gave it more throttle, the sea frothing and churning above what Erica imagined were frantically spinning wheels. If anything, the tractor was sinking backward, digging itself into the seabed as sure as the tide was rising to drown it. A ripple of excitement ran through the crowd as the machine folded itself in the middle, thrashing for grip, burying itself further still.

The crew abandoned ship then, piling out of the back of the trailer and swimming to shore as the tractor driver flipped open the escape hatch above his head and stood on his seat with his arms raised in a helpless shrug.

Erica laughed, a genuine laugh, for the first time in weeks. If ever there were a clumsy metaphor for her life right now, she was sure this was it.

She stood, rubbing heat into her bare arms as she made her way to the ramp and turned her back on the unfolding debacle.

It was warm in the caravan, and the gas bottle was full and the water and power supply connected and working, for which she gave some small thanks to Carla's need for a bolt-hole.

She boiled herself some pasta and stirred in a jar of green pesto, which she ate at the lounge table overlooking the sea. Afterward, she sat with a cup of tea, sharing her attention between the book she'd picked up on impulse from the supermarket and the farm tractor towing the stricken lifeboat rig from the water.

Finally, as the sun dipped below the horizon, she grabbed a double chocolate Feast from the freezer, flipped on the lamp in the bedroom, threw her clothes all over the floor and lay and read in the soft yellow glow until her eyelids grew heavy.

This place had been Carla's one and only act of defiance. She'd never told Richard, and Erica knew that meant she'd never betray it to anyone else, either. She fell asleep smiling at the thought that no one would ever find her here.

At first, she thought the postcard on the doormat was some kind of bizarre mistake. The house number was the same, but the street name was different and the village in question was miles away. And she'd never known anyone with that name.

She stared at the card, perplexed, as she filled herself with bacon, eggs, fried bread and sweet tea. She picked it up and tilted it against the glaring early-morning sunlight, comparing the craggy coastline depicted on the front to the one outside her window.

It was only when she turned it over in her hands for what must have been the tenth time that she groggily realized there was a message in the bottom corner, opposite the address. An instruction.

Her heart stopped. She turned the card back around and looked at the photo again. Later, she'd look the place up and confirm what she already knew. But for now, she'd just hide it under a book, and drink her tea, and hyperventilate a little, and cry, and ask herself the question to which she was sure she didn't want to know the answer:

Who was Annie Fisher, and what had she done to deserve this?

CHAPTER 17

Wednesday, 6:30 a.m.

Annie woke up drunk again, on the sofa, three hours after she'd fallen asleep, with sunlight streaming painfully into her eyes from between her haphazardly thrown-together curtains. She lit a cigarette, and smoked it where she lay, gingerly turning her neck to crack the kinks out of it and trying to distract herself with things that didn't frighten her. Laundry: she had a lot of laundry to do. That wasn't frightening. Pizza: the Domino's ground beef, sweetcorn and jalapeño pizza she'd forced herself to eat in a break from Carla Cockburn's interview at Thetford police station at ten o'clock last night had been tasty and filling. In fact, her appetite for it had grown with every bite, until it was only with snarling reluctance that she'd shared a couple of slices with the uniformed staff.

What else? The ten-year school reunion group she'd been added to on Facebook, by someone she'd forgotten she was even friends with and hadn't thought about in years? No. No, that was scary. Everyone had a hard time at school in one way or another, she'd come to realize. Some kids had unrealistic expectations foisted upon them by overbearing parents. Others were shy or introverted and had difficulty relating to their classmates. Some were ashamed of who they were, and so pretended to be someone else every minute of every day. Some were hopeless at sport and were the last to be picked for team games on the rare occasions they failed to get out of PE lessons. Others still were subjected to years of daily torture and torment, perceived as weak, or annoying, or stupid, or just plain different. And some, Annie knew, ticked all of those boxes and more besides. And those people, she reflected now, stubbing her cigarette out on the coffee table because she couldn't reach the ashtray, did not attend ten-year school reunions.

And so Annie thought about the emerald-green Jeep she'd once owned, a symbol of another time, when her life had been filled with love and laughter and her career had seemed like it had a future. She wondered where that Jeep was now; whether the festering cockblanket who'd stolen it had stripped it down and sold the parts, or exported it to Uganda or somefuckingwhere, or whether someone else was happily driving around in it at that very moment, making their own joy-filled memories.

She concluded that in all probability it had met the same fate as the love, the laughter and the career, and so she lit another cigarette and thought about making a cup of tea instead.

Inevitably, though, by the time she'd managed to lever herself upright and stand with an alarming crack from her lower back and shuffle through to the kitchen and flick on the kettle, she'd run out of happy thoughts. She tried to focus on Carla Cockburn—specifically, the immediate change in her demeanor upon learning that her husband had been murdered right in front of Sarah Abbott's house.

It had been, for want of a less tired analogy, like flipping a switch. The trembling and the crying had stopped with such startling suddenness that it was as though her own throat had been cut. Her horizontal shoulders had dropped, her rod-straight back curling into her chair, and her clenched jaw had relaxed such that it changed the shape of her whole face, from square and lined and hard to soft, slim, youthful. In an instant, whatever she'd lost and however keenly she'd felt it, Carla and Annie alike had known that she'd been set free. And from that second onward, she hadn't uttered another word.

Annie thought about that freedom while she made herself a cup of coffee and some toast with thick-cut marmalade. She watched the birds outside her window and wondered how she'd feel if her own freedom came at the cost of someone else's life. It would, she concluded, have to be someone nobody would miss—check—and who'd taken their own share of human lives—check. But could she be the one to pull the trigger, or plunge the knife, or just deliver the firm nudge that would send the bastard windmilling from the clifftop to be dashed against the rocks below and washed out to sea and eaten by the crabs and fishes and hungry mermaids? Sure, she thought, if she were drunk enough.

There was one thing, though, for which she knew she wasn't drunk enough—hadn't been last night, certainly wasn't this morning, and probably never would be.

There wasn't enough vodka in the world that would make the thousand pounds in cash on her coffee table okay.

CHAPTER 18

In my dream, which had featured, among other things, a new species of spider named Trump and a car made entirely from human bone, Erica Shaw was ranting accusations at me while dismembering herself limb by limb when Jenny Riley woke me with the phone and said, "We've got a break. We've had a call from a member of the public who thinks his dog has found an elbow."

The jumble of thoughts that flooded my brain was conflicting to say the least. On the one hand, if Erica had been chopped into pieces, then she most likely wasn't our killer, in which case I felt somewhat vindicated. On the other, if Erica was the innocent victim I'd believed her to be, then I'd failed to protect her and everything was fucked. And now I wasn't really listening to anything Jenny was saying, because I was furious with her for describing Erica's defiled corpse as a "break," and because how the hell do you find a severed elbow, anyway?

I was crying by the time she hung up, my head filled with photos of Erica in her sixth-form uniform and a rolling replay of my encounters with her at That Man's house: her in a dressing gown, looking for somewhere to plug in her hair dryer, startled as I walked right into her; my hand tight around her throat, hers tight around mine, as we rolled together on wet gravel, wrestling for a gun.

Hindsight, I reminded myself, helped no one; had I known then what I knew now, then of course I'd have been able to save her. But I didn't. And as simple as that was, the reality of it just made me cry harder, and harder still until I began to choke and cough and retch in the shower.

It was a half-hour drive at that time of the morning, but I made it to Two Mile Bottom in twenty minutes with my heart in my mouth and my white fingers clawed painfully into the steering wheel. Jenny had sent me the location in Google Maps, and I found the forest access road without any trouble. The constable on guard duty swung aside the single-bar gate to allow me onto a rutted gravel track, along which I navigated the Alfa at a speed unsafe for wildlife and wheel rims alike.

A quarter of a mile in, the rows of tall, still pines seemed more dense, the shadowy places between them tighter, darker. And then they weren't.

On the left of the road was a clearing, an intersection with a narrow tract of grassland that backed onto a railway line. Adjacent to this junction, a ring of trees marked the edge of a dell, maybe a hundred meters across; how deep, I couldn't see.

A pair of patrol cars marked the spot, and the CSI van, and a Focus from the car pool, but there was only one person in sight: Kevin, standing beside his car with a large plastic bag in his hand, staring blankly at his phone as I drew up and launched myself from the car, struggling for breath.

"Where is she? Where's Erica?"

Kevin looked at me like I'd lost my mind. "Well, that's the million-dollar fucking question, isn't it?"

My brain froze, and my mouth with it, wide open, the hot, thick air stinging the raw patch at the back of my throat. I looked from Kevin's narrowed eyes to the bag and back, mind wheeling between confusion and hesitant relief and fear and back to confusion. "You mean..."

It dawned on him then what I was asking. "Oh," he said, waving the bag at me. "You thought... Yeah, this isn't hers."

It wasn't an elbow, not as such. It was an arm, severed just below the shoulder and just above the wrist and folded *at* the elbow to fit inside the bag. The torn skin and ragged flesh were blackened, the bone protruding. I felt bile rising in my ragged throat. "Thank fuck," I panted. "Whose is it?"

I half expected him to play on my obvious distress, to torment me with a bit of showmanship, drag out the dramatic tension before the big reveal. He didn't, though. He just turned the arm around to reveal the lower section of a tattoo—some kind of Celtic band, edged in gold. "Well, that's what I was just looking at," he said, wiggling the phone in his other hand. "I *think* it's Samantha Halloran's."

My stomach flipped. I was dangerously close to throwing up, and Kevin knew it when my cupped hand flew to my mouth in an effort to hold it in.

"You alright?" he said, although it was quite obvious that I wasn't.

I nodded. "Show me."

He hesitated just for a second, eyes narrowed, judging me. Finally, he nodded back and said, "Got some wellies?"

The crime scene was on the opposite side of the train tracks, which meant finding out how deep that hole went. Quite deep, as it turned out, though the slope of the ground, a well-beaten path and a helpfully raised perimeter tape made a relatively easy walk of it.

"It's a flint pit," Kevin informed me, though I hadn't asked him. He led me to the mouth of a tunnel under the tracks, where water trickled through between a small pond in the base of the crater and whatever was on the other side. "They used to haul it away by boat. This goes to the river." He pointed to the far end of the tunnel, where all I could see was mud and overgrown weeds. I turned around, surveying the steep, tree-lined walls and the impenetrable tangle of brambles and fallen branches within.

"Creepy," I muttered, both to myself and as a lazy acknowledgment of Kevin's history lesson. "We're going through there?" I scanned the arch above us: crumbling brick pinned through with giant russet-colored bolts, presumably to stave off collapse. It looked as though it had been unattended for decades, though the facing wall was adorned with newish signs appealing for reports of damage.

Kevin nodded and beckoned me to follow him, which I did, splashing through the shallow stream and emerging into what I can only describe as a swamp. "Up here," he said, clambering up a steep bank, up to his ankles in wet mud.

"I'm not sure I can," I said, but he didn't stop and help, the bastard.

My leg was throbbing by the time I'd clambered over three fallen trees and sunk twice almost to the tops of my boots in the marsh. The white forensic tent, however, was erected on a flat, level, relatively firm patch of ground, which at least allowed Kevin to dress me with some degree of dignity, albeit in front of an amused uniform and Leila Solomons, the duty crime scene tech, who just looked vaguely baffled.

"Sorted?" he said as I flexed myself inside the paper suit

and smeared Vicks under my nose and slipped the mask over my face, pointedly ignoring my audience.

"Net noo it," I said, and slipped inside.

There were two bags in the tent—large, green, heavy-gauge rubble sacks with tied handles. One had been neatly slit along its side, spilling a mat of hair and a slippery, curled-up hand into the weeds. The smell, even through the mask and the Vaporub, was almost overpowering. I only took a quick look before I tapped Leila on the arm and said, "Alright, if you're finished recording, open them up," or some muffled version of it, and then I turned around and got the hell out of there.

It was no better after two cigarettes and a cup of rancid tea from Kevin's Thermos, but I doubled up on Vicks and breathed through my mouth and thought hard about the smell of my mum's linen, fresh from the washing line.

Leila had opened the bags and artfully arranged their contents on a plastic groundsheet. The parts made one complete body, give or take, but laid out in order, its condition was striking.

She was relatively intact—desiccated flesh still covered her limbs and most of what remained of her torso, though her skin had split and slipped along the paths of least resistance. Her scalp lay beside her skull on the sheet, but she still had a semblance of a face. Her legs had stripped clean to the bone, though, and she didn't appear to have any feet. Comparing the whole to the mugshots and family-supplied photos on Kevin's phone left me in little doubt that we'd found Sam Halloran.

I called Leila over and asked her what the story was with the legs.

"First impression," she said, seeming much better able to enunciate clearly from inside a mask than I am, "she spent some time in the open before she was wrapped up. The condition's fairly consistent across the rest of the body, which ties with the first bag only being split open this morning. Otherwise, it's thick plastic, tough, airtight. There was nothing alive in there with her."

Kevin looked like he was going to throw up in his mask. I sympathized, and so I clapped him on the back and beckoned him back outside.

"Okay, two things," I said, flipping off my mask again and taking a breath of clean air. "Firstly, who the hell walks their dog in a swamp?"

Kevin shook his head and shrugged. "I don't know," he said.

I nodded. "And why don't you know?"

He looked baffled by this question, so I gave him a clue.

"Kevin, where's the witness?"

"Oh," he said. "Yeah, I don't know. Anonymous call."

"Male or female?"

"Male."

"How did you get hold of the...elbow?"

"He told us where the dog dropped it. Uniform got here first and recovered it from the nettles."

I pointed to his phone and said, "Bring up the map," and he did so, zooming in on the pulsing blue dot that more or less marked our location. I took the phone from his hand and spun it around, zoomed out a little. Turned around and watched the landscape rotate with me, the roads and the railway and the nearby river forming a shape that I instantly recognized. And there, maybe half a mile away as the crow flies, was a spot I'd pinpointed on my own map at least once or twice.

Heart pounding, right leg aching sickeningly to the bone, I waded back through the stream to the flint pit, and levered myself between trees as I scrambled up the steeper southern face, and, with Kevin in hot pursuit shouting, "Ali, what's going on, what have you found?" I strode out to the top of the railway embankment.

"Look," I said, and let him follow my outstretched hand across the tracks, and the wide, murky river, and the dense belt of trees, to an open field in the middle of the forest. From up here, it was just possible to make out the mouth of a driveway, and the outline of a cluster of buildings shrouded in heat haze: a barn, and a four-car garage, and a two-bedroom stone cottage constructed sometime around the turn of the last century.

My body turned cold, as though That Man had reached up from his house in the woods and opened up the top of my head and filled me to the brim with ice water. I turned slowly around on the spot, peering out into the cool, dark spaces between the trees across the trail, suddenly hyperaware of the silence, the gloom, and the eyes of every creature in the forest upon me, breath held fast, muscles twitching, poised to run. Watching. Watching *me*.

"He's here," I said. "Somewhere. He's close."

Kevin followed my stare along the track. I was determined that I'd see him; that he'd slip out onto the trail and glance back at me with a nod and a wink before melting into the haze.

"What do you mean?" he said.

"That Man." I looked up at the limp treetops and sniffed the air. It smelled of heat and death and Vaporub. The sky was a deeper blue than I thought I'd ever seen, like an impossible memory of a summer from so many years ago, of Mum and Dad and Reena and me, in a hot, stuffy car in the south of France, looking for our campsite, Mum wrestling an upside-down map with all the windows down while the two of us kids drank Fanta the temperature of tea and tried not to be sick.

"Reed?" Kevin said.

I nodded. "Whatever you want to call him. He's here. Watching."

Kevin spun around, just as I'd done, presumably torn between ridiculing me and pointlessly demanding that the entire forest be locked down immediately.

"You won't see him," I said, peeling the paper suit down over my arms and shivering as the sweat on my neck met the air. "But come on, you think it's a coincidence? That some mystery dog walker happens to stumble across Samantha's body, right now, today, in the middle of everything that's happened? What do you think the odds are? A hundred to one? A thousand? A million? No way did this just happen," I said. "Trust me. That Man is back."

EPISODE 4

CHAPTER 19

The morning briefing was chaos, the incident room buzzing with confusion and enthusiasm and a strange kind of voyeuristic excitement that I'd never seen there before and which unsettled me slightly.

Jenny was a juddering mess of caffeine and bed hair as she stood at the front of the room, looking like she was ready to sweep everything from the incident boards and start over. I wouldn't have blamed her; if she hadn't been out of her depth before, she was in well over her nose now.

"Right," she shouted, a little louder than was necessary to gather our collective attention. She seemed to make herself jump, and had to take a deep breath to collect herself. I felt for her. "Sorry. Right, we've got a bit to get through. Um..." She had a handful of printouts, but she didn't seem to know what to do with them. She flipped through them once, then waved them above the desk beside her as though willing her hand to open and let them go, and then she closed her fist on them so tightly that they crumpled all to hell. "Sorry," she said. "I've had a lot of coffee. Okay, first things first. At 5:37

this morning, we received a call from a member of the public, advising us that his dog had found something he described as a human elbow on an area of marshland beside the Little Ouse River, off the A134 between Thetford and Mundford. This—" she straightened the bundle of papers and held them aloft to display a photo of Samantha's bagged limb "—is the offending article. It's part of an arm, approximately midbicep to midforearm, with elements of a tattoo clearly visible." She flipped the photo to the back of the stack, and held up the next. "Two cars responded from Thetford, and found two partially buried refuse sacks, one of which had been torn open, ostensibly by the dog." She flipped to the next photo, a close-up of the opened bag. "In and around the bag, they saw what they deduced, given the presence of the arm, to be a quantity of dismembered human remains, which, on closer inspection, we believe to be those of Samantha Halloran." She stepped aside then, and pointed to Samantha's mugshot on the board behind her. "I know you all know this, but to recap, Sam was last seen on..." She scanned the board for the date, but it wasn't there and she couldn't remember it. I glanced at Kevin, who looked like he was trying to divide big numbers in his head. "Last seen in February," she continued, her voice wavering, "in King Street, where she was working as a prostitute. Sam was also known to Kerry Farrow, whose DNA was subsequently found in a cage on the property of the individual known to us as Thomas Reed." Flip to a printed Ordnance Survey map of a section of the forest, with the railway bridge and That Man's house circled in red Sharpie. "Given the proximity of that location to today's crime scene, I'm going to hazard a wildly pie-in-the-sky guess that it's not a coincidence, and that Sam isn't the only missing woman who was buried in this marsh. Therefore, I've asked for a radar survey and excavation of that location, which has been authorized. Kevin, I want you to get in touch with Dr. Galloway at the university and get wheels rolling on that as soon as we're done here."

Kevin was still staring at the mugshot, and took a second or two to register his own name. He did so now, and acknowledged her with a nod. I scribbled a note of Jenny's instruction, in case he hadn't been listening and asked me what she'd said, and then raised my hand.

"Have we traced the dog walker who supposedly found the remains?" I asked.

"Not yet."

"It's going to be a prepaid, unregistered mobile, isn't it?"

"What makes you say that?"

"Well, having been to the scene," I said pointedly, "it's a bit of a trek to get to it, not an obvious place to walk a dog at all. I'd imagine that's why they were buried there in the first place. The forest is full of walking trails, and that's well away from any of them, so what was this so-called dog walker up to that he needs to be anonymous?"

Jenny shook her head. "I don't know," she said, with more than a hint of nervous impatience, "but it doesn't really matter, does it?"

"It does if Reed alerted us to the body himself to point another finger at Erica and tie up our resources for a few more days while he tracks her down," I pointed out.

She flinched at that; it clearly hadn't crossed her mind, because she said, "Point the finger how?"

"I don't know. Maybe he's cottoned on to you blaming everything he's done on her and he's running with it? Like, 'Hey, look, I know where the bodies are buried'? Bearing in mind how much of her DNA we found in Mark Boon's flat, where I don't believe for a second she ever set foot, what's the betting we'll find a load on Samantha? If we do, he's playing right into your narrative by giving us the bodies, *and* by killing Richard Cockburn." I didn't know if any of that made sense; it did in my head, but I was speaking faster than I could think.

Apparently Jenny didn't think so, or maybe she just didn't appreciate me pointing fingers at her, because she gave me a hard stare before she looked over at Dan Hooper and said, "Fine. Dan, when you're done with Samantha's parents, see if you can get a fix on the phone. Where was it sold and when, and where did the call come from?"

"Guv." Handsome bastard.

"Moving on." She took a deep breath, and I put my elbows on my knees and my burning cheeks in my hands and gently stroked my eyebrows with the tips of my little fingers. "We've finally had Malcolm Lowry's postmortem results back from Wales," she said. "Dr. Kubica has reviewed them this morning in the light of yesterday's incident and determined with a 'high degree of probability'" (she made quote marks with her fingers, and I cringed on her behalf) "that both Mal and Richard Cockburn were attacked with the same style of weapon, if not *the* same weapon."

A sharp collective intake of breath whistled across the room. No one spoke, though a question hung in the air, almost palpable. Jenny gave me a pointed look and then answered it.

"The comparison with Eli Diaz is inconclusive," she said. "But the pattern of wounds across all three is very similar. One cut, clean across, right through to the bone, with something similar to this." She shuffled her papers and raised a photo.

My spine convulsed. The silence was thick enough to bite. It was some kind of machete, or hacking knife, or I don't know what, but it was all purpose and no style. A tan plastic handle with a hex bolt fixing, and a narrow, straight blade, perhaps a foot long and tapered upward to a point. Not a subtle weapon by any stretch of the imagination, nor easily concealed. The sight of it brought beads of sweat to my brow, but I couldn't look away.

"Approximately a thirteen-inch blade, perhaps two to three inches wide, with a nonserrated cutting edge, drawn across the throat from behind, from left to right. So, in a right-handed manner."

That last part pinged an alarm bell in my head. I scribbled a note—*right-handed?*

"I'll email this to everyone, by the way. Thirdly, Kevin's updated me this morning on the hunt for the Abbott family. So far we've come up with absolutely nothing whatsoever, which is shit, but we do now have a magistrate's warrant to enter the house. Uniform are standing by and Sandra's on her way back there as we speak. Ali, if you and DC Fisher could do the honors? I'm looking for any sign that Reed was in that house or is known to the family, and I want to know where Carol and David Abbott have disappeared to."

I looked wearily past Kevin to where Annie was sitting wide-eyed, listening intently. She felt my eyes on her and blushed back at me with a slow nod. Her own eyes were glazed and heavy-lidded. She'd had a late night, I realized, interviewing Carla Cockburn alongside me—but then so had I, and with a rudely early wake-up call to boot. Her brow was also glistening, her cheeks a deep crimson. Tired, yes, but Annie was either highly flustered, or drunk, or both.

"Ali, as I understand it, Richard Cockburn's wife has been released on bail, yes?"

My turn to blush again. I'd thrown everything I had at Carla, but she wasn't going to give her daughter up for any of it. And rightly so, to my mind. I liked to hope I'd be that unwaveringly protective in her shoes. I nodded. "She definitely knows where Erica is, but we could waterboard her and she still wouldn't tell us. Under the circumstances I can't see any value in asking her the same questions over and over again, so I sent her home."

Jenny looked crestfallen, and I guessed I knew how she felt, although not for the same reason. She wanted Erica found so that she could charge her with murder. I wanted her found so that she wouldn't *be* murdered. As with all stories, the truth of her situation likely fell somewhere in between those two scenarios, but whatever the case, we at least agreed that finding her fast was critical.

We also, I'm sure, agreed that our current tactic wasn't working. The incident room had received a hundred and thirty-eight calls since Jenny's press conference had hit the six o'clock news. Every one of them had to be logged, reviewed, triaged and followed up. Not one of them bore a credible sighting. Erica, to all intents and purposes, was as much of a ghost as That Man, and as things stood, we had zero hope of finding either of them. We needed a miracle, and Jenny Riley wasn't going to be the one to deliver it.

CHAPTER 20

The locksmith was busy chatting up Sandra when Annie and I pulled up in front of the Abbott house. The street was otherwise quiet and still, save for a twitching of net curtains in the upstairs window at number thirty-three.

We stood beside the car for a long moment, surveying the crime scene tape lying in the grass; the tire marks from the generator that had run the floodlights after the sun went down; the long rectangle of swept tarmac from which Richard Cockburn's Volvo had finally been recovered in the early hours of the morning. Annie was silent, her eyes unfocused, hands trembling ever so slightly.

"You okay?" I asked her.

She jumped, and stood to attention, nodding a little too convincingly. "Yeah, fine," she said, and smiled at me. It was a prettily shaped smile, but there was no sign of it in her eyes. All I could see there was pain.

"You sure?" I was trying for my soothing voice, but it cracked and I sounded like a thirteen-year-old boy instead. I was always the cool chick at school. "If there's anything you want to talk about, you don't have to bottle it up, you know." I ducked into her dipping line of sight, and smiled reassuringly, gesturing to the car. "We can sit and talk right now if you want."

She smiled again, though it was more of a wince. Shook her head. "No," she assured me, "I'm okay. Just...you know. Fresh in my mind." She pointed at the spot where Richard had met his grisly end. "I've never seen anything like that before," she said.

I had, but I was, for once, grateful that I couldn't actually remember it, because no one was asking me if I needed to talk about it.

"It's why I packed this in and retrained as an analyst," she said. "I don't seem to handle trauma very well."

"I know what you mean," I laughed, walking her up the drive to where Sandra was shooing away the locksmith. "Same reason I got divorced and retrained as..." Yeah, no, now's not the time. "Morning, Sandra."

"Ah, is Morgan Freeman and Miss Daisy." Sandra reached in through the open window of her van and hooked out a cardboard tray containing two McDonald's coffees. "Is probably cold but get your own next time." She went back in and came out with a brown paper bag. "You want McMuffin?"

It took longer to spread grease all over the paperwork than it did for the locksmith to get through the lock. I thanked him and saw him safely out of the drive, and then we cleaned ourselves up and let out our respective belches and got to work.

I eased the door open, bracing myself for the olfactory assault I was sure was coming. To my surprise, though, it wasn't too bad—just the musty, dusty smell of old, moldy food. I stepped aside and let Annie and Sandra follow me inside, paper shoes swishing on the terra-cotta tile, loud in the overwhelming silence of the house.

"Makes me feel better about my kitchen," Sandra said, barely above a whisper. Annie suppressed a smirk.

I skirted around the large, empty pine table in the center of the room, its four chairs tucked neatly in. Of all the surfaces in the kitchen, the table was the only one that was clean—incongruously so, in fact, albeit scattered with half-opened envelopes, corners torn away in hasty triage, contents still trapped inside. The wood had been scrubbed hard with bleach at some point, its lacquer rubbed away almost entirely in a circle radiating from the center, so that only the corners still reflected the light from the window, like an inverse vignette.

"That's weird," I said.

Sandra found a light switch by the door and flipped the overhead lights on. "Electric still is on," she noted.

I took in the stack of fossil-encrusted dishes on the worktop, the pile of bulging bin bags beside the door to what I guessed was the downstairs toilet. "What's in there?" I said to Annie.

She looked the door up and down, and reached out and opened it. I was right, there was a toilet and a sink inside, and the frosted window with the chipped frame, but we weren't going to get in there to examine it just yet. The room was full to waist height with empty-looking boxes and bags full of bags and a car tire and a selection of winter coats and God knows what else.

Sandra bent over the table, her nose an inch from the dull wood, and gently breathed in its aroma. I wasn't sure whether she was being scientific or just weird, so I nodded for Annie to follow me and moved on into the hallway that led to the front door and the stairs.

The doormat was buried in mail. I dug my hand into the pile and scooped some letters out from the bottom. "These are from the beginning of April," I said. More than three months ago. I dropped them as Annie squeezed past into the sitting room, and followed her into the gloom.

The mantelpiece was piled with unopened birthday cards. Sarah had vanished the day before she turned nineteen, or the day before she would have, depending on what happened thereafter. On an adjacent table, in the corner opposite the window, a small pile lay unopened beside three large silver picture frames: a straight-A exam certificate, an Oxford University acceptance letter and a studio portrait of Sarah, her fine blond hair draped artfully across her shoulders, blue eyes shining, her smile radiating confidence with a subtle note of mischief.

Annie and I stood in silence for a long moment, transfixed by a face filled with life and promise and beauty, until Annie broke it with a whispered, "Shit," and I looked at her and saw that she was crying.

I didn't know what to say. I wanted to put my arm around her and give her shoulders a squeeze, but I didn't know how she'd feel about that, so I just gently touched her back, and felt her stiffen and stop breathing, and then left the room, embarrassed. "Sandra, I'm heading upstairs," I called.

"Gloves, don't touch anything," was her terse reply. She knew I was wearing them; she'd seen me put them on, so either it was for Annie's benefit, or she thought I was an idiot, or she'd just officially designated this a crime scene.

I didn't hang around to find out. I climbed the stairs, feeling the familiar pain begin to creep into my hip, and paused at the top to consider the layout. One room to the left, the door closed. A bathroom and what looked like a box room, side by side in front of me. A fourth door to the right, slightly ajar.

I turned right, and then wished I hadn't.

★ ★ ★

The master bedroom was dark and chilly, its heavy curtains drawn, but there was enough light from the window above the stairs for me to make out a shape in the bed. I froze, electrified by fright, eyes fixed on the recumbent form, willing it not to move as I waited for my heart to slow down and the goose bumps to settle over my body. They did, and I remembered to breathe, and felt the wall behind me for a light switch. My fingers found it, but it was already on; no amount of flicking it up and down shed any new light on the subject.

Momentarily, having reassured myself that whatever was in the bed was not going to spring up and cut my throat, I foot-swept my way to the window and took a curtain in each fist and jerked them apart along a sticky plastic rail.

Sunlight, to the immediate protraction of my regret, flooded the room.

On the high table beside the bed, there were two teddy bears. They sat side by side, leaning into one another for support with their feet dangling over the edge and their fur matted with dried blood as they watched over the body in the bed.

I could see that it was a woman. She was wearing a nightie, which had ridden up at the bottom and soaked itself flat at the top, such that the specifics of her anatomy were apparent in spite of her mummified state.

Above, however, the clues stopped. The remains of a pillow covered her face, crusted black. A fan of feathers spread like angel wings around her, matted to the headboard and the wall and the dried-out puddle of sickly mulch that had previously been her head.

I stood still for a moment, trying to control my breathing and to not focus on her tight gray skin or the horrifying way it stood out against the wide black stain on the sheet beneath her. I glanced around the room, but it was impossible to tell whether anything had been disturbed. Clothes spilled from drawers and baskets and the built-in wardrobes. The floor surrounding the bed was a minefield of mugs and pill packets and used tissues and tiny brown husks and a hundred and one other things that probably had some use in some other context. Every raised surface was covered in ashtrays and drink cans and stacks of pennies and dog-eared books and overturned nail varnishes, lipsticks, mascaras, the spaces between black with dusty-winged corpses.

My throat was too dry to shout, so I focused on the open doorway and returned to the landing. Everything in me screamed *Don't open any more doors!* but of course, opening doors is my job.

The room opposite the master bedroom was, as I'd assumed, a box room, and had been used as one quite literally. It was comparatively orderly, too—cardboard filing boxes stacked neatly along the far wall, spanning the room to the height of the windowsill, and larger, irregularly sized retail boxes along the right side, slotted together like puzzle pieces, microwave beside printer below television above flat-pack display unit.

I closed the door and checked the adjacent bathroom. Dripping tap, smeared mirror, bathtub full of shampoo bottles. It may have been the scene of a struggle, but I guessed probably not.

Finally, soothed somewhat by the sound of voices drifting up from downstairs, I opened the fourth door.

This, evidently, had been Sarah's. It had been kept tidy, in spite of all its bustle. The walls were painted lilac over old patterned wallpaper. The one to the right, above the single bed, was hung with a pair of *Wolverine* film posters. To the left, a dresser and a pair of floating shelves about as long as my wingspan displayed a startling collection of beautiful stuffed bears, each one posed—I hoped—to look at me as I walked in.

The view of limp trees in the woods behind the house added to the quiet sadness of the room, and I tried to imagine Sarah in here, laughing and texting and posting her wittily passive-aggressive Facebook statuses, but it was impossible. I kept my eyes on what I determined to be the head bear, a small but lustrous specimen that was a hundred years old if it was a day, as I backed slowly out of the room. It was either that, or look at the shotgun on the floor and the fountain of dried blood and brain and skull that coated the bed.

"Look at it from other way. You see?"

Annie was bent over the kitchen table when I walked in, holding her hair in a bunch at the side of her neck so as not to drape it over the surface. Sandra stood in the center of the room, her phone pressed to her ear. I could hear hold music over the rustle of her impatiently tapping foot.

"All okay?" I asked, the words husky from the abundance of saliva in my throat. I hadn't been sick yet, but I was still tempted.

Sandra nodded. "Knife marks," she said. "In table. They have blood in them."

"You're right. Bloody hell." Annie straightened and let her hair down, and turned to look at me. "Shit, are you alright? You're white as a..."

The hold music stopped. A tinny voice said, "Hello?"

Annie looked at Sandra, who looked at me, and then they both looked up at the ceiling.

"Are you still there?"

"Tell them to call the coroner," I said. "I think I've found the Abbotts."

CHAPTER 21

The ground-penetrating radar arrived in the marsh beside the train tracks just after noon on Wednesday, and ran under floodlights into the early hours of Thursday morning. By dawn, the data had been downloaded and roughly analyzed and a dozen points of interest mapped. By 8:00 a.m. the forensic archaeology team was assembled, fed, watered and grimly eager to excavate.

By three o'clock on Thursday afternoon, the search was complete, and five women had come out of the ground.

Like all of us, Jenny Riley was in a grim mood. What had seemed like an impossibly confused and confusing situation was now verging on a complete clusterfuck.

She was pacing the room with a pained expression when I arrived with Annie, and she was still pacing, on and off the phone, for some time after the team had assembled and sat down and stopped chattering. Finally, as the exchange of nervous glances threatened to reach fever pitch, she strode to the middle of the circle of dragged-up chairs, held aloft a plastic bag containing a bloodstained sheet of paper and said, "What the fucking absolute fuck is this?"

No one moved.

She flipped the bag around to display the contents of the note to the team. Six words, scrawled diagonally across the page in blue biro: *I'm sorry Sarah. God forgive me.*

"This note was found beside David Abbott's body," she said, "right after we found knife marks containing type B negative blood in a table in his house. It says, 'I'm sorry, Sarah, God forgive me.' It's looking like Mr. Abbott probably wrote this sometime between blowing his wife's head off with a shotgun, and lying down on his daughter's bed and putting said gun under his chin. "'I'm sorry, Sarah. God forgive me.' What the fuck does that even mean?"

The silence was long and uncomfortable, Jenny just standing there in front of us, haunted eyes darting from face to face. It was Dan Hooper who eventually, tentatively, broke it.

"That he couldn't take the guilt of not being able to protect his daughter?" he suggested, his piercing blue eyes already screwed into a wince.

Jenny's shoulders sagged, the plastic envelope slapping against her skirt as she bowed her head and let out a weary sigh. "Yes," she said. "Thank you. But no." She tossed the note onto the desk beside her. Pulled out the chair. Sat heavily. "What it *means* is that we now have to consider the possibility that it means something else. Specifically, that David Abbott murdered his daughter, and if, as seems likely, one of the bodies at Two Mile Bottom is Sarah's, that he therefore murdered Sam Halloran and four other women, too. And if we entertain that idea—which we fucking have to—then we also have to entertain the idea that Thomas Reed therefore *didn't* kill them. Which then will beg the question of whether or not he has in fact killed anyone at all, and if so why, and if not, where the hell is he? Because for all we know, he could be dead, too."

I opened my mouth to interrupt, but nothing came out. I looked over at Annie, and saw the horror I was feeling reflected in her face. I was momentarily taken aback; the last time she'd expressed an opinion, she'd been as keen as anyone else for Erica to be guilty.

I looked at Dan: at his furrowed brow, at the straight, white teeth nibbling at his bottom lip.

I turned to Kevin, his fingers scratching the bald spot on the top of his head. *Say something*, I screamed silently. But neither of them did.

"I don't necessarily believe any of this," Jenny continued. "Honestly, I don't know *what* I believe. But we have to consider the possibility that as far as Mal Lowry and John Fairey and Julian Keith and Eli Diaz and, for God's sake, Richard Cockburn are concerned, Erica Shaw is the one we're looking for. And God knows she has a motive for the latter. Someone. Anyone. Say something."

I tried. There were words in my head, but they were jumbled and drowning in panic. This couldn't be happening. It couldn't. I didn't know all the answers, but I knew what I knew. I was there, for fuck's sake. That Man had tried to kill me. I *knew* it.

Everyone was looking at me. Annie looked puzzled. Kevin's eyes were full of sympathy, and maybe a touch of embarrassment. Dan just nodded, slowly. Oh Christ, how much had I said out loud?

"Ali." Kevin leaned forward in his chair, rested on his knees so that he was looking up at me. "It was Erica who made a dent in my skull, and she was going to shoot you if Reed didn't stop her. He was the one who saved your life, remember? And why would he kill Erica's stepdad? She's the one with the obvious motive for that, not him. Why are you so convinced she's not the one coming after us?"

Jenny leaned forward and placed a hand on my knee. It felt cold, made me squirm. I could feel myself crumbling. Couldn't be here. Had to get out.

"Ali," she said, "I know what you're going through. Believe me, I do. But everything we know about what happened to you is based on an assumption. You saw Erica drive away after she tried to shoot you, and then what? Where did she go after that? She had a twenty-minute head start, and everyone was looking for her in the direction you pointed them. How do we know that was where she went? How do we know she didn't loop around through the woods and come right back for another go? We don't *know*, because you don't *remember* what happened inside that house."

Well, that hit a nerve. I swatted her hand away, startling Annie and Kevin back in their seats as I snapped in Jenny's face. "So this is my fucking fault now, is it?"

She flinched, but held her gentle tone. "That's not what I just said, Al—"

"No," I shouted, louder than I'd intended, but nowhere near as loud as I wanted. "No. You don't get to do that. You don't get to change my narrative. You don't know. *You* don't know, because you weren't there, were you? You weren't anywhere. Have you even been to the fucking crime scene?" Another flinch told me no. "You haven't met Erica, have you? You haven't met that man. Apart from Kevin, I'm the only one of us left alive who's even seen his face, let alone talked to him, but you lot think you've got it all figured out, don't you? Well, let me tell you, you know exactly nothing about him. *Nothing.* You don't know where he came from, you don't know where he is or what he does, you don't even know his fucking *name*, for Christ's sake. You keep calling him a ghost, but now it's like you don't even know *that* about him. He had a cage under his garage, Jenny. A fucking *cage*. But sure, Annie knows a word that sounds scientific, and she found you a picture of Erica driving a van, so now obviously she's some kind of criminal mast— Actually, fucking hell, Annie, who even *are* you?" Annie was pressed into the back of her chair, eyes wide, and she began to stutter as I jabbed a finger at her. "Seriously, where did you come from? You just waltz in here with your coercive fucking control smelling like a distillery, you do basically fuck all except swan around in the DCI's car, but suddenly this whole case is upside down and back to front and Erica's running around the country cutting the heads off coppers. What exactly is your motivation here, Annie? What do you know that the rest of us don't?"

"Okay, that's enough, Ali, thank you." Jenny was on her feet, sweeping her chair back out of my reach. "I'll listen to a reasoned argument, but I'm not prep—"

"Fuck you, Jenny," I spat. I looked at Kevin's bowed head, and the tears threatening to spill from Annie's eyes. "And fuck you two, as well." I stood too quickly and whirled to face the rest of the team: a sea of blurred faces, their names spinning around so fast in my dizzy head that I couldn't read them. My face was flashing hot and sweating cold and my mouth filled with tangy bile. "I need some fresh air," I said, and then everything went black.

CHAPTER 22

Annie Fisher had seen her share of dead bodies before the start of this week, not counting funeral home viewings of grotesquely embalmed grandparents. The first was an eighteen-year-old student who'd gone out to celebrate his exam results, belligerently insisted to his friends that he was entirely capable of walking the two miles home, and fallen into the estuary. He'd turned up on the beach the next morning, looking fresh and clean and almost serene, albeit pale and with sunken eyes. She'd found him tough to look at in spite of his relatively good-looking corpse, and very much harder still to touch. Indeed, her relationship with dead things had always been somewhat strained. Her cat, whose name was Stupid Cat, had fulfilled his own legend by strolling in front of a street sweeper. He, too, had been relatively unmangled, dying of a swift blow to the head that left the merest trace of blood around his grimacing mouth. And yet, despite having loved that cat and held and stroked and kissed and been licked all over her scrunched-up face by him for the best part of a decade, she couldn't bring herself to touch his still-warm fur, or carry his limp form from the side of the road. She'd put on a pair of gardening gloves and scooped him up with a shovel, wincing at the dead weight of him as he rolled over, dead legs akimbo, dead fur rippling over his dead white belly, and dumped him straight into the hole she'd already dug between the hydrangeas. Poor Stupid Cat.

And it was the same with her hamster (whose name she could no longer remember) when she was a kid, and with the baby birds that had fallen from the nest in the park, and all of the mice that Stupid Cat had brought home to lovingly present as a token of his being an utter shit.

She knew that as a police officer, she had to suck it up. It was part of the job. It was what she'd signed up for. And her second experience had lulled her into a false sense of security. An eighty-two-year-old gardener who'd suffered a sudden and immediately fatal heart attack while pruning a privet hedge. He'd been fit, muscular and tanned, but equally he'd been an old man, and death is something of an occupational hazard for old men. Annie hadn't been shocked, or even particularly sad, but even so, she was glad of the lunchtime drinks she'd knocked back when it came to looking for the poor bugger's pulse.

The third time, she'd made sure to have a few swigs from the bottle in her locker before hustling out to the car. She'd needed them, too—a twelve-year-old girl, knocked down by a driver distracted by the hurry he was in. Her head had penetrated the windscreen and the top of the frame had broken her neck before flinging her ten feet into the air. By the time Annie and—what was his name again? Stuart? Stefan? Sim—no, Rob, that was it. Rob McLean. He always smelled like a Magic Marker and his wife was having it off with one of the desk sergeants. Annie didn't blame her; he was the most boring individual she'd ever had to sit in a car with. All he talked about was football, and Annie didn't know the first thing about football and couldn't have been less enamored of it if it had conned her out of her life savings and left her with a dug-up driveway. Anyway, the little girl had landed in the road folded double, but had been moved to the pavement and covered with blankets by a crowd of local mums by the time she and PC McTedious had got there. Annie, not realizing the extent of the girl's injuries, had leaned in to check for signs of life and to try to stabilize her neck, upon which her head had lolled unnaturally to one side and given her a close-up view of the back of her brain.

Annie didn't stop drinking after that, and she couldn't remember much about any of the others.

This, though: this was different. Photographs of severed arms were one thing, and they were nothing she hadn't seen before. She'd seen plenty of crime scene photos, dozens of postmortem records. She had the same access to the internet as anyone else, and yes, she'd watched all of those videos. Some of them had even made her feel sick, and one, from some war zone or another, had kept her awake for a night. But nothing came close to the slideshow scrolling through her mind right now: the pin-sharp pictures, direct from her own memory, of decomposed feet and hands and thighs and torsos and heads. Oh God, the heads.

The hip flask of vodka had done nothing to dull those images. Annie had a distressing feeling that nothing would erase them; that that was it, she was doomed to carry them at the front of her mind from here on in. But that didn't mean she wasn't going to try.

She stopped at home for a change of clothes. The usual trick: a slow pass of the house, a few minutes' surveillance, senses on high alert as she approached the door. Dread at whatever gift she was going to find inside today. Just like

Stupid Cat, she realized, which made her laugh a little too loudly halfway up the drive.

There was nothing, though. No trinket on the table. No crockery drip-drying on the draining board. No footprints on the mat, no unfamiliar outdoor smell, no steam on the bathroom mirror. No sense of being watched, or of having been violated, at least not here. The house was empty, and had been since she'd left that morning.

Annie threw her shirt and trousers into the laundry basket in her bedroom and covered herself in a thick mist of deodorant. It did nothing for the smell that lingered in her nose, of earth and decay and violent death, or the image of empty eye sockets staring into her, or the sense that they could somehow see her more clearly than any living thing.

She stripped and ran for the shower, shivering under cold water for a long moment until the heater got with the game and turned it almost instantly blisteringly hot. The two extremes made her queasy, and before she could stop herself, she'd liberally thrown up all over the tiles in front of her, gasping for breath and clutching at her stomach as jets of water from the scaly shower head rinsed thick streams of vomit down the side of the bath to swirl around her feet. *Living the dream*, she thought. *Living the dream.*

At some point, Annie found herself dressed in a pair of old but comfortable jeans and a Sonic Youth T-shirt she didn't remember acquiring and was certain she hadn't bought, despite it fitting very nicely. She gave her hair a cursory brush and drew on some eyeliner, and that was enough. The words *polish* and *turd* sprang to mind, and she felt guilty for it; objectively, she realized she was probably being unfair to herself, but as it had been for the longest time, the reflection staring out of the mirror at her was, to Annie, a study in banality, the proverbial picture beside the dictionary entry for *average*.

This time, though, the thought startled her as it elbowed its way around her head, jostling for space with the severed limbs. She knew there was nothing actually wrong with her, and that even if there were—even if she looked like the back end of a broken-down bus, as her mother used to say—it would have no bearing on her worth as a human being. She knew that. She'd been told it a thousand times as an awkward, gangly teenager.

And yet. Those poor girls—the ones in those bags, cut into pieces and buried in that marsh—Annie would have bet her last pound that they'd all been perfectly beautiful. And if they were who they appeared to be, and it was James or Thomas or whatever the hell his name was who had violated them in that way, then what did that say about Annie? After all, she'd been alone with the man. She'd even shared a bed with him. But not only had he not tried to take advantage of her, he'd declined so intently to kill her that he'd gone as far as *rescuing* her from such a fate. So, maybe there was something wrong with her after all. Maybe she wasn't pretty enough, or witty enough, or full-on *Sex and the City* enough.

So Annie, she figured, had a simple choice. She could choose to believe she was so undesirable that she couldn't even get herself murdered by a serial killer, or she could continue to stubbornly deny, in spite of the evidence to the contrary, that he was one.

She studied herself intently: her tired, faintly bloodshot hazel eyes, neither too close together nor too far apart. Her nose, a little dry and red but neither too big nor too small. Her dry lips, neither plump nor thin. The frown lines on her forehead, neither too many nor too deep. Her eyebrows, unsculpted but neat, and one above each eye like anyone else's.

Her dimples, which she guessed were cute but which hardly counted as a distinguishing feature. Just an ordinary face, framed by ordinary hair, tied in a bun with a plain, ordinary band.

Ordinary. Unremarkable. Average.

Overlooked.

Not worth killing.

Annie sighed, and hooked her phone out of her pocket in the laundry basket, and called for a taxi. It would be half an hour, the dispatcher said, and so she moped down the stairs and rinsed out a glass and poured herself two fingers of vodka, crushed ice from the freezer and a top-up of cranberry juice as a token effort at heading off the water infection she planned on giving herself.

She'd drunk two of those by the time she heard the car horn sound outside. She fetched her bag and dropped in her phone, squeezed her purse to make sure it was there and silently narrated herself locking the front door and zipping the keys into the inside pocket, to imprint on herself that she hadn't forgotten. Then she walked to the old Mercedes at the curb in front of her house, and took hold of the door handle, and opened the door.

CHAPTER 23

"I feel like I'm going mad. Like...what if everyone else is sane and reasonable, and it's me who's completely batshit? I mean, I took a bit of a beating, didn't I? Maybe it screwed me up more than I thought? Maybe I'm wired up all wrong? It's either that or there's some kind of conspiracy going on. Is that what it is? Kevin? Is that what I'm missing? Is it a conspiracy? Are we in one of those films where it turns out one of the good guys was the bad guy all along? Is that what's happening? Is Jenny the bad guy?"

Kevin set my coffee down on the low table beside the couch I hadn't yet struggled up from, in the family interview suite a floor above the incident room. The doctor had given me a cursory check over and prescribed lying down and chilling out for a while, so that was what I'd done. I didn't know how long I'd slept—there were no windows, and I couldn't reach my phone—but I felt somewhat refreshed, if no less frustrated.

"What you need to remember," Kevin said softly, "is that we're all in this together and we all want to do the right thing. Jenny's not the bad guy, she's just in way over her head. You knew that. Anyone who had any in-depth understanding of any aspect of this case either didn't write anything down, or they're dead, or..." He looked vaguely at the top of my head and gave me one of those poor-puppy expressions. "Until today, we didn't even have any bodies. And that note from Abbott doesn't change anything—it just means we've got a shitload more threads to tie together. But we'll get there, yeah?"

"I don't know." I really didn't. "I just..." I creaked up onto an elbow and reached for my coffee. Kevin pushed it closer and turned the handle toward me. I blew across the top and took a sip. "That's not bad, for once," I said.

Kevin smiled and looked at me expectantly.

I raised my eyebrows and acted quizzical.

"You were halfway through a sentence," he said.

Shit. Was I? "I..."

"You can't remember, can you?"

"It probably wasn't important."

"No." He slipped off the adjacent settee and knelt on the carpet beside me. "What I mean is, you can't *remember.*"

I felt a flash of panic in my chest, but I was too zoned out to deal with it. "What do you mean?" I said, perhaps a little too defensively.

Kevin reached into his pocket and pulled out what, in spite of the evident loss of my faculties, I recognized as my note-book. "You dropped this," he said, and placed it gently on the seat in front of me.

Did I fuck drop it. He took it out of my pocket, is what he did, the slippery shit. "Really? Did I?"

He thought about it, and then shook his head. "No, but that's not the point. Look at it." He flipped the cover over to display the first page. I sipped my coffee and looked at it.

Your name is Ali Green, a note that, for the first couple of weeks of my recovery, had seen a lot of action.

Below that, my address.

The make and model of my car.

Lock the front door. Key ring!

"Ali. Mate."

"I…"

"You keep blurting out random shit that's in your head. You get halfway through a sentence and forget what you were going to say. You just told the entire team to go fuck themselves, and then threw up in Derek Burke's lap and blacked out. Either you're a raging wino or…for fuck's sake, Ali, I'm worried about you!"

Worried. Was that what he was? He didn't look worried. He looked angry. His voice was calm, but his hands were shaking and his face was red and he was trying to tell me I was mad. That was it, wasn't it? This man was trying to convince me I was going insane. Why? What had I done wrong? Why was he doing this to me?

"Jesus Christ, that's not what I'm doing at all and you know it! We're meant to be mates, aren't we? Look out for each other? How long have you known me?"

"Is this where you remind me you're one of the good guys?"

He clamped his mouth shut and bowed his head, took a few deep breaths through his nose.

"I'm not mad, Kevin," I said. Was I? "I wasn't ready to come back, but I'm here, and I'm trying to get on and do my job, however hard you or anyone else tries to convince me I don't know what I'm doing. Understand?"

He sighed, and nodded. "Okay," he said. "You're fine, then. That's good. That's all I wanted to know." He stood and headed for the door, turned and looked at me. "You might want to know that forensics can't recover any DNA from the bones in Fairey's car. They're going to have to put them together like a jigsaw puzzle and come up with a best guess. Oh, and we've got another potential tat match on one of the girls in the marsh. Anja Jankovic, one of Hertfordshire's. The weird thing being that Kerry Farrow's covered in the damn things, and we can't seem to find a single one of them. So the plot thickens." He turned and opened the door. Hesitated. Closed it again. Didn't look at me, but spoke quietly. "I'm not going to tell Jenny about you," he said. "But I am going to make sure you do something about it. I'm not trying to piss you off. I just want you to be alright." Then he left, and I was, both literally and figuratively, on my own.

So. Hertfordshire.

For all I couldn't remember, I did know that David Abbott had been a regional sales manager for a company selling, fuck, I don't know, pots and pans or something, and if even I knew that, then Jenny sure as hell did, and she'd be jumping up and down at the obvious clue.

I guessed it was down to me, then.

I felt around under the settee for my bag, and retrieved my phone, and scrolled through my contacts until I recognized Edith's picture. Dialed her number. Got her voicemail.

"Can you come over tonight?" I said. "There's something I need your help with."

CHAPTER 24

Annie jumped as the car horn blared behind her, and she turned to see the minicab idling at the curb on the opposite side of her driveway.

Heart in her mouth, she ducked down low enough to see a pair of legs in the driver's seat of the Mercedes and forced an amiable laugh and said, "Shit, I'm so sorry—wrong car." She closed the door gently—too gently, as it only clicked onto the first latch, so that she had to open it again and say, "Oh my God, I'm such an idiot," and slam it shut.

Feeling like the world's biggest fuckup, she took a shuddering breath and walked as steadily as she could to the waiting taxi, in which she was relieved to see a familiar face.

"What are you like?" he said. His name was Mo, and he lived two villages away. Four times out of five, whatever the time of the day or night she called for a cab, Mo was the one who'd turn up. He had a kind face, and what Annie thought of as a typical taxi-driving physique, in that he looked like a man who lived on whatever he could buy from a twenty-four-hour petrol station. As willing as he was to drive in silence if she wasn't in the mood to talk, she knew that he'd been married for over forty years and had seven grandchildren, on whom he doted unconditionally. It warmed her heart, in spite of the painful envy.

"I'm losing the plot," she sighed, buckling herself in.

Mo smiled knowingly. "Oh, Annie. The whole world has lost the plot, my darling. If anything, you're slow to catch on! Where are we going tonight?"

"Anywhere you like," she said. "Somewhere different. Somewhere I can sing songs and drink myself to death."

She could tell from the long, sad pause he took to look at her that he wanted to reach out and help her. If she'd seen that expression on one stranger's face, she'd seen it on a thousand. But she didn't want Mo's help. She didn't want anyone's, not anymore. She just wanted to drink.

This was one of those nights when Mo drove in silence.

Annie didn't bother reading the sign above the door. In fact, she wasn't even sure there was one, but it was of no consequence. It was a gloomy shithole two streets from the North Sea, with a sticky carpet and an overbearing smell of stale sweat and spilled beer, and as she walked in, a greasy, ponytailed mountain of a man she could have sworn was the Comic Book Guy from *The Simpsons* was caterwauling a rendition of "I Will Always Love You" into the karaoke machine. And nobody was listening.

The place was bustling, mostly with tired-looking men intent on shouting over one another, but it wasn't uncomfortable. She took her two double vodkas to a free corner table and sat, necking the first one as she scanned the room for faces she might recognize, either friendly or hostile. A couple might have rung a bell, but they didn't set off any alarms. She could relax at least.

The singer, for want of a better word, had moved on through Jennifer Rush's "Power of Love" and Berlin's "Take

My Breath Away" by the time Annie returned a second time with two more drinks. And this time, someone noticed.

"Been stood up, have you?" He loomed over the table out of nowhere, a full pint of something dark and frothy in one hand and what looked like a vodka and tonic in the other.

Annie looked up from the man's shiny brogues, past his ironed jeans and his more than adequately filled out rugby shirt, to the receding hairline that framed his cocked eyebrows and overconfident grin. He wasn't anything special—certainly not the type she'd pick out across a crowded room—but even as her conscious brain was recoiling, something locked somewhere deep inside it was shrugging and saying, *Yeah, fine, whatever, he'll do.*

For the second time that day, she stuttered, trapped between two responses. *Apparently not anymore.* And *Fuck off and jump in a fire.*

"Cat got your tongue?" he said.

Annie felt the pressure building in her head, her pulse accelerating, fight-or-flight charging the muscles in her limbs. Two words replaced all of the others on the tip of her tongue: *panic attack.* A vision flashed through her mind, of her hands on the rim of the table, flipping it, glasses flying, her elbow connecting with the man's sternum as she fled for the door.

"I'm Jason," he said, smiling, oblivious. "Let me see if I can guess your name."

"Is that one mine?" A woman's voice. A hand on one of Annie's drinks. A body on the bench seat beside her. A wave of perfume. A wet kiss on her cheek. An arm across her shoulders. "Sorry I'm late, babe, work was murder. You two know each other? Jason, was it?"

Jason shifted from one foot to the other, sloshing a few drops of ale onto the carpet. "Right," he said, but he didn't move. "Right. You two..."

"Oh God," said the voice in Annie's ear. "Were you trying to chat her up?" She laughed and took a sip of Annie's vodka. "Awks."

Jason looked over his shoulder, presumably to check that none of his mates were laughing at him. They were—three similarly douchey-looking rugger buggers, two of them with their polo shirts tucked into their jeans, sniggering and raising their glasses to him from the bar. "Fucksake," he sighed, and put the vodka down on the table. "You might as well have that."

"What have you put in it?"

"What do you mean?"

"Exactly what I said."

"Vodka and tonic, same as what your girlfriend ordered."

"If you could take it away, that'd be great."

He looked confused, and a little overoffended. "What, you think I've spiked it?"

"Don't get upset," she said, "and don't be a dick. Just take the drink away, give it back to the barman and have a nice evening, yeah? Better luck next time, and all that."

Jason huffed, and then he puffed, and then he shook his head and snatched up the drink and hissed, "Whatever. Fucking vagetarians."

A laugh. "Uh-oh. I hope this karaoke's got Cyndi Lauper, 'cos I can see your true colors shining through, mate."

Jason exited, stage right. The arm withdrew from across Annie's back, leaving goose bumps in its wake. The drink hit the table, slid, clinked against its twin. "Sorry," the woman said. "Hope I didn't overstep. I could see you about to go into panic mode."

Annie unclenched her fists and her teeth, sucked in a lungful of air, blew it out slowly and deliberately as she felt her new companion shift over on the seat to give her space. She nodded and tried to force a smile, her eyes shut tight in an effort to keep the tears in. Finally, she gave in to the sting with a gasp and let them spring open, blinking her cheeks wet and her vision blurry. "God, you must think I'm pathetic," she said, attempting a laugh as she looked around at her rescuer.

Whatever she'd been expecting from the hard-edged voice, the weight of the arm, the self-confident swagger, the *presence* beside her, she'd been wrong. To Annie, she looked like little more than a girl, ostensibly at least. Her arms were slender, her waist wasplike, her poise angular, but her face, framed by dark hair that looked too straight to be God-given, had a youthful softness to it, and she didn't look entirely comfortable in her frame, as though she were unused to her own waifishness. She wouldn't have placed her far beyond eighteen or nineteen, were it not for her eyes. Annie squinted into their dark depths and felt a spark of recognition, a reflection of the scars it had taken her more years to accumulate than she might otherwise credit this girl with having lived. Her smile, though, didn't hurt at all.

"'Course not," she said. "The world's a dangerous place to be a girl. If we don't look out for each other, no other fucker will."

Annie laughed. "I'll drink to that," she said, as though she needed any excuse. She slid the second vodka back toward the stranger across the otherwise empty table. "You're welcome to join me."

The girl smiled again and picked up a bottle of Coke with a straw in it from the seat behind her. "Driving," she said, and took a sip. "But knock yourself out."

"That's the plan." Annie tipped her glass to clink it against the bottle, spilled a little over her fingers and licked it off. The girl watched her for a moment, just a beat longer than Annie was comfortable with. She felt heat spreading through her face as she tipped a little too much of her drink into her mouth and half choked.

"Well, you're going the right way about it," she laughed, a glimmer of mischief brightening her eyes.

"Listen." Annie took another swig, emptying her glass. "I don't want to be rude or anything, but..."

The girl nodded. "You're right," she said, reaching for her bag. "I didn't mean to interrupt."

"Oh, no, I don't mean that." Annie slid her empty glass away and picked up the full one. "No, I just... I mean, I'm..." She clocked the girl's raised eyebrow, and flushed with embarrassment. Took a deep breath. "I'm straight," she said.

The girl laughed. "That's not really any of my business," she said. "I mean, so am I, so...high five, I guess."

"Oh God."

"I mean, I could probably put it to one side for that...the girl who plays Wonder Woman, what's her name?"

"Lynda Carter?"

"Lynda Car—I'm twenty-one."

"Right. Sorry."

The girl laughed and slurped her Coke. "So," she said. "What *is* a nice girl like you doing in a place like this?"

"Ha. I don't know. Running away?"

"What are you running away from?"

"Life. You?"

"Man."

Annie snorted. "I'll drink to that, too. Last guy I liked turned out to be a psychopath." And there it was. She'd said it out loud.

"Been there." The girl held up her hand for a real high five, and Annie obliged.

"You, me and every woman in here, probably. You want another drink?"

★ ★ ★

An hour and three more doubles later, the question was the same, albeit a little more slurred, and the answer was, "Sure. Can you sing?"

"What?"

The girl jabbed a thumb at the middle-aged woman with the '80s hair and the tasseled biker jacket who was at that moment murdering "Because the Night." "Can you sing?"

Annie laughed. "Fuck no."

"Can you sing better than *her*?"

"Definitely not."

"Quality. You get the drinks, I'll get the track list."

So Annie stood at the bar, thinking about how much she liked this strange girl who'd appeared out of nowhere and shared so little about herself. She hadn't even asked her name, and it seemed a bit late to do so now, so she figured she'd casually introduce herself when they said their good-nights. Or maybe she wouldn't mention it at all, and would instead remember her as some sort of guardian angel, neither real nor imagined. Mythical, perhaps. Like a unicorn, or a...

Annie didn't know what. Whatever it was, it was childishly fanciful—she was lucid enough to know that much. And this girl was definitely real, because Annie knew she wasn't the only person in the bar who'd seen her. Moreover, there was something nigglingly familiar about her, though for the life of her she couldn't think what it was. Something in her eyes, she thought, or her mouth, or the shape of her face, or *something.*

It would come to her later, in a brutal, horrifying flash, when she heard the ladies' room door swing shut and the footsteps stop outside her stall, just as she was thinking about how much she hated pub toilets and how vulnerable she was, alone in a cold, damp afterthought of an outhouse with her knickers around her ankles.

But not now, because the girl was beckoning to her excitedly from the little stage at the end of the room, and Annie was putting down their drinks on top of the monitor, and then a microphone was in her hand and she didn't have time to think about much else. And that was how Annie came to spend her last few gloriously carefree minutes as the Kenny Rogers to Erica Shaw's Dolly Parton, singing "Islands in the Stream" in a dive bar two blocks from the docks, in front of precisely no one who gave a shit.

EPISODE 5

CHAPTER 25

I expected a fight, but Carla showed no emotion when she opened the front door of her house to find me on the doorstep, rehearsing my defensive speech. She had keys in her hand and one of those environmentally friendly shopping bags looped over her arm, but she didn't so much as proclaim herself busy; she just stopped, looked me blankly up and down and stepped aside to let me in.

I stood in the kitchen doorway as she dumped the bag and keys, filled the kettle and fetched a pair of mugs from the cupboard. Then, perhaps sensing my awkwardness, she told me to "Go sit down, I'll bring it through."

I did as I was told, tiptoeing through the house like I shouldn't have been there. Which I shouldn't have, obviously. I'd skipped the office and come straight here, although I had at least called and left a message with Dan to tell Kevin to tell Jenny where I was, if and when she asked. I'd wanted to speak to Annie, too, but she wasn't in; apparently she'd called at four in the morning to say she was sick. None of that surprised me, though I did feel a small twinge of guilt, partly for being of the mind to drag her into something that would probably get her into trouble, but mostly for having been a bitch to her the previous afternoon. If I'd driven her to a drinking binge, then I only had myself to blame for having to lone-wolf it this morning. But even so: bollocks.

When Carla eventually joined me, she sat on the edge of the settee, back straight, composed, and smiled. It was the first smile I'd seen from her, and the difference it made to her face was striking. She looked youthful, relaxed—far from the wound-up bundle of tension and snot that was the picture of her in my mind.

"Thank you," I said. "I'm sorry I didn't call ahead," although that strategy hasn't always worked in my favor in the past.

"It's fine," she said. "I'd have been back in twenty minutes, anyway—I'm not doing a big shop today."

I returned her smile, and nodded gently, and then felt self-conscious and stared into my coffee. "How are you feeling?" I asked her.

She huffed a little half laugh and said, "Well, the bruises still hurt, but I haven't got any new ones."

I looked at her sleeves, pulled down over her hands as they had been on Tuesday. I'd seen what they were hiding that night. She'd be sore for a time yet.

"It's funny," she said. "Usually when someone loses her husband, after the funeral it's like a barrage of Hallmark moments, isn't it? Anyone who'll listen. Out come the photo albums. It's all sunsets and wedding dresses and 'Did I ever tell you about the time we...?' and 'Oh, look at him, he was always having so much fun!'" She sipped her tea and pointed at my lap, or rather, I quickly gathered, the seat beneath it. "Richard strangled me until I passed out, right there," she said, and looked at the coffee table where I now rested my mug. "One time he pushed me over and I cut my head open on the corner of that table. I lost count of the number of times he raped me on this carpet. I can't remember us ever..." She hesitated, smiled apologetically, waited for me to nod my approval before finishing her sentence. "I can't remember the last time I had sex because I wanted to, when I wasn't crying, or screaming, or trying to keep the weight off whatever part of me he'd just broken. *Those* are my wake stories—not the happy memories. I don't think I even have any of those anymore, not yet. But I will, because that man isn't here to make sure I don't." She smiled again, and this time there was a light in her eyes. "So I'm sorry if I don't seem very helpful, but I'm glad Richard's dead. Just...relieved, you know? And it doesn't matter that you know that or how terrible it makes me sound, because we were both right here when it happened. All I care about, Ali, are my daughters. And I know you think Erica did it, and that she killed your friends and whoever else, but I'll never, ev—"

"Actually, I don't," I said.

Carla held the word in her mouth for several long seconds, studying my face, presumably for a sign that I was playing a trick. I held her stare, but I thought about what I was going to have for dinner instead of what my eyes were doing. One self-conscious twitch would have blown it. "You don't?" she said finally.

I shook my head and swallowed a mouthful of coffee. "No, I don't. Not personally. I'll be honest with you—" or semi-honest, anyway "—most of the people I work with disagree. They think she's an accessory at the very least. But listen to me, Carla, very carefully. The man they think she's colluding with—the man I believe held your daughter prisoner for three months in a cage, and murdered my friend Eli and put me in hospital—that man is not her friend, and he's going to catch up with her before I do unless you help me. I'm not playing you here, Carla. This isn't a trick. I've got plenty of questions for Erica, but my absolute priority is keeping her alive, and whatever you think, whether you think she really did kill three policemen, whether you think it was her who slashed your husband's throat, I honestly couldn't give less of a shit right now, because that man will cut the life right out of her without a second thought. And I don't think it *was* Erica who did it. I think it was him, and that means he was right here outside this house two days ago. And we both know Erica was here too, Carla, so what I really need right now is for you to help me save her life." I reached into my pocket and drew out Edith's card and placed it on the table in front of her. "Call that number," I said. "She's a criminal lawyer, a good one, and a personal friend. She'll represent you free of charge, and if you do everything she says, then all of this'll go away, I promise you that, but the condition is that you do everything *I* say, right now. So tell me."

Carla had curled in on herself, hugging her mug and drawing her knees up to her chest. I gave her a moment to process what I'd said, half worrying that I'd gone a bit too far as she gazed at the school portrait of Erica on the shelf way behind me and chewed her lip. Eventually, she sighed and drained her tea, and put down her empty mug, and said, "I don't suppose you want to buy a load of old brass shit, do you?"

I waited her out. Listened to the tick of a clock that I couldn't see. Thought about calling Edith when I got home. Stared into Carla's eyes and willed her to tell me the fucking truth. And finally, she did.

A hundred miles an hour isn't inherently troubling; speed in itself never killed anyone. When the roads are full of half-wits incapable of using their mirrors, however, and when your right hip is numb and you don't know where your foot is, and you can all but hear the disapproving tuts of other road users as you elbow your way past them in the inside lane, it starts to feel stressful. When you're only doing a hundred out of deference to some spurious notion that a hundred is Too Fast—a measure of bravado, an automatic ban—and the urgency is such that nothing short of warp speed is fast enough, it's exponentially more so.

And I know there's no logic to it. I wasn't racing against time, not really. There was no countdown. No tangible evidence of any immediate danger. That Man was not, as far as I knew, advancing upon Erica's bolt-hole at that very moment. If he knew where she was, then chances were he'd already been and done and gone again, and I was risking my life and others' in a frantic chase to recover a two-day-dead body. And if he didn't, and hadn't, then Erica was probably sitting in her vest and knickers watching *Pointless* and eating a Rustlers Rib, and I might as well just stick to seventy. What I'm saying is, this scene contains no suspense.

And yet by the time I'd circled the city I was swimming in sweat and tears, and my throat was hoarse from yelling. The open roads out toward the Broads were no better; I had four near misses overtaking tractors and trucks and casual motorists seemingly with nowhere to go and all the time in the world to get there. As the lanes narrowed coastward I took blind bends at lethal speed, missing oncoming vehicles by inches, my fingers white around a wheel I could all but feel bending in my terrified grip.

The car was earth-brown to its door handles and smelled of hot rubber and clutch smoke when I finally brought it to a stop in a shower of gravel and threw myself out, seat belt buckle cracking off the window as I discarded it, door bouncing back off its hinges and thumping me in my bad hip. I stumbled but didn't fall, gritting my teeth against the bolt of pain that shot up my side and rattled my teeth. Now was not the time for this.

Behind me, a row of old prefab bungalows followed a narrow track along the clifftop. I couldn't remember which of them I was looking for, but Carla had drawn me a diagram across two pages of my notebook, and I'd wedged my phone in to mark the page. That was all the phone was good for; I had nothing even resembling a signal. *Emergency calls only*, it said, which made my stomach flip.

I turned side-on to the searing sun and righted the map with the sea on the left and the track straight ahead, and surveyed the houses. Postwar scaled-down ranch-style affairs, each different but somehow the same: all porches and woodworm and dusty glass, muted yellow or blue or might-have-once-been-white. The first two had cars parked on their lawns. The third had an empty, depressed look, like no one had crossed its threshold in a decade. I didn't like it. The silence seemed louder than the roar of breaking waves down below, and my body was racked with chills. I told myself the breeze was chilling my damp shirt, but it was a lie; there was no breeze. I was just afraid.

Carla's map, though, was not frightening. It was drawn in pencil, with smooth, confident strokes and beautifully to scale. I could see the gap in the houses, the plot she'd boundary-marked with bold lines, a hundred yards from the car, and so, taking a few deep breaths and telling myself everything was fine, I started to walk.

The thought did cross my mind, at that point, that I might have been wrong, that Erica's innocence was only a matter of faith, and that I was the only one who had any. There was every chance that she was watching me, just waiting for me to blunder within striking distance and expose my throat. But I didn't believe that, not right then. And my legs certainly didn't; the right was too preoccupied with trying to function as a leg, and the left was busy doing both of their work, and before I'd had time to consider their conspiracy of betrayal against my mounting trepidation, they'd carried me to the edge of the empty lot.

Erica's father's static caravan was, as her mother's diagram predicted, broadside to the sea within feet of the cliff edge. There was no way to approach without being seen from one of the three wide windows along its flank. With an open cornfield at my back, I was as conspicuously exposed as if I'd been carrying a flag and an air horn. At first scan, though, there didn't appear to be much of a threat. There were no vehicles on or close to the wide grassy plot, no faces in any of the windows that I could see, no sign of movement anywhere within my line of sight.

I scanned the borders of the neighboring plots. They were marked by scruffy rows of weed and shrub and a low single-wire fence. The bungalows on either side were as exposed as I was—no trees, no bushes, no piles of anything that might adequately conceal even a crouching, tightly bunched assailant. No tension in the still air. No hairs erect on the back of my neck. Nothing to stop my legs from pressing on.

It would have been neither a shock nor a surprise had I been pushed off the cliff as I limped around the perimeter of the caravan. I was more than aware of the irresponsibility of my actions as I checked again for the phone signal I knew I didn't have and stood three feet from a lethal, rocky drop, staring at the map, and the mobile home, and the beautiful blue of the sea and the sky and the perfect golden sand on the beach, and the note in my pad that read *Key in l/h pocket.*

There was no one home; that much was obvious, even before I thumped on the door and all of the windows and called Erica's name and peered into, under and all around the caravan. But someone had been, and recently. There were dishes in the sink and the bed was unmade, and that was all the probable cause I decided I needed, so I dug out Carla's key, complete with its old, corroded RAC fob as retrieved from behind a drawer in her kitchen, and steadied my breathing, and rubbed some feeling into my right thigh, and let myself in.

CHAPTER 26

"That fucking bitch! Who the fuck does she think she is?"

Kevin moved his hands away from his tightly closed eyes, dragging them hard across his face and through his hair to the back of his neck, where he massaged himself with a groan as Jenny swept random items of stationery into her desk drawer, just so she could slam it shut. "I'm staying out of it," he said.

"The fuck you are. You're supposed to be her partner. What's going on with her? And what the fuck does 'Gone to find Erica' mean?"

He shook his head and unscrewed his eyes. "I've barely worked with her. Lowry put us together about three days before she got hurt."

"But you're mates, right?"

Kevin blew out a sigh, and shrugged. A week ago, he'd have said yes. A week ago, he'd have taken a bullet for Ali Green, although the one opportunity he'd had to do just that, he'd spent rolling around on the floor with the top of his head split open. But now? "You know what she's been through," he said. "You can't expect her to be..."

"Be what?" Jenny came around her desk and perched on the edge, ready to feed Kevin whatever prompt he needed to spill the beans. "Herself? A good copper? Anything other than a liability?"

"That's not fair," he snapped. "You don't know her." He bit his tongue, apprehensive of his tone, but pride swelled in him just the same.

Jenny nodded. "So tell me. You like her, right? Respect her?"

"Yes."

"So what's with all the frost? The pair of you haven't made eye contact in days, so there's clearly something not right. What did she do, turn you down?"

Kevin felt his heart speed up, and made an instinctive grab for his ring finger before he could stop himself. "What do you mean?" he spat, knowing it was a redundant question but happy to bat the ball back into Jenny's court regardless.

She didn't answer—just sat there, fiddling with her stapler and staring at him with a cocked eyebrow.

He folded. "There's nothing like that," he said. "I'm married, and she's..." What, exactly? Not interested? Not his type? Not into men? He didn't even know; he was just scrabbling for evidence of propriety, although Jenny hadn't asked for any. He knew he was protesting too much, that he should have just gamely laughed and said, "Ha ha, yeah, that's it," appending an eye roll and a rapid change of subject.

Or should he? Maybe he'd actually played this perfectly, taking one for the team entirely by accident. It wouldn't be the first time. He hung his head and closed his eyes again, blocking out Jenny's stare and wondering whether he could make himself blush.

He couldn't, but Jenny seemed to accept his answer, at least for now. "That's tough," she said. "Believe me, I know. I've had my fair share of unrequited crushes." She gave a nervous laugh, trying to sound companionable, he guessed, but it came off as strained.

Kevin gave the floor a slow nod, confused thoughts trickling through his brain. "Can we not?" he said finally.

She rolled her eyes and changed tack. "So," she said. "What do *you* think? Do you think she's right? Do you think I am too objective?"

Oh God. What part of "I'm staying out of it" didn't she understand? Kevin shrugged in spite of himself, and met her stare. "I don't know," he said. "I mean, it's hard for me to be objective, isn't it? I've met Erica, once, when she cracked me over the head and threatened to shoot me, but whether or not that means I think she's behind all of this is another matter."

"And do you?"

That was the million-pound question, wasn't it? "I don't know," he said. "Do I think she somehow drove Reed to kill those girls? No, probably not. I think the man's exactly what Ali says he is. I think he probably… I've forgotten the word. Coerced?"

Jenny nodded and gestured for him to continue.

"I think he probably coerced her into helping him get rid of Fairey and Keith, but that doesn't mean she killed them."

"Doesn't mean she didn't, either."

"No. I mean, maybe she's got that…what's it called? There's a name for it, isn't there? When kidnap victims start sympathizing with the—"

"St—"

"Well, anyway, you know what I mean. I'm not saying she's innocent, but I'm not saying there isn't any more to it than she's guilty, either. And look, she's five foot four and ten stone, she's not exactly the Predator. Which, yeah, I know, doesn't mean she's not capable of cutting anyone's throat, but… I don't know, I'm just not really feeling it. And Ali's definitely right about one thing."

Jenny shifted uncomfortably on the desk, her jaw set hard, stapler discarded. "What's that?" she muttered.

"Well, it's true, isn't it? You're the only one on the team who hasn't stood in Erica's shoes. We've all done the same courses, right? But Ali was there. I was there. I saw how scared that girl was. I stood in the cage, Jen. And today I stood in a swamp and watched those girls come out of the ground in bin bags. It's..." He shook out a heavy sigh, felt a sudden tiredness wash over him. The bald spot on his crown was itching. He knew he was crossing a line, but somewhere, deep down and well hidden, it felt good to cross it. He hadn't crossed a line in a very long time. He threw his hands in the air like he just didn't care, and scattered the remains of his caution to the wind. "You just don't know what you're talking about," he said.

Silence descended. Jenny watched Kevin through narrowed eyes, her lip trembling just a little, her hands pale where the edge of the desk dug into her palms.

Kevin didn't know what else to say. He thought about getting up and letting himself out; he figured he was about to be angrily dismissed, anyway. He'd left it too long, though, and the more he thought about what to do, the later and the worse it got until he just felt awkward and small and of a mind to begin systematically questioning all of his life choices, starting from this precise moment and working backward until somebody stopped him.

"Right," she said, snapping both Kevin and herself out of the moment by springing from the desk and snatching her bag from the floor behind it and striding directly for the door.

Kevin watched her go, thinking about how many seconds

he'd wait before following her out of the office, and how nonchalant a face he could pull off in her furious wake.

When she turned back to him, however, there was lightness in her features, and an unsettling hint of a smile on her lips. "Come on, then," she said. "Let's fucking do it."

Jenny, as it turned out, much to Kevin's dismay, liked Whitney Houston. A lot. Indeed, she knew all of the words to songs that he'd never even heard before, which made him feel somewhat left out as he watched the verge scroll past in silence. Mercifully, she at least had a pleasant voice.

It was faintly unsettling, though, given his uncertainty as to the mood she was in with him, that she seemed so manically cheerful as she aimed the BMW south, floored the accelerator and belted a power ballad almost directly into his right ear.

Twenty minutes later, she finally put a lid on it, turning the music off and the sat nav volume on as she left the dual carriageway and pointed the car out into the middle of the forest.

"So come on, Kevin." She shifted in her chair, adjusting to the undulating rhythm of the road. "Talk to me. Tell me something about you. Who'll be waiting at home when you get in?"

Kevin took a moment to process the abrupt change of pace, and the ringing in his ears. If she was trying to make peace, he thought, she had a funny way of going about it. "Um..." And it seemed like a strange time to suddenly want to get to know him. If this were a cop movie, he thought, then this was the bit where the rookie partner opened up about her family, right before getting shot. Anyway, "Okay, yeah," he said, awkwardly, "So, Gemma's my wife. She's a fighter controller at Marham."

"How long have you been married?"

"Seven years. But we've been together since high school, pretty much."

"Oh," she cooed. "That's really sweet. Any little ones?"

Kevin winced. If they'd been pushing their luck before, this was going to clinch it. "We're getting there," he said. "We've been trying for five years, and we just found out...well, it looks like we finally nailed it. And I haven't told anyone at work yet, so keep it under your hat, alright?"

"I won't tell a soul," she said, through a sparkling grin that Kevin thought looked genuinely joyful. "Oh, Kevin, congratulations!"

He let himself smile then, more with pride than anything else. "It was a long five years," he said. "We needed a lot of... help. You know. Anyway, what about you?"

"Oh, my husband's a writer," Jenny laughed. "Or he says he is, anyway. He's basically a fucking layabout, but there we are. His name's Kevin, too," she said, and they laughed at the coincidence, which Kevin half took to mean she thought *he* was a fucking layabout as well. "Kids are grown up and gone, and he's basically nocturnal and barely talks to me, anyway. Seriously, I could die tomorrow and it'd take him a week to notice. But at least I get a king-size bed to myself, which is lovely. It's got a memory foam thing on it. Have you got one of those?"

"No."

"Oh my God, it makes such a difference. I used to have terrible problems with my back, but not a sausage since I bought that. Really soft. Lovely."

"That's—"

The sat nav lady interrupted Jenny's foreshadowing, instructing her to take a right in half a mile. And a minute later, Kevin was unclipping his seat belt and stepping out of the car and drawing back the bolt on the gate at the foot of That Man's long, dark, winding driveway.

The memory of the last time he'd done this flooded his brain, and he took a moment to steady himself. He focused on the strand of blue police tape hanging limply from one end of the crossbar, dirty and rumpled no doubt from the dozen or so intervening visits by crime scene techs and detectives; aside from the clear blue sky, it was the only tangible reminder that this place was different now.

He walked the gate aside and let it hang, took a long look at the fifty yards of driveway he could see before it curved away into the woods. He scanned the trees to either side, squinting between shadows and shafts of dusty sunlight. He listened to the wood pigeons cooing among the branches, and turned to follow the rustle of an adder as it melted into the shade of a log beside the track. He stepped aside as Jenny let off the brake and the car rolled between the gateposts. Then he took a breath, strolled around to the passenger side, settled back into the car, and said, "Okay. Let's go take a look."

Jenny didn't seem nervous at all.

CHAPTER 27

The caravan had been occupied, and recently. The bed was unmade, the sheets rumpled and kicked aside, one pillow on the floor. Someone was a restless sleeper.

A mug containing half an inch of tea, curdled and skinned but not yet moldy, sat on the table in the lounge.

In the kitchenette, a plate, knife and fork were soaking in cold water in the sink. On the counter, a jumble of groceries—tea bags, bread, biscuits, sugar, a bag of apples—sat opened and toppled in the puddle of the carrier bag that had been peeled down around them in situ. In the fridge below, I found fresh milk, juice, butter, marmalade, bacon, eggs. All the major food groups plus grain, fruit and dairy, John Fairey would have said. John Fairey was an idiot.

I returned to the bag and gently moved aside pasta and a jar of sauce and a pack of croissants, feeling around in the bottom for a receipt. I found it. It was dated three days prior—Tuesday, about an hour after Richard Cockburn's death.

I made a note to have the store's CCTV examined, and tucked the receipt into my notebook. However stretched the viewing team was, it would be quicker than sending that mug away for DNA testing.

Mug.

I was thirsty.

I found a clean mug—there was a cupboard full of them—and made myself a cup of tea. I put it down beside what I presumed to be Erica's and slid in behind the table.

The view from the picture window beside me was spectacular. I could all but look directly down the cliff face onto the wide golden beach; in the distance, I could see the face itself as it curved seaward. The beach was far from empty, but it had none of the flamboyant bustle I would have expected from a hot day in July. I was half tempted to go down there myself, under the auspices of looking for a sunbathing fugitive. But I knew she wouldn't be there, so I sipped my tea and stared at the sea, and debated with myself whether it would be a massive waste of my time to just stay here and wait for Erica to show up. "Probably," was my conclusion.

It was nice here, though. I wondered if Erica would mind if I had something to eat. I was sure Carla had raised her to be hospitable. A full English might be pushing it, but I was sure a couple of slices of toast would be alright.

There was a book on the table. I slid it across to me and read the cover. It carried a picture of a young woman on a country road, staring purposefully over her shoulder at an unseen threat. It was called *You Can't Hide.* The *Independent* called it "a captivating thriller." I took a mouthful of tea and picked it up to read the blurb on the back, revealing a postcard tucked underneath. A view of a sun-kissed beach crisscrossed with streams. A verdant ridge curling into the sea beneath a beautiful clear blue sky. A caption: Three Cliffs Bay.

I flipped it over. A message inscribed in the bottom left-hand corner. *E: Not safe here. Take care of Annie.*

The card was addressed to Annie Fisher. I was now covered in tea.

I bolted from the caravan as fast as my fucked-up stupid leg would carry me, checking my phone five times before I got back to the car as though any ten square yards of clifftop were any more likely than the next to give me a signal.

I strapped in, hit the starter and sprayed gravel over three or four parked cars as I gunned it, silently apologizing to everyone whose alarm was now going off, and to everyone whose relaxing day at the beach had just become a lot louder.

I punched the postcode from the envelope into the sat nav as I navigated the single-track lane back to the main road, far faster than I knew was sensible. I may have run over a rabbit, I'm not sure.

As soon as a bar of signal appeared on the Bluetooth display, I shouted at the car to dial Annie's number, swerving around a tractor and narrowly missing an oncoming scooter as it rang. And rang. And rang.

I hung up and tried Kevin. Same result.

"Call Jenny," I barked. Her voicemail cut in right away: "Hi, this is Jen Riley. I can't get to the phone at the moment, but do leave a message and I'll call you back as soon as I'm free."

Bland, I thought. Just like you, Jen Riley. Bland! "Jen, it's Ali. Call me as soon as you get this."

I used my hazards and horn to bully a Volvo out of the way. A fucking pool car would have been nice. I voice-dialed the incident room and got through to Dan Hooper, who always seemed to have one, the bastard.

"Dan Hooper," he said casually as I misjudged a turn and bounced two wheels over the grass verge.

"Dan, it's Ali. Who spoke to Annie Fisher this morning?"

"Fucked if I know."

"Okay, never mind that. I'm going to give you an address and I need local uniform there in a hurry. You ready?"

"Ali, what's going on? Are you alright?"

"Just write this down." I read him the address. "I need two cars to assist with a welfare check, but I need them quietly, and I need them a hundred meters either side of the house. Got it?"

"Two cars for a welfare check?"

"Please?"

"Okay, I've got it. Is Jen with you?"

My heart skipped. "No, why?"

"Oh, she stropped off somewhere with Kev this morning and we can't get either of them on the phone."

"They left together?"

"Yeah. You don't think they're—"

"No." I hit the brakes for a stop sign. Checked both ways. There was a car coming. I went anyway, and was treated to a blast of horn and a wanker sign.

"Fuck off," I spat.

"Oh, right."

"Not you, Dan. Please, just sort this for me and I'll ring you back as soon as I get there, okay?"

"Ali, are you on your ow—"

I cut him off, and floored it.

Apparently Dan did have it, because in the twenty-four minutes it took me to arrive at my destination, he'd managed to corral two patrol cars from somewhere and position them discreetly two hundred yards apart in Church Road. It wasn't all good, though, because my leg had cramped up by then, I couldn't brake properly and I knocked the mirror off one of them. There goes my pension.

I managed to stop the car with the handbrake, and extricate myself with a modicum of grace. I limped over to the squad car I'd just crashed into, wherein the two guys in uniform were staring at me in disdainful disbelief. "Sorry about that," I said, dangling my warrant card in front of the open driver's window with one hand and passing the severed mirror through with the other. "Hi, I'm Ali."

The two men nodded silently. The one in the passenger seat frowned and tossed the mirror over his shoulder into the back of the car. He looked like a man who just couldn't even.

"Okay," I said. "So listen, there's nothing to get hyped up about. I'm going to carry out a quick welfare check, and if everything's okay I'll come back and buy you all an ice cream, but if you hear me shouting, or if anyone comes barreling out of that house, then just...be there, alright?"

The driver nodded. "Are you expecting anyone to do that?"

"Fucking hope not," I said, and took out my phone. "What's your number?"

He recited it, and I dialed it and hung up so I'd have it to hand. "Cool. What are your names?"

"Jim."

"Col."

"Great. Can you let the other guys know what's going on?"

"Will do," Col said.

I didn't like this frosty air of monosyllabic disapproval. "Let's not wrong-foot this," I said. "I appreciate you getting here so fast, and I'm sorry about the car." I smiled as best I could and gave them two thumbs-up and Jesus Christ I was overacting and why did this shit always need to be so bloody awkward?

I walked away, pausing to turn my engine off, which I'd

forgotten to do. Apart from the hedge behind which Col and whatever the other one's name was had concealed their car, there was no cover for me to approach the house, but by that point I didn't care.

I strode the remaining seventy-five yards, focusing on the birdsong to tune out the blood rushing around my head as I scanned the front of Annie's cottage.

Two windows at the bottom, two up top. Door to the left at the head of the driveway. Tatty Renault parked there. Three other cars parked in this stretch of the road, all empty. I nodded at the two women in the far patrol car, and stepped into Annie's drive.

The house looked quiet, empty. The windows were all closed, the curtains half-drawn. I couldn't see anything inside. Fifteen feet to the door. Nothing happening. I thought about trying to call her again, but I realized my hands were shaking. *Come on, Ali, sort yourself out.*

I reached the door, and listened. Heard nothing. Took a deep breath, steadied my fist and hammered three times.

Something shattered. A short, sharp crash from inside the house, between the second and third knocks.

I pounded on the door again. "Annie?"

My stomach flipped, my temples pounding now. I took a step back, ready to kick the door, but my right leg was jelly. Something at the corner of my eye, a glint behind the window.

I thumped on the wood again, and grabbed the handle and shook and twisted it and shouldered the door and it swung inward, sending me stumbling into a darkened living room, clipping a tall table by the door and scattering its contents on the floor.

Annie Fisher was on the sofa, eyes wide, mouth agape, hands raised, squealing, *"No no no no no."*

On the coffee table in front of her, a gun.

CHAPTER 28

It was a house just like any other: a simple, tidy brick-and-flint box, maybe a hundred or so years old, with a quaint little pitched-roof porch and modern double-glazed windows.

Its incongruities, however, were glaring. For one, it was half a mile from the nearest road, and considerably more from the nearest neighbor, set as it was at the edge of a twenty-acre forest clearing.

It also had a detached garage block, wide enough for four cars, its footprint almost as large as the house itself. And along a rutted track, halfway between the house and the tree line, stood a tall barn, its weathered wooden doors ajar, pitch darkness within.

Jenny drew the BMW up to the head of the driveway, a wide gravel square swept and ridged from the tires of a regular stream of heavy vehicles over the past weeks. She swung the car around to face the garage and cut the engine.

Kevin shuddered in his seat, gazing sadly at the patch of gravel in front of the left-hand garage door where, on his last visit, he'd watched a young woman bleed to death, his own blood mingling with the torrential rain that poured down over his face and into his eyes.

"You okay?" Jenny nudged him with her elbow and unclipped her belt.

He nodded. "It looks different." He wasn't sure how. The sunshine, maybe.

"You okay to do this, or do you want to stay in the car?"

Yes. Kevin very much wanted to stay in the car, but then what was the point in him being here? "Nah, I'm cool," he said, and unstrapped himself and stepped out of the car, a chill trickling through him in spite of the heat. He turned around on the spot, taking in the house, the barn, the empty field between and around them, the wall of pines that marked the boundary on all sides. Beyond, he could just make out the hill above the railway line, at the rim of the flint pit—the gateway to those five girls' grim and lonely resting place.

Kevin reached into the car and took the bunch of keys and the evidence-bagged garage door clicker from the glove box. He pressed each button in turn until both doors clunked and hummed and rolled up and over into the roof. "You ready?"

"I was born ready."

The garage was empty, save for a few cobwebbed garden tools and a ladder hung on the wall. At the far side, where there'd once been an array of rolling tool chests and a false-backed wooden cupboard, there was now only an open doorway onto a flight of stairs.

Kevin led, feeling around the corner for the light switch and illuminating their descent. He did the same at the bottom and a set of LED spots blinked into life, flooding the room into which Jenny now followed him, digging her nails into her palm and trying not to let her claustrophobia overwhelm her.

In the center of the room, all but filling it, was the cage. Twenty feet square, built from ten-gauge steel wire with a two-and-a-half-inch diamond mesh and one-and-a-quarter-inch channel frame. A door, five feet wide and seven feet tall, with a self-locking mechanism and, somewhere back at headquarters, a reinforced titanium padlock.

Jenny hovered in the doorway as Kevin strolled into the cage. There'd been a metal bedframe bolted to the floor the last time he'd been down here. It was gone now, along with the thick rubber matting and the little en suite in the corner that consisted of a toilet, sink and pull-around curtain. It reminded him now of the booze cage out back of the shop he'd worked in, the summer after school.

"You coming?"

Jenny shook her head, shivered quite noticeably. "No, I can see it," she said.

He smiled reassuringly, and nodded. "You can't get shut in," he said.

She hesitated, took a few deep breaths. Walked shakily to the cage door. Examined the frame as though she might find anything noteworthy. Gave up and stepped through.

Kevin beckoned her to stand beside him in the center of the cage. "Single bed over here—" he pointed "—complete with shackles. Toilet in the corner. He gave her a kettle, a fridge, a microwave, although that was broken."

"I've seen the pictures," she said.

Of course. This wasn't her first day on the job. "Pictures are pictures," he said, and walked to the door. "Here's what you don't get from pictures." He stepped outside, swung the door to. Jangled the keys at her, though he didn't click it shut.

Jenny froze before she could react, her face rigid with horror.

"The door's not locked," he said. "You're fine, nothing bad's happening. You're safe. You can walk out any time you like. Erica couldn't. She was down here for three months."

"Kevin, could you open the door, please."

He stepped aside and swung it back. "What was that? Ten seconds? Imagine three months, and tell me you wouldn't come out shooting."

"Don't ever pull a trick like that on me again."

"You needed to see it."

"Yes, fine, and you made your point. Thank you."

Kevin unlocked the front door of the house and opened it onto a bare whitewashed lobby. A door to the right, beside the stairs. A door to the left that led into the kitchen. A third dead ahead: a storeroom, now empty. He showed Jenny through to the living room, where they stood for a moment, watching the dust swirl in the splinters of sunlight that poked in through gaps and cracks in the boards covering the windows. A thousand pinpoints of light, like disco balls.

There were no seats. What furniture there was had been shuffled to the far corner of the room, ornaments and lamps and books and electronic gizmos stacked around it on the floor.

At Jenny's feet, one of two circular imprints in the cream-colored carpet, the pile lighter and thicker between them—the back feet of a settee. There were no front feet.

A wide rectangle had been cut from the carpet and underlay, revealing a trace of a stain on the concrete floor beneath.

Kevin crossed the room, fetched a low side table and placed it between the settee marks, two legs on carpet, two on concrete. "Have a seat," he said.

Jenny looked from Kevin to the table and back again and sighed heavily, her patience clearly waning. "What did I just say?"

"It's not a trick."

She blew a loud breath out through her nose and sat, her

feet apart so as not to rest them on the stain. "You don't have to teach me empathy, you know," she said. "I'm not a robot."

"I know." Kevin leaned against the windowsill and considered his boss, perched awkwardly on a coffee table on the spot where Eli Diaz had been slain on an unseasonably tropical May Day bank holiday. "It's just...you've been jumping to a lot of conclusions lately, and they might look different with a bit of perspective. You know?" She looked up at him, one eyebrow cocked, but in a receptive way, he thought, not threatening. "Ali nearly died on that sofa," he said, emboldened. "Eli did die, right at your feet. And out there, where you parked the car, that's where Rachel Murray died. And Kerry Farrow, she was in that cage, just like Erica was, and we don't know where she died or where she is now, but you know what? The common denominator isn't Erica. It's Tom Reed, or James Faulkner, or whatever else you want to call him. And I'll bet good money the same goes for those five women up on that marsh, and the more we get caught up trying to pin things on that girl, the farther we get from holding him to account for what he did. It's disrespectful to those women, it's disrespectful to Ali and it's disrespectful to the four officers we've lost to this case. So far." He shuddered a little at that last bit, but he didn't think Jenny had noticed. She was staring at Eli Diaz's bloodstain and chewing her tongue. "I need a piss," he said. "I'll meet you back at the car." Then he left the room before she could give him the bollocking he'd just asked for.

For all his bravado, Kevin didn't like being alone in that house. He started to regret his decision before he was halfway up the stairs, but Jenny was at the bottom and he didn't want to lose face after speaking out as he had, so he told himself not to be so stupid and carried on climbing.

Though the house was empty, he closed the door behind him, and turned sideways-on to the toilet in order to keep half an eye on the handle. It wasn't that he felt stalked, watched or shadowed, it was…well, he wasn't sure what it was, but it manifested as a tickly knot at the base of his spine, and he was relieved in more ways than one to finish peeing.

He didn't waste time exploring once he was done. He eyed both bedroom doors as he crossed the landing, and kept his back to the wall on the way downstairs, and darted across the hallway and through the open front door, mentally kicking himself for being a scaredy-cat.

Still, he thought, at least he hadn't freaked out in the cage like a…

Like a…

Kevin came up short. Not only did he now feel like an arsehole for his instinct to mock a woman's reaction to an underground cage designed to keep women hostage, but he had a virtually unobstructed view of twenty acres of land, and he couldn't see said woman anywhere.

The boot of the BMW was open, though.

Kevin didn't get a Bad Feeling just then, not as such. But he was sufficiently unsettled as to put his hand in his pocket for his phone, and to feel a mild surge of alarm upon realizing he'd left it in the car.

He took a breath and admonished himself for a third time. "Don't be a twat, Kevin," he said. That anything could have happened to Jenny in the past three or four minutes, here of all places, was plainly the stuff of horror movies. And Kevin, as he'd taken quite adequate pains to establish, wasn't in one of those. Kevin was a die-hard lethal weapon, and as such he was more than equipped to handle a little jump-scare when Jenny popped up from wherever she was hiding.

Even so, he stopped and listened at all three corners of the house before poking his head around, and, having arrived back at the front door none the wiser, he made a full circuit of the garage, too, just to make sure no one was hiding there, either. Now he felt even more of an idiot.

He returned to the BMW to retrieve his phone and call her. That was when he started to get the Bad Feeling. He stared at the place where it had been for a full fifteen seconds, and then he checked the glove box and under the seat and under the car and then stared at it again, as though it might change its mind and appear before his very eyes. But his phone wasn't there.

He stood, and looked at the vertical boot lid. He couldn't see inside from this angle; he'd have to move closer. He willed his legs to move for an uncomfortable amount of time before they complied, edging him toward the opening, his eyes fixed, unblinking.

It wasn't empty.

"Jen?" His voice was barely a squeak. His eyes ached from the strain of trying to see through the steel haunch of the car. "Jen, are you there?"

She was wearing blue. Whatever was in the boot was blue. But it was impossible; that was what he kept telling himself. They were alone here, miles from anywhere, the only vehicle in the driveway, on a random visit, unplanned before the moment they'd left. No one had followed them here, he was sure of it. He'd taken to *making* sure of it since the team had started losing their heads. So it couldn't be Jenny in the boot. Unless she'd climbed in there herself, which, for a split second, he conceded she might just do in order to get back at him. Maybe she'd seen him edging up the stairs, heard him talking to himself in the bathroom. She did have a sense of humor, after all, even if she didn't air it often.

That was it. It had to be. And so even as it occurred to him what a stereotypical horror-movie thing it was to do, he got ahold of himself and forced a laugh and said, "Very funny, Jen, you can get out now," and stepped around to the back of the BMW.

She wasn't there. It was just a cool box and a spare petrol can.

He turned and took in the cracked-open doors of the barn. Wondered how she could have gotten over there so fast, and why, before the hairs on the back of his neck told him she was standing behind him.

"Okay, you got me," he said as he spun around to face her.

He just had time to register, as she swung the blade at his neck two-handed like a baseball bat, that it wasn't Jenny he was looking at.

CHAPTER 29

"It's not mine, I swear!"

"Annie, don't you fucking touch that gun!"

"I haven't touched it! I'm not going to touch it! It isn't mine!"

"Annie, get the fuck away from it and keep your hands up over your head!" I was on my back foot, fully into the room with nowhere to go and nothing to hide behind, cocked into a shooter's stance more by luck than judgment, with one hand hovering at my throbbing hip as though I had a weapon there, which I did not.

Annie shifted to the opposite end of the sofa, hands up, panicked eyes on me. "It's not mine, Ali, I promise."

"Whose is it?"

She just sat there, shaking her head, and started to cry.

"Annie, talk to me," I barked. There was someone else in the house. Shit, there was someone else in the house, wasn't there? I scanned the room: open plan, stairs leading up from an alcove, archway through to the kitchen, French doors from the dining room out into the garden. Four uniformed officers within a hundred-yard radius. No other help for miles around. And something else. Something else. "Annie, who else is here?"

That gun. I'd seen that gun before.

"Don't fuck about, Annie. Who's in the house?"

I'd stared down the barrel of that gun.

"Ann—"

The penny dropped. Annie, who'd been so pleased with herself after finding that photo. Annie, who'd been so keen to advance the theory of Erica's complicity. Annie, whose name was fucking *Annie*, for Christ's sake.

My head swam. I felt the heat and the bile rising again. *Not now. Not now, Ali.* I forced myself to focus. "It's you, isn't it?" I said. "You're the witness. You know him, don't you? You know That Man." She was sobbing now, shaking her head, hugging her knees. "Annie," I said, hard-edged, no time for compassion right now. "Is he—is *that man* in this house right now?" *Say no. Say no. Please say no, Annie.*

"No."

I stared at her, crying her little heart out, looking toward the kitchen, and I knew that it wasn't her who'd spoken. She couldn't have said a word if she'd tried.

"It's mine." The voice was soft, feminine; a little hoarse maybe, but it was loud, well-projected—a chest voice, not a head voice. It sent a chill right through me.

I didn't go for my phone. I went for the gun instead, taking two long, painful strides and snatching it up from the table, regretting the forensic faux-pas even as I stepped clear of the furniture and leveled it at the center of the archway. "Erica," I said, my voice cracked and breathless. How was this happening? What *was* happening? "It's Ali Green. I'm alone. I'm armed. I want to see your hands."

"I haven't got anything."

"Show me." Why hadn't Annie gone for the gun? Why had Erica left it on the table? Was it even loaded? The last time I'd seen it, in Erica's hands, it had only had one bullet left in it. The faint scar on my cheek began to burn. A memory of her clawing at my face. A vision of scraps of my skin lodged under her nails.

Erica slid sideways into the archway—a silhouette at first, blocking the light from the window behind her. She held her hands out in front of her as she stepped into the room and resolved into color, and her appearance startled me. She barely resembled my memory of her, or the photos pinned to the incident board, or propped against my computer, or stored in my phone. She'd lost at least a stone, her limbs bordering on gangly, her hips sharp and narrow, and she'd ironed the tumbling curls out of her hair.

There was no mistaking her eyes, though. Erica stared into mine along the rib of the revolver, just as I had hers the last time we'd met. "Touché," she said. And then between us, held up between her forefinger and thumb, a bullet, copper-jacketed with a brass case. "I don't keep it in there."

"Stand still."

"I am."

I thumbed the chamber release and let the cylinder pivot out of the gun. Empty. Snapped it back in and lowered the weapon. "Give it to me."

Erica took a step forward and placed the cartridge in my outstretched hand. "I didn't come here to hurt her. Or you."

"Sit down."

She didn't.

"Why are you here?"

She glanced at Annie, who'd buried her head in her hands.

"Don't look at her," I said. "I've been to the caravan. I saw the postcard."

She sighed and dropped her hands, making me flinch. "Mum," she said.

"Yeah, to protect you."

"From what? You?"

"I th—"

"Does Richard know?"

My breath caught in my throat and I bit the side of my tongue painfully. I stared at her, and she stared back.

"Ali, does he know about the caravan?"

"You don't know," I said. I glanced at Annie, who silently shook her head.

"Don't know wh—" She startled. Her eyes grew as they darted between us, panic flashing through them. "What's happened to her? Annie?"

"Erica, sit down," I said.

She threw me an incredulous glare and then, in one smooth movement, she swept up a leather bag from the floor at the end of the sofa, slung it over her shoulder and walked straight through me on her way to the door.

"Erica, stop!" I managed to get a hand to the bag and pull it back; she jerked around to face me with a fist already raised and I stepped into it before she had the chance to swing, blocking her arm with mine and sweeping her feet from under her with my leg. "Just stop," I shouted, Erica struggling to regain her feet even as she hit the carpet. "She's safe. Nothing's happened to her, she's fine."

She slumped, let go of my leg, sat on the carpet, panting. "What don't I know?" she said.

"There's a picnic site on the other side of the woods. People use it for dogging. There was some old bloke sitting in his car, playing with himself. I told him I'd call the police if he didn't give me a lift back to town, so he did. I went home.

Mum helped me. My nan died while I was…away. Did you know that? She lived on her own, out on the Fens, middle of nowhere. They haven't even cleared the place out yet. That's where I've been. I was kind of hoping you'd have found him by now, or he'd have come looking for me. I thought it wouldn't take much for him to find me, but then you didn't, either, so I don't know."

"Why did you want him to find you?"

She nodded at the empty revolver on the table between us. "That was what the bullet was for."

"So what made you come back?"

"That policeman. The one who was looking for me. I panicked when I heard what happened to him. And then Mum told me what you said and I figured every copper in the country was going to be looking for me. She said Richard'd turn me in so I couldn't stay at hers or go back to Nana's. That's why she sent me to the caravan. He didn't know about it. It used to be my dad's. It was her safe place, although I was still pretty sure *he'd* find me there."

"What happened?"

"You saw the postcard. It was under the door when I woke up. Fucker followed me out there, came right to my door when I was asleep and didn't do me in. Just left me a note. *Take care of Annie.* So that's what I'm doing, because a) God knows she needs a friend right now, and b) I figured sooner or later he'd stop believing his own hype and realize I wasn't going to do his dirty work for him, and I'd be here waiting when he came to do it himself." She gave Annie a pointed look. "Except I got that wrong, didn't I?"

I felt Annie deflate beside me. "Wrong how?" I said.

"Tell her, Annie. Show her the money."

I looked at Annie. She sighed and dragged her hands through her hair and gave a tight nod. Stood and crossed to the kitchen. Took the lid off a cookie jar. Returned with a wad of twenty-pound notes and dropped it on the table. "I didn't know what to do with it," she said.

"Annie, what…?"

"That's where I found it. It's all there."

"What do you mean, that's where you found it?"

She collapsed back onto the sofa and just sat there, shaking her head.

Erica uncrossed her legs and stood. "I'll get you a drink," she said.

"It's not my money. I didn't ask for it. I didn't ask for anything."

Oh God, Annie, what have you done? "He's paying you?" I said.

Annie's face was a knot of frustration. I could all but see her tongue tying itself in knots.

"Drink this." Erica came from the kitchen with a glass brimming with ice and what I assumed was vodka. She took one of Annie's trembling hands and gently curled the drink into it. "He's got a key," she said, sitting back down and tucking her legs under her. "He's been coming here when Annie's out. He left her the money. He doesn't want to kill her, else he'd have done it weeks ago. Fucking idiot thinks we're all on the same side."

"Oh, for fuck's sake, Annie." It was all I could muster. I watched her drain the glass, and hold it out to Erica, who got up and took it back to the kitchen.

Too much to deal with. Pressure building. Pain in the back of my head. I had to get out. "Stay here," I said. "Sit down."

I left the front door open and walked to the car. Reread the postcard. Rooted around in my bag and found three tenners and a business card. Took them to the patrol car parked ten yards behind and gave them to Tim or Bill or whatever his name was. "Buy everyone drinks and ice creams," I said. "Panic's over. Everything's okay. Sorry I kept you. Put my name on everything, I'll square it all away, alright?"

The two of them looked at the crumpled notes in Jim's (that was his name) hand. "You sure you're okay?" he said.

"Yep!" I gave him my toothiest grin and patted the roof of the car. "Have a great day, guys. I really appreciate your help."

I waved as they passed me on my way back to the house, and then I collapsed against Annie's car and wailed silently into the blackness of eternity.

CHAPTER 30

Kevin was looking down when he turned around, expecting a face half a foot lower than his, so the machete blade struck him on the chin, splitting the bone as it knocked him off his feet and opening what he imagined, in the strangely calm and lucid second before he hit the ground, to resemble a second mouth directly below the one to which he was accustomed.

It didn't hurt yet, at least not as much as the back of his head where it hit the gravel, and the blood wasn't running into his eyes, so he was able to think fast enough to kick his leg up and stop a second downward stroke with his foot. He felt it go in, but it didn't go through, which was a positive.

The man he knew as Tom Reed pulled back the blade and said, "For fuck's sake, Kevin, keep still so I can kill you."

"No." Kevin figured he was probably in a lot of trouble right then, but if he was getting butchered, he was getting butchered alive until he ran out of limbs to fight with.

Reed kicked his worryingly numb foot out of the way and brought the foot-long machete down tip-first, aiming straight for his heart. Kevin, on autopilot, threw his arms out straight, his hands going for Reed's but catching the blade instead, just below the hilt. He stopped the blow, but he might have lost a finger or two; he wasn't sure. He couldn't feel anything but rage and fear.

"Stop it," Reed said.

"Why are you here?" It didn't seem like the time to ask, but he really wanted to know.

Reed put all of his weight behind the knife. "It's my house, dickhead. Why are *you* here?"

"Where's DI Riley?" Arms buckling.

"Is that who that was?"

"If you've killed her—"

"You'll what?"

"You're going to have to take my fucking hands off if you don't want to die, you piece of shit."

"Fine." Reed pitched up suddenly, slicing Kevin's palms deeper and releasing the knife from his grip and swinging it at his right hand.

Kevin managed to snatch it out of the way, and took the initiative while his assailant was off balance. He aimed a kick with his uncut left foot and managed to land it on the inside of Reed's knee, folding it. He scrambled up as Reed went down, trying not to count his fingers as he used his elbows and one leg to lever himself more or less upright.

Reed lashed out with a backhanded swing, taking a notch out of Kevin's calf. He barely felt that, either, and it was the one he was rapidly repurposing as his spare leg, not his hopping leg, so it wasn't going to slow him down any.

His thoughts, however, *were* slowing down with every cup of blood that poured out of his face, so he didn't think about the consequences of aiming his bisected foot at Reed's head until it was too late to stop the swing.

He felt that. The pain was so immediate and so visceral

that he swooned briefly before suddenly and uncontrollably throwing up in the boot of the car as he fell against it.

Then Reed was up on his feet again, with victory written all over his face. "Good shot," he said, and pointed the knife at the cool box in the boot, now dripping in blood and vomit. "On both counts."

Kevin's stomach turned over again, but he kept it in. "What do you mean?" he panted.

Reed shrugged. The bastard was just standing there, playing with him now. He knew he'd won.

"Oh, come on." Kevin's head swam. He was losing too much blood. His foot was probably severed inside his shoe. He'd definitely lost a finger somewhere. His chin was literally hanging off. Christ, he hoped they glued him back together before they let Gemma see his body. *Duct tape. Anything. Don't let her remember me in pieces.* "Oh God, what's in the box?" he gurgled.

"Open it and see."

He knew what Reed was doing. He wanted him to turn his back. Lean forward. Offer his neck. Let him lop off his head with honor. Well, fuck that. Kevin didn't take his eyes of the man standing before him as he fiddled the handle of the box with his knuckles and hooked his wrist under it and lifted it onto the lip of the boot.

It was moderately heavy—about five kilos, he thought—and whatever was inside was one big lump that slid around and thumped on the sides. "What is it?" he said. "What's in the box, Tom?"

"Open it."

"No."

"Alright. Well, look, I need to be getting on. I only came back here to pick up the rest of my shit." He laughed. "It's the first chance I've had when no one's been around. I mean, what were the odds, mate, seriously? Your timing's impeccable, I'll give you that. Anyway, whatever, hang a lampshade on it for now. I really just need you to die. Sorry. Nothing personal. Gotta go. Shit to do." And with that, he flicked the machete up over his shoulder, and brought it around in a fast, sweeping arc, straight at the top of Kevin's head.

Kevin was ready, both shredded hands gripping the handle of the cool box, and with a grunt he swung it at the incoming blade.

They connected. Kevin saw the shockwave travel through Reed's shoulders as the machete stopped dead, and before the other man could react, he pitched the ten-pound box at the center of his face.

It wasn't a perfect shot, but it was good enough. Reed got a hand to it, but it punched him in the nose and cheekbone and sent him back three steps, four, an angry "Ow" his immediate response.

It wasn't a lot of space, but Kevin took it, hopping around to the driver's door of the car, leaving a thick smear of blood from his hands across the windows. He got two of his good fingers to the handle and threw the door open, roared through the pain as he scrambled inside and punched the lock button as Reed made a grab for it. "Fuck off!" he yelled, trying not to watch as Reed drew back the machete and aimed it at the window.

They both noticed at the same time that the passenger-side door was still open. Reed bolted for it as Kevin hoisted himself over the center console and grabbed the handle and pulled it shut.

The key was still in its slot. Kevin jammed his foot onto the brake pedal and stabbed at the starter with a knuckle, waking the engine; he knocked it into Reverse with his wrist and stamped on the throttle with his left foot, pulling Reed across the driveway as he backed clear of the garage and knocking him down again when he hit the brake. He tipped the lever into Drive. Floored the throttle. The rear wheels spun in place, the big BMW squatting and fishtailing and leaping forward.

He jerked the wheel. His palms opened up and he sucked in a sharp breath, the pain flooding his senses as his hands slid uselessly around the leather rim.

Kevin froze as the car punched through the garage door, tearing it off its rail and smashing the windscreen a split second before it hit the far wall at thirty miles an hour. The wall didn't give, but Kevin did, folding in half like a ragdoll and mashing his torn face into the air bag and his knees into the dashboard. His lungs filled with smoke and his head filled with pain and *now* he had blood in his eyes as well as everywhere else.

Reed was on his feet and advancing on the car. If Kevin was still alive in there, he'd be a damn sight easier to kill now.

Kevin *was* still alive and, more crucially, still semialert. He twisted around to look out through the back window and saw his furious would-be assassin crossing the driveway apace. He tried the starter again, despite the front end of the car being crumpled into a pile in front of the windscreen. No go. So he did the only other thing that entered his head.

Kevin shouldered the door open and pitched himself out of the car, crawling on his elbows and knees for the door not ten feet away in the center of the garage wall. He didn't look back; he knew it wouldn't help to know what was there. Instead, he dragged himself to the top of the basement stairs and, using his three good fingers and one working foot, pushed himself over the precipice.

Every stair on the way down put a dent in one of his ribs. His hands were all but useless for the task of stopping him at the bottom, and he accordioned when he hit the floor, flipping onto the top of his head and crashing down on his back.

He could see the top of the stairs from where he lay; see the shadow fall across them as Reed's frame filled the doorway.

Kevin summoned the last of his strength to roll over onto his front and dragged himself, commando-style, along the concrete floor. Reed was halfway down the stairs by the time he got his backside into the cage, and was at the bottom as he pulled his legs in and swiveled around to reach for the door.

It was heavy, too heavy for a man with hands like Kevin's, but as Reed made a dash for it, he managed to get it to move.

Reed's fingertips were brushing the door as it slammed shut and the twin locks clicked into place. And then they were both on their knees, foreheads all but touching through the mesh, Reed hissing furiously, Kevin blowing blood bubbles out of his nose and both of his mouths.

"Fuck you," Kevin said.

Reed blew out a breath and nodded. "Fuck you too."

"You're not killing me today, you bastard."

"I'm not even bothered," Reed panted. "I just don't care enough not to. Where are the keys?"

"In my pocket."

"How are you going to get out?"

Kevin looked up at the lock. There was no keyhole on the inside. The mesh was too small to get a hand through. "Shit," he said.

"I didn't take a spare. Your lot have got them all."

Kevin looked at his hands, his shoe, the blood pooling under him on the floor. *I'll make a stain like Eli*, he thought. "Doesn't matter. I'll probably bleed out. You win anyway."

Reed looked him in the eye, and smiled. "Nah," he said. "I'll give you that one. Round's over and you're still alive."

"Awesome." *Make sure you tell my pregnant wife that; she'll be fucking thrilled.*

"Tell me something." Reed sat back on his feet, regarding Kevin with something that looked like childish curiosity, but surely wasn't. "Your head. Where Erica hit you. Does it hurt when the weather changes?"

In spite of himself, Kevin shook the offending head. "No."

"Oh." Reed looked…disappointed? "My arm kills me when it rains," he said.

"Good."

Reed laughed. "That's fair." He considered him for a moment, and then said, "For what it's worth, she didn't kill anyone. The things you've been saying about her? All me."

"That's what I thought."

"Well, sometimes it doesn't matter what we think, does it? It's all about what we can prove. You know that as well as anyone."

Kevin stared at him through the cage door, and wondered what the hell he was trying to say.

He didn't elaborate, though. He just sat there, thinking and watching him until Kevin started to feel faint and needed to lie down.

Whether Reed sensed he was about to die or simply grew bored, Kevin couldn't tell, but a minute or two later, he stood. "She'll come looking for you," he said. "Maybe she'll get here in time. Maybe I'll even still be here." He smiled sadly through the mesh. "I hope not. I don't want to have to kill her, as well. I still feel bad about…you know. Anyway. Better get on," he said. "No hard feelings, eh?"

And then he was gone, and the lights went out.

EPISODE 6

CHAPTER 31

I don't know how long I'd stood there, or how much vodka Annie had put away by the time I'd collected my thoughts and ducked back inside the house, but she seemed eerily calm, perched on the edge of the sofa beside her empty glass, her eyes dry, her back straight and her hands wedged between her knees like she was about to tell a story. Lost for words, I waved a "WTF" at Erica's angelic little face.

"Yeah, that's totally normal," she shrugged. "She's high-functioning. What can you do?" She smiled and gestured to a mug of coffee on the table. "Not sure how you like it," she said, "but it's warm and wet."

Same way I like my women, I thought, and tried and failed not to giggle. Erica was biting her lip. She totally knew.

"I'm sorry about before," Annie said.

I nodded. "So talk to me. Just the facts, ma'am."

Erica gave me the side-eye.

"Just…tell me what happened, in small words and short sentences. And make it convincing, because right now it's looking really, really bad for you, Annie."

She nodded. "I was all ready to tell you, you know. I thought I was being sent to headquarters to get fired. I was going to tell Riley everything, but…well, the next thing I knew, I still had a job, and then once I'd not said anything, it was too late to say anything, wasn't it? I could have handled going to jail if I'd had nothing left to lose, but not then."

"So tell me now."

"Mark Boon," she said.

The dead sex offender in the flat smeared in Erica's DNA. I looked at Erica; it didn't seem to register. "Okay."

"I was on a date in the city. I got stood up. I went for a walk and ended up down by the river. It was the middle of the night, there was no one around. He came at me."

"Mark Boon did?"

She nodded. "He knocked me over and started trying to pull my trousers down. I just…froze."

This wasn't the opening I was expecting—the one where I realized I had no idea of anything this woman might have been through.

"And then *he* was there. James. Or Thomas Reed, as you call him."

"Or Rob, if you're me," Erica said.

"He dragged him away, might have hit him with something, I don't know. But he rescued me, at any rate. He was really kind. Brought me home, made sure I was okay. Didn't try anything on, didn't make me feel unsafe in any way. He just looked after me, and then he left. And no, I never asked him what he'd been doing there that night."

My heart sank. This was not what I wanted to hear, although it explained why Annie might not have considered him a viable serial killer.

"Your DI, Fairey. He came here a couple of days later, asking questions. I told him James… Reed—" she glanced at Erica with a sympathetic smile "—Rob, whatever. I told him he'd been with me all night, because as far as I knew he had. He didn't seem to like that."

"He wanted him not to have an alibi?"

She nodded. "I think so, yeah. But I told the truth, as far as I knew. I passed out at some point and didn't wake up until lunchtime the next day, so I had no idea what time he'd left. I had no idea who he was. I just thought he was a nice guy. And then, a while later, he came back saying he needed my help, and I figured I owed him, so I said okay."

"To what?"

"I said he could stay here for a couple of days, like, officially. That if anyone asked me, I'd tell them he was here. But no one ever asked."

"When was this?"

"When Mark Boon was killed."

I looked at Erica again. She looked at me. "Who's Mark Boon?" she said.

"A dead rapist who had your knickers in his flat."

She was blank for a moment before her face drained of color. Then, a spark of recognition. "Wait. Rob said something to me about framing me for murder. I thought he was—"

"Google him," I said. I turned back to Annie. "So you're saying that the night Boon died, you agreed to give Reed a false alibi?"

She flinched, but nodded. "He left his van here, and some other stuff, but he was gone for at least a day and a night."

"Did he stay here with you at all?"

"Yeah, he was in my bed when I came home the second night. But…nothing happened."

"What do you mean?"

"I mean he didn't even try to touch me or anything."

Erica raised a hand. "Me, either. Well, apart from… Well

anyway, he didn't try to rape me. I don't think he could, to be honest."

"Could what?"

"Like…get it up."

"Wait," I said. "Apart from what?"

Erica shrugged. "Well, I let him give me a bath. I thought it might make my life easier, but he just fumbled about and started crying, so…"

"And that was it? That was all that happened between you?"

"Mate, he kept me in a cage, in case you didn't get that memo. I might be batshit but I've got *some* self-respect. He killed Sarah and Kerry. I tried to shoot him, remember?"

"You know he killed Sarah?"

"I didn't see her. I only saw a pile of bin bags before he knocked me out. He told me later she didn't suffer, though. So yeah, I know."

"So Sarah and Kerry… Wait." Kerry. A surge of excitement. "What do you know about Kerry?"

"She was my roommate for a few days. She wasn't much fun. Then he took her away to play some sort of game with her."

"A game?"

"I don't know, but she didn't come back."

I put my head in my hands and tried to rub the insanity out of it, but to no avail. I gave Annie a long, hard look, and asked her, "When did you last see him?"

"That was it," she said. "But he's been here. He's still got a key. He keeps leaving things. That money was here a couple of days ago."

"Why haven't you changed the locks?"

"What's the point? I didn't want to make him angry. I hoped I'd just prove he isn't a monster and make everything okay. He's the only guy who's ever been nice to me." She laughed. "God, I'm so lame."

Erica nodded her agreement. I considered her for a moment. She looked so small sitting there, curled up like a little girl. But she wasn't small. However much Annie had screwed up, the image she'd pulled out of ViPER was no less real. I had to know the answer. "I've got a picture of you," I said. "Driving that Transit van, the day my partner disappeared."

Erica didn't look shocked, or frightened, or even dismayed. She just shrugged and said, "Yeah, probably."

I waited a beat, but that was her whole answer. "Explain," I said.

"He made me drive it there. He said he wanted to get rid of their car. I was scared if I didn't do it he'd kill my mum or my sister. I bought petrol, I drove it to where he said, he set fire to the car, then he took me back and let me sleep in the house for being good."

"It was him who set the car on fire?"

She paused, perhaps a moment too long. Her mouth said, "Yes," but her eyes said no. "And I didn't know there were bodies in it, before you ask."

"But you knew there were bodies somewhere?"

"I knew they'd been to the house. I didn't know what he'd done to them." She held my stare, unblinking. Didn't back down. Finally, she said, "I'm sorry for what I did to you."

The air left me like I'd been punched in the chest. I felt Annie stiffen beside me. Jenny's crackpot theory about loops through the woods flashed through my mind. An image of Eli Diaz, his head flopping uselessly in the puddle of blood in my lap. "Tell me what you did," I gasped.

Erica's face didn't change. There was nothing in her eyes, no more menace than remorse. "I didn't want you to die," she said. "But I knew you would if I left you. And I left you anyway. I'm sorry. I can be a bit of a bitch sometimes."

Annie put a hand on my back and held it there silently as I collected my breath. "It's okay," I said. "You did what you had to do."

She laughed and shook her head. "Not yet, I haven't. I ran away instead. But hey, I'm not running now, am I?"

I looked at Annie. Annie looked at the gun.

"Don't even," I said. "Jesus Christ. What am I going to tell Jen?"

Annie shrugged. "The truth, I guess. It's either my career or both of ours, right?"

My career. That was a funny one. How much of a career did I have left? Sure, I'd caught up with Erica and uncovered Annie's secret, but I could barely walk or remember my own name, so really it could go either way right about now.

I needed to talk to Jenny. God alone knew what I was going to say, but all of the bullshit had to end, right now. I stood and took my pad and pen from my back pocket. Flipped to a fresh page and wrote down everything I'd just heard while Erica went to the toilet and Annie guzzled another vodka. Then I dialed Jenny's number and, again, reached her voicemail.

I tried Kevin. No answer.

Where the hell were they?

I rang the incident room and got through to Dan again. "Is everything alright?" he said.

"I'm fine. No panic. Have you heard from Jen or Kevin yet?"

"No, I was about to ask you the same thing."

I tried to keep my voice steady; did a better job than usual. "Do me a favor," I said. "See if you can get a ping off her car if it's tracked, or failing that, either of their phones. Straight through to mine, if you can."

"I'll do my best."

"You *are* the best," I said, and hung up without saying goodbye, like all the cool cops do. I didn't feel very cool, though. I felt sick. "Annie," I said. "Get your shoes on. Something's happened to Jen and Kevin."

Erica frowned and reached for her bag despite not being invited.

Annie looked down at the shoes she was already wearing, turned the color of swamp water, and threw up on them.

"That's normal too," said Erica.

I looked at the pair of them, and at myself in the mirror, and tried very, very hard not to cry.

CHAPTER 32

"Are you sure this is a good idea?"

I wasn't, not even remotely, so I looked at Erica in the rear-view mirror and said, "It's the only idea," which I realized answered the question as well as if I'd just said, "No."

We'd been five minutes from headquarters with our stories finally straight when Dan rang.

"They're on the marsh at Two Mile Bottom," he said. "There's a Vodafone mast right across the road. Last ping came from there about twenty minutes ago. Probably left their phones in the car."

My gut feeling told me that wasn't what had happened, but I couldn't let myself imagine that any Bad Thing had happened, not with my harsh words to Jenny still bouncing around in my head. Of all the things to be able to remember, that was simultaneously both the most and the least helpful; it made sense of Jenny being at the crime scene, but if anything had happened to her, then it was on my head, and I really didn't want to think about that.

In any case, they were either alive and fine and hadn't heard their phones ringing, or they were dead; That Man didn't waste time standing around explaining his dastardly plan. He'd have cut their throats through to the bone and left them where they fell.

Nevertheless, the plan changed, and I mashed the pedal to the metal and set a course for the center of the forest.

There were vehicles parked on the access road: two CSI vans, a support unit and a panda car. Neither Jenny's BMW nor any of the unmarked pool cars were anywhere to be seen.

I pulled the car up to the head of the path leading into the flint pit and told Annie to go check. Her shoes were already wet, after all.

"Are you thinking what I'm thinking?" Erica, from the backseat—the first words she'd uttered since Dan had called.

I didn't answer. I waited for Annie to come back and tell me what I already knew: no one had seen Jenny or Kevin all morning. "We're looking for bodies now, aren't we?" she said.

I didn't answer that, either, though I thought she was probably right. Nor did I get out and walk up the hill to take a long, meaningful look over the treetops to the house in the distance. I just brought up the map on my phone and pinpointed the house and gambled on the fastest way of getting there.

The track ran parallel to the railway line and the river, the forest both looming beyond and flashing past my window at sixty miles an hour. Passing the row of shuttered railway cottages on the left, I hit the brakes and swung the Alfa across a narrow footpath and a clump of protruding tree roots and squared it against the pedestrian tunnel under the tracks. For a brief, gutting moment I didn't think it was going to fit, but give or take some paint on my already-scuffed door mirror, I managed to squeeze it through.

"Left," Annie said, pointing my phone to the right.

I stopped the car. "My left or your left?"

"That way."

I went right, blowing down weeds and startling a flock of Highland cattle, pinning the throttle open just far enough that the pitch and roll of the road felt only mildly unsafe until I reached a T-junction. "That way?"

Annie opened her eyes and checked the screen. "Yeah, then again at the next turn."

I didn't need directions after that. There was no mistaking the mouth of that driveway, or the shade of the darkness as it curled away into the trees.

"Okay," I said, the car idling between the gateposts. I tried not to think about my pulse or my breathing or the smell of burned oil and brake dust or Annie's trembling hands or Erica's wild, frightened eyes in the mirror or the open gate or the menacing shadows or the memory of what had happened the last time I'd driven into them. I had no idea of what we were going to find at the end of the drive. Maybe two dead police officers. Maybe nothing at all. Maybe I'd completely lost the plot. Maybe I was about to walk into a trap. Maybe I should call for backup, and embarrass myself even further. Maybe I was just sitting in a car with a fugitive and a corrupt alcoholic detective and the joke was entirely on me.

"Ali?"

I looked at Annie, aware that I'd probably said all that out loud. "I guess there's one way to find out, right?"

She nodded.

Erica sighed from the backseat. Leaned forward and poked her startlingly sweat-drenched face between us. "Are we nearly there yet?" she said. Her mouth was joking, but her eyes most certainly weren't.

★ ★ ★

The high sun was no match for these woods. They were darker than I remembered, dense at the top and dense at the bottom with ferns and brambles, dead branches and fallen trunks. You could hide pretty much anything you liked in there and no one would ever find it.

That thought made me shudder even more than the sudden cold inside the car, so I shut it out of my mind and concentrated on following the track. Behind me, Erica was pale and deathly silent, her eyes darting between the trees, probing the shadows, peering up to look for the sky. I dreaded to think what those eyes had seen in this place. Sooner or later I'd have to ask her, or someone like me would, and she'd have to see it all over again. She was strong, there was no doubt about that, but her strength was neither here nor there. I'd signed up, implicitly at least, for what I'd been through. Erica had signed up for a day out with her best friend, and she'd been punished for it every day since.

And Annie? Well, Annie had signed on the same dotted line I had. Wherever it had gone wrong for her, whatever had driven her to the drink that had led her here, and whatever I thought about the way she'd dealt with it, she knew she'd done wrong, and I knew she'd find a way to atone for it without my interference.

And that thought filled me with dread, too, because on top of everything else I knew, however much I tried to kid myself, however much I ran the numbers in my aching head, I knew in my gut that we were driving once more into a situation for which we weren't remotely prepared.

Erica knew it, too. "I don't like this," she said. "I've got a bad feeling."

Annie reached over her shoulder, offering her hand, and Erica took it.

"You'll be fine," I said. "Nothing's going to happen. Just

stay in the car and if anything's even slightly out of place we'll hunker down and call in backup. And if anything *does* happen, don't hang about, just get to the police station in town. You'll be okay, I promise."

I caught her eye in the mirror. She wasn't stupid—she knew I couldn't promise that—but she smiled anyway, and said, "Okay."

And then there was light at the end of the tunnel. The trees ended abruptly and the sun blazed into the car, blinding me for a second. I blinked it away, squinted out at the house as its familiar ordinariness spread across the windscreen. I clocked the open door as I brought the car to a halt and silenced the engine. As my stomach began its descent toward my pelvic floor, I turned my head and took in the missing garage door and the tangled wreckage of the white BMW. I saw the open boot and the blood smeared across the rear bumper, the shattered glass and the crumpled wing and the wheel folded in at an awkward angle. I saw a flash of That Man's van, in the warehouse at headquarters—the incongruous stillness, the explosion of violence frozen in place. And then it was me who was frozen in place, staring at the car, dragging my unwilling eyes toward the door of the house, the door I'd walked in through and been carried out of, and I was suddenly, horribly aware that I was belted into my seat, entirely vulnerable to whatever horror might hence unleash itself.

There was a stunned silence in the car for a long, tense moment.

Erica was the first to take a loud, gasping breath. Annie was the first to say, "Oh, fuck." And I was the first to know someone was going to die.

CHAPTER 33

"Okay, so we call for backup."

I stared at the door. Counted ten seconds, listening to the blood rushing through my head. Annie was right. Call for backup—that was what I'd said. I nodded, tried to find the words to agree, but my hand was already on the door handle and all that came out was, "Erica, stay in the car."

"Fuck no," she said, scrambling out faster than I had, her feet on the ground before Annie was even out of her seat belt. "We're already a walking horror-film cliché. You're not leaving me alone. We're not splitting up. If anyone's going in there, we all are."

I ducked back into the car and took the revolver from the glove box. Cracked it open and took the bullet from my pocket and slotted it into the chamber. Turned the cylinder to next-up the round and clicked it shut. "I've told you what I want you to do," I said. "If you don't do it, it's on you."

"What else is new?"

Annie came around the car as I scanned the windows, the tree line, the distinctly uninviting barn, before starting for the garage. I kept to the left, indicating to Annie to watch the side wall of the building while I peered into the darkness within.

"I don't like this," she said.

I rolled my eyes. "None of us like it. We're only going to check the car so we know what we're dealing with. Okay?"

"What if there's no one in there?"

"Then we're too bloody late," I said, and raised the revolver and pivoted around the door frame and pressed my back to the wall and swept the garage with the gun sight. "Okay, it's clear." I crossed to the BMW, keeping the gun trained at first on the open boot and then, as I sidestepped the rear of the car, each of the windows in turn. There was no one inside. "Fuck," I said.

The BMW almost looked like an old-school motorway patrol car, a thick red stripe running most of the length of its bright white flank. Someone had lost a lot of blood.

"What's that?" Erica, huddled beside me, pointed at the driver's door, just ahead of the handle, where the smear of blood ended in what looked for all the world like an arrow head.

The air fell thick with dread as three heads turned to the pitch-dark opening in the garage wall.

Annie leaned in close and whispered, "What's in there?"

"That'll be my room." Erica took two steps toward the doorway before I managed to catch her arm.

"Trap," I said, and held her back as I edged quietly to the threshold. I touched a finger to my lips and held my breath and listened.

Birds. Annie, breathing. My own heartbeat.

Erica tapped my shoulder and mimed reaching around the doorway and flicking a switch. I closed my eyes and listened some more, to the hairs on my neck and the tingling in my spine. There was someone there; I was almost sure of it. Right on the other side of that wall, listening, holding their breath, waiting to cut off whatever part of me was first through the door. I could *feel* it.

I motioned for Annie and Erica to stand back, and then I took a step away from the wall and held the gun close to the door frame and cocked the hammer. Took three deep breaths and summoned my voice.

"Armed police," I said, loud enough to startle all three of us. "Place your weapon on the ground where I can see it, and come out slowly, hands-first." I had no idea if that was right; I'm not authorized to carry a gun, and if I had to fire it I'd be in a world of shit, but at that moment I didn't care. Every nerve in my body was on edge, every muscle rigid, my eyes focused on the ridge of the revolver and the darkness beyond, an urgent memo scrolling through my brain: *Check before you shoot. Check before you shoot. Check before you shoot.*

No movement. No sound.

"I repeat. Throw down whatever you're holding, and follow your hands slowly out the door."

Nothing.

I looked back to Annie and jabbed a finger at the car outside and mouthed the word *torch*. She nodded and Erica watched her as she darted out to the Alfa, grabbed the Maglite from the glove box and hurried back inside. I took another step back and gestured to her to take my position against the wall.

Silently, "Okay?"

Nod.

"Three. Two. One."

Annie flicked on the torch and angled it around the frame, bathing the stairwell in sudden and blinding light as I stepped in and swung the gun around the corner, finger tight on the trigger, heart pounding, ears already humming in anticipation.

There was no one there.

I reached in and flicked on the light switch and waved to Annie to turn off the flashlight. Stood for a moment, just breathing and trying not to succumb to the dizziness threatening to tip me down the thick carpeted stairs. I kept the gun trained on the doorway at the bottom, the room beyond now filled with bright white light. "Kevin?" I yelled. "Jenny?"

Nothing.

I started down the stairs, instinctively spreading my weight and rolling my feet, though I knew the steps were concrete and wouldn't creak. I could feel Erica behind me, and hear Annie's unsteady breath behind her. A chill ran through me from bottom to top and lodged my heart in my throat. This was wrong. We shouldn't be here. Whoever wasn't hiding behind that wall was waiting for me at the bottom of these stairs. And I was scared.

And then, halfway down, a faint gurgling groan from below. I recoiled. Erica hit me from behind and grabbed my shoulders to stop me from falling.

I swallowed the lump in my throat and forced a breath and said, "Who's there?" in a trembling voice that made me hate myself.

Another wet groan, this time with what sounded like a "Help" attached.

"Who's down there?"

A cough. "Ali?"

Jesus. "Kevin?"

"Help."

"Are you alone?"

"Alone… Det-Detective constable f-four-seven-t-two… K-Kevin McManus. Assistance r-r…" He gurgled again, coughed up what I guessed was a puddle of blood. "Assistance required," he said.

Good enough. I bolted to the bottom of the stairs, swung

the gun around the door in a cursory sweep and stopped dead in my tracks.

I'd never seen the cage before. Pictures, yes, but I'd learned about it from my hospital bed. It was bigger than I'd imagined, dominating the space. I've stayed in far smaller hotel rooms with worse facilities, although they generally had windows and the option to check out, and none of them had had their fixtures and fittings replaced with the shredded remains of my colleague.

"Annie, watch the stairs. Kevin, we're here." I went to him, tried the latch. No go.

"You need the key," Kevin said.

I took in the blood-soaked shoe, the smudged stain soaking into the concrete, the sticky handprints. And his face. Jesus Christ, what had he done to his face? His lower jaw was split in two, his chin hanging at a crooked angle, the skin slipping away from the bone. His face was entirely covered in blood, and it was oozing out from the crack below his mouth at a worrying rate. "Fucking hell. Okay, where is it? And where's Jenny?"

"I don't know. He took her." He brought his right arm out from under him, leaving a new trail of drips from the wide-open gash in his palm. A bunch of keys hooked over his third finger. The fourth one missing. "I don't know which one," he muttered.

Erica knelt by my side and said, "Hi, Kevin."

He looked up at her, blinking blood from his eyes, and attempted a smile. "Hi, Erica."

"Show me the keys," she said. "Spread them out."

He nodded and dropped the bunch onto the floor and began fanning them with his fingertip.

I put my arm across her shoulders and asked if she was okay. She nodded. "I need to call an ambulance," I said.

Kevin coughed, spraying flecks of blood, and said, "He might still be here."

I considered that for a second, and knew there was nothing much I could do about it. I needed to get backup out here an hour ago, and I needed to go outside for a signal. "Erica, listen. Annie and I will be right upstairs, okay? If he is here, we'll be right between you and him. Get this door unlocked, I'll be back in a minute."

Erica was shaking—God knows what she felt, being down in that basement—but she agreed.

I picked up the gun and let it lead Annie and me back up the stairs, backs to the wall, hyperalert still to every corner and shadow. I skirted Jenny's car, covering every square inch of the floor with the revolver until I was satisfied the garage was empty.

"He's not going to make it, is he?"

I kept to the east wall, out of sight of the house, and took out my phone and dialed the number. "I don't know. We need to clear this place and find Jenny."

The phone rang, startling us both. Jenny's name flashed across the screen.

"Shitting hell." I swiped the answer button. "Jen? Where the hell are you?"

A pause. A voice, alien, and yet horribly familiar. "She can't come to the phone right now."

The floor fell away from beneath my feet, leaving me floating, spinning, flailing in space. My nerves lit up like fireworks, sparks and crackles and a thousand tiny explosions spreading through my body from the center out in waves. I felt myself falling, though my eyes told me I was petrified, feet welded to the floor, muscles locked, unmoving.

"I guess you found Kevin," he said. "Is he still alive in there?"

Annie was staring at me, alarm and confusion loud on her face, shrugging a question at me. I couldn't move.

"Ali? Are you alright in there?"

In there. He was watching me. I willed myself to breathe and my eyes to move, squinting against the sunlight, scanning my field of vision. Trees. Barn. One or the other.

"Well, look, while I've got you and you're letting me talk, I just want to tell you I'm sorry for what happened between us. I really didn't want it to come to that, and honestly, I don't want it to come to that again, either. I'm really glad you're okay, but I'm afraid to say you've got me a little bit cornered."

The house. If he was cornered, he had to be in the house. I looked at Annie, managed to signal toward it with my eyes. Watched her face change, her eyes darken, her jaw set.

"What I'd really like is for you to stand down for a minute, turn away, go back downstairs, talk to your friend. Give me a head start. What do you say?"

I forced the words out of my throat. "Where are you?"

"Over here," he said.

I looked out there again, trying to see into the dark places. Nothing moved. He wasn't standing there waving. "Over where?"

"I'm in the barn."

The doors, ajar. Black inside.

"I'm watching you through a rifle scope. Say hi to Annie for me. I guess I couldn't rely on her, after all. It's a shame, she's a nice girl."

"Bullshit," I said. "We've got all your guns." Didn't we?

"So what I'm thinking is, if you just stay well over there for a minute, I can be on my way and not have to kill you both."

"No." He was bluffing. If he was in the barn with a rifle, he wasn't cornered. He was in the house and unarmed. I willed life into my limbs and gestured to Annie to get out of earshot and get on the phone. "I want Jenny back."

"Who?"

"You know who."

"Oh, her. You don't want her back."

"Then you're not leaving. I want Jenny, and I want answers."

"Answers to what?"

"Fucking questions, dickhead."

He sniggered. "Well, why don't I call you when I get where I'm going?"

"That's fine," I said. "You're going straight to the nick, in about twenty minutes, unless you really have got a gun, in which case you'll be going to the morgue. Either's fine with me, but I want Kerry Farrow's body and I want my detective inspector back, so you might as well give them up while we're waiting." Emboldened, I stepped out of the garage onto the gravel driveway and looked over to the open door of the house. "I don't like talking to you on the phone," I said. "Come out so we don't have to come in after you, there's a good b—"

The rear window of my car shattered, the explosion of glass followed a split second later by a faint crack.

Annie was running before I hit the ground, and was out of the garage and in That Man's sights before I could stop her.

CHAPTER 34

I'd never seen a sky as blue as the one I stared up at as I lay on my back on the gravel beside the car, trying to figure out what hurt. I didn't know what *kind* of blue it was. Azure? Sapphire? Cobalt? Those are the usual words people use to describe it, but I didn't really know what any of them meant. It was just blue. The purest, deepest blue I'd ever seen or imagined. It was peaceful and beyond beautiful, certainly worthy of being the last thing I ever looked at.

It wouldn't be, though. Annie saw to that when she threw herself down beside me and stuck her face in the way and shouted, "Ali, Jesus, are you hit?"

I wasn't sure. I didn't think so. "I'm alright," I said. "Stay down."

She was already on her feet, though, and then she was hurling herself into the driver's seat of my car and the engine was running and before I could react, the wheels were spinning and she took off backward across the drive.

I could see what she'd reacted to, then. I glanced across to the barn to see the big wooden doors crash back off their hinges and in front of them was a van, surging out of the darkness and onto the dirt track that would lead it to the mouth of the driveway.

I knew what she was going to try to do, and that it wasn't going to work. The van was huge; it looked like one of our old riot control vehicles, a full-size twin-wheel Sprinter with bull bars and window guards and, oh God, a secure cage in the back.

I scrambled to my feet and screamed vainly after Annie, watching helplessly as she spun my Alfa through an admittedly impressive J-turn and gunned it for the tree line, closing the distance faster than That Man could, maybe two or three car lengths in it, the van bearing down on her with twice the weight, twice the momentum.

I was off and running, adrenaline and fear and fury in full control, my only objective to be close enough to that van to mount it if it stopped.

Annie beat him to the tunnel in the trees. Then, a flash of brake lights and my car swerved first to the right and then to the left, the rear wheels locked as it yawed sideways into a slide. The back end hit first, slamming against the first tree on the right. The front end followed suit a beat later, the Alfa coming to a dead stop in a billow of smoke and plastic and air bags, wedged tight across the mouth of the track. I saw Annie fling the door open, and then the van was on her, no brakes, no hesitation, slamming into the side of the car and folding it as though it were made of paper.

But it held. The back end of the van leaped five feet into the air and slammed down hard as the front plowed into the car I hadn't finished paying for and stopped in the space of about a yard.

I was still a hundred feet away when That Man kicked open his door and slid down from his seat, pulling a rifle out after him. He walked around to the front of the van, raised it to his shoulder and aimed at the ground somewhere beyond the wreckage. I yelled, reached for the revolver in my back pocket. Found the pocket but not the gun. Skittered to a halt as That Man lowered the rifle without firing and turned to look at me.

There it was: the face my brain had been unable to render since the day he'd crippled it.

It was bland, expressionless, a generic collection of generic features, no more memorable than the e-fit pinned to the notice board in the incident room.

Nothing came flooding back. There was no magical moment of recognition or mutual understanding. Nothing. He just shook his head, and raised the rifle, and fired.

I took a reflexive staggering step backward as something bounced off my hip; it stung and made a tiny hole in my jeans, but that was all it did. I watched as he gave an exaggerated shrug and dropped what was clearly an air rifle into the weeds. He reached into the van, pulled out a long black bag and what looked like some kind of bow, and threw me a childish wave, and melted into the trees.

I caught hold of my senses before the adrenaline could wear off, and darted around the other side of the van to where it had buried itself in my car.

The Alfa was toast; it was three feet wide and bent like a banana. It was also empty.

I clambered up over the top of it and jumped down onto the track. Annie was lying some twenty feet away in the dirt, and as I reached her side she sat bolt upright, wild-eyed, and said, "Fucking hell, I wasn't drunk enough for that."

"How bad is it?" I looked her over for missing or right-angled limbs, but she was intact.

"Did you see me fly?"

"No."

"Oh, well. I'm not doing it again. Which way did he go?"

I pointed.

"You hurt?"

"No."

"Got the gun?"

"No."

She gave me two sarcastic thumbs-up and said, "Awesome. You had *one* job." And then she was on her feet, pain and anger radiating from her face, and she hauled me up by the armpit from my squat and said, "Now what?"

Now we wait for the backup to arrive, and we call for a rolling perimeter on the surrounding roads, and air support. That's what now what. But twenty minutes is twenty minutes. "I don't know," I said. "Stop fucking about and chase him, I guess."

Kevin sorted slowly through the keys one by one until Erica recognized the one that fit the cage.

"That's it," she said. "The brassy one. Can you get it off the ring?"

Kevin looked at her, bemused, and held up his hands. "Not in a hurry," he said, "but I'll try."

She watched anxiously as he fumbled with the split ring, his fingers slithering all over as he deposited more and more blood on it. "I can't do it," he coughed.

"Let me try. Hold it up here."

He levered himself a little upright, groaning as his head swam and his foot dragged on the floor; jammed the bunch of keys ring-first against the mesh wall of the cage.

"No, you need to wipe that, don't you."

He sighed and nodded and feebly rubbed it against the least bloody section of trouser cloth he could see through his sticky scarlet filter, and then presented it to her again, far from clean but workable at least.

Erica pulled the required key through the mesh and set to work rotating the ring, looking for the ends, which she found eventually. She could just get a nail to it, but had neither the hands nor the room to turn it as well. "I need you to help me. If I hook it on, you turn it, okay?"

Kevin grunted his agreement, and spilled some more blood from his palms as he manipulated the ring. They dropped them and had to start again twice before they finally got the key hooked into the spiral and the ring turned all the way around and then it was free, and Erica fell back against the wall behind her and laughed.

"I'm glad you're enjoying it," Kevin gurgled, slumping against the door.

"It's either that or cry," she said. "You know there are two locks, right?"

The second key was easier, now that their routine was more practiced. Finally, Erica pushed herself to her feet and slid the first key into the top lock, pulled it out and tried it in the bottom. A moment later the cage was open, and Kevin spilled out into the room.

"You think you can walk?" Erica suggested optimistically.

Kevin laughed despite himself. "I was hoping you could carry me."

"Oh, well, I'll see you later then," she smirked.

"Fine, fine, help me up."

Erica looked like the end of *Carrie* by the time she'd manhandled Kevin to the top of the stairs. His blood was in her hair, on her face and hands, streaked across her T-shirt and down one leg of her jeans. She could remember being this desperate for a bath before, but only once, and it was a memory that made her shudder.

She maneuvered him through the doorway, and draped his arm across her shoulder again and led him past the crashed BMW to the threshold of the garage.

Then she dropped him.

"Okay, what the fuck?" She walked out into the sunshine, to the spot where the Alfa had been and no longer was. "Where the f—" She spun around, her toe catching the revolver lying on the gravel, and took in the scene at the edge of the clearing. The van, canted over to one side, with a twist of bright red metal protruding from one end. "Ali?" she shouted, turning to look up at the house out of some vain hope.

"What's going on?" Kevin tried to crawl out to join her, but she stopped him.

"Stay here," she said. "Get out of sight. I'll...find something to keep you warm."

She picked up the gun, and then kept her eyes on the van as she sidestepped over to the door of the house. It was still wide open, and she pressed herself to the frame and peered inside. "Ali?" Nothing from the living room. "Annie?" She slid in through the door, and ducked her head into the kitchen. Nothing.

She put one foot on the bottom stair, but she sensed there was nothing up there for her. She knew that house, knew what it felt like empty.

Hurriedly, and without a second glance at the missing square of carpet, Erica crossed the living room and took the edge of one of the curtains in both hands and ripped it from the rail.

Kevin had the full-on shakes when she got back to him. She draped the curtain over him, bunching it up under his head to make a pillow, and ran her fingers through his matted hair. “You’re going to be alright,” she said. “Help’s coming. I’ll be back.”

“Don’t leave me,” he slurred.

She stood. “There’s something I’ve got to do,” she said, walking to the back of the BMW. “I’ll be as quick as I can, I promise.”

And with that, she checked the gun was secure at the small of her back, lifted the can of petrol from the boot of the car, and went for a walk.

CHAPTER 35

Annie kept up, panting into her phone to redirect the response teams to the surrounding roads on the premise that we'd do our best to herd That Man in their direction. Between us, we were armed with two mobile phones, a notepad and a biro, so I could only hope we didn't catch up with him first.

He wasn't hard to track; he was a big man, and his crashing progress through the undergrowth was both indiscreet and destructive, leaving a trail of bent and broken ferns in his wake.

In a matter of minutes, though, both the brush and the treetops began to thin out, and the ground turned hard and brown—a carpet of dead leaves and twigs, an obstacle course of moss-covered fallen trunks. There was light here, as well as shade, glittering shafts of sunlight breaking through the canopy and casting a golden glow across the forest floor.

There was also silence.

I held up a hand and signaled for Annie to stop. Put my hands on my knees and sucked in air and spat out the raspy crap coating the back of my throat. The pain in my leg was coming back now, my right knee trembling under my weight.

Beside me, Annie squatted and surveyed the scene, her eyes more focused than I'd seen before, like a hawk's, alert to the slightest movement. "Where the hell did he go?" she whispered.

I shook my head, trying to steady my breathing. "I don't know. He was right in front of us."

"Have we fucked up here?"

I nodded. "Yeah, I think we might have."

"Shit."

I reached out and clapped a hand on her back. "Which way's the road?"

She waved off to our left, vaguely. "Over there somewhere. If we keep going this way, we'll come to the river, I think."

Good. "Good. Then we'll do that, try to stay this side of him, and hopefully we don't have to catch up to him, someone else can."

She announced her agreement by offering a high five. I didn't leave her hanging.

"Keep moving?"

I started to nod, but something wasn't right. "Wait," I whispered. It was too quiet. Far, far too quiet. That feeling, the one of being watched. "Turn around," I said. "Watch our back. Try not to breathe."

Annie turned slowly, the only sound the sole of her shoe grinding a dead twig to dust. Nothing else. The birds weren't singing. The rabbits weren't rabbiting. There was just silence, for a long, oxygen-starved moment.

And then, something. A scratch. Metallic. To the right of us, I realized, away from the road. *Shit.* A beat, and then a repeat, longer this time. The range impossible to gauge.

The range.

"Annie," I whispered.

A bow.

"What?"

A rustle, louder, and movement, fifty feet to my right, a large, dark shape rising from behind a fallen tree.

Erica's words, ringing in my ears. *A game.*

"Fucking run," I said.

Annie fucking ran, and so did I, the first arrow whistling through the space vacated by our parting heads at the precise moment I realized what was happening.

I sprinted straight ahead, leaving my progress up to blind luck as I craned my head to see That Man nock a second arrow, his eyes on me for a split second before he turned and aimed somewhere behind him.

I ran straight into a tree, of course, and it hurt, but not as much as an arrow to the face was going to hurt, so I bounced right up again and pinned myself to the trunk, frantically scanning for Annie.

I couldn't see her, but I could hear her, and I could see That Man tracking her, bow drawn, ready to shoot.

"Annie, get down!" I screamed, and he loosed the arrow and turned and glared at me, reaching into the bag he'd slung like a quiver across his back.

"You could have just fucked off, Ali," he called. "I told you I didn't want to hurt you."

I almost laughed. Shouted instead. "Is this what you did with all those girls? Is this what you did with Kerry?"

"Why not?" He drew back the third arrow. "You've got to admit, it's kind of fun."

I ducked back behind the tree, and a second later felt the thump as the arrow buried itself in the trunk. "Where is she?" I shouted.

"Who?"

"Kerry."

Silence. I gave him ten seconds, and then the thought that

he might be advancing on my position grew too strong, and I risked a look. He hadn't moved; he was just standing there, bow in one hand, arrow in the other, his head bobbing from side to side like he was weighing up his answer. "Sure, okay," he said. "Emily's Wood. There's an old wooden carriage, or what's left of it. She's under there. Are you going to run, or what?"

Where the hell was Annie? If she had any sense, she was running as fast as her legs could carry her out of these woods, but no sooner had that thought crossed my mind than I spotted her, fifty yards the other side of That Man, edging from tree to tree. "No," I said.

His shoulders dropped. The bow hung limply at his side. "Why not?"

"Because you can't get me if I'm hiding behind this tree?"

He seemed to consider that for a moment, before coming to the quite correct conclusion that it was stupid and that I'd be dead if he came any closer. "That's stupid," he said.

But that wasn't the real reason.

I stepped out into the open, and faced him. Took a step toward him, and another. "Actually," I said, "the reason I'm not running is that I'm coming for you, not vice versa."

Still, he didn't raise the bow. I took another step, and another, and then I didn't stop. "You don't get to hunt me," I said, trying hard to ignore the fact that, unarmed and alone in the woods, I didn't have a leg to stand on, either figuratively or, to all intents and purposes, literally. "I get to hunt *you*. It's *my* job. I'm the fucking hunter here, not you."

He was looking at me with increasing bewilderment, the bow twitching at his side. "Stop," he said. "Don't come any closer, Ali Green."

"Why? What are you going to do?"

"What are *you* going to do?"

It was a good question. I didn't know the answer. All I knew was that I was twenty yards away and the bow was coming up from his side.

And then, Annie answered the question. She appeared from behind a tree already at full tilt, homing in on him with terrifying purpose.

I knew she wasn't going to make it. I saw the change in his face as he heard her, and broke into a run as he started to turn. We were twenty feet either side of him when he released the arrow, and I was on his back with my arm clamped tight around his neck before she'd finished spiraling to the bracken carpet, two feet of shaft protruding from above her right breast.

I attacked his face with my free hand, pushing my fingers hard into his eyes; he dropped the bow, clawing at my arms, spinning and bucking with a primal roar. I squeezed his throat tighter, my bicep burning, nails locked into my own shoulder. I didn't know what the fuck else to do but squeeze the life out of him.

And then he reached back and grabbed a fistful of my hair, and he pitched forward and twisted and pulled, and I was airborne, his face whirling past my eyes as I headed for the ground, landing on the back of my neck with a crack that I thought for a second signaled Game Over, but my arm was still tight around him and he came down with me, headfirst into my belly, punching the wind right out of me as he collapsed across my body with his belt in my face.

I couldn't breathe. I felt bile rising in my throat and knew that I was going to throw up, and that if I didn't move I'd choke on it, and I dug all of my nails as deep as I could through his shirt into the small of his back, and broke three of them off in him as I dragged a tortured wail out of his throat.

Then he elbowed me hard between my legs, and I was all but done. He knelt on the side of my face as he scrambled over me, and I grabbed for his leg and missed, and then he was crawling for the bag that had fallen from his back and was up on his knees and that thing was in his hand—the thing I'd seen a picture of, the knife, the one that had killed Lowry and Diaz and Carla's husband and God alone knew who else, and I knew that if I didn't get up right now, I was dead.

I rolled over, gritted my teeth, pushed myself up and got a foot underneath me. The pain thumped up through my body and I retched, a thick string of bile spilling from my lips, but I was moving, scrambling to my feet, knocking That Man into the dirt as I ran over him to Annie's side. She was conscious, back arched, face bathed in sweat, teeth grinding in agony, but it was either one or both of us and I had to do what I had to do. I heard the scrape of the machete as he drew in his arms to push himself upright. I said, "Be brave, Annie." I planted my foot on her collarbone and pushed it flat to the ground, and I took the shaft of the arrow in both slippery hands, and I locked my elbows and heaved with my back and pulled the arrow out of her chest and flipped it in my hands and turned to meet him as he came at me, machete poised to swing right through me, to take my head clean off my shoulders. I ducked and charged and pushed up with all of the strength I had left, and we collided, me and That Man, the arrow piercing the top of his throat and where it stopped, I didn't know, but my fist was under his chin and the machete was spinning uselessly to the ground and as my leg gave out and I twisted and fell away, he collapsed beside me with little more than a grunt.

Annie's scream was loud in my ears then, and I crawled to her side and took her face in my hands. Her pulse was racing, her breathing shallow and ragged, her pupils dilating and constricting in time with the blood throbbing out of her chest.

"Don't panic," I said. "You're going to be okay. I'm going to get you out."

She put a hand to my head, pulled me closer to her. "Fucked up a bit, sorry," she rasped.

I nodded. "Saved my arse, though."

"Yeah." She winced and groaned as a spasm tore through her shoulder. "Totally worth it, th—"

A shot. I jumped, spun around, fell back on my tail.

Erica stood beside That Man, the gun in her hand, a wisp of smoke drifting from the barrel. She looked at Annie and me, her face as calm as the breeze that tickled her hair. "He moved," she said. Glanced down at him, at the rapidly expanding pool of blood at her feet, and back to me. "I'm pretty sure he moved."

An alarm bell rang somewhere in my head, but I was past caring. "Fucking hell, Erica," I said.

"She alright?"

"Not really."

"Need some help?"

"Yeah, ten minutes ago."

She shrugged, and tucked the empty gun into the back of her jeans as she stepped over to Annie's side. "Sorry," she said. "Better late than never, eh?"

CHAPTER 36

The house was fully ablaze when Erica and I carried Annie out of the woods, her shirt torn into strips and tied tightly around her chest.

Erica's instruction to "Follow the smoke" hadn't really registered over the effort it took just to put one foot in front of the other, so the wall of flame that greeted us stopped me in my tracks.

Erica didn't notice, and carried on walking until Annie loudly reached the limit of her extensibility, whereupon she stopped and looked over her shoulder and said, "What?"

"Erica, what did you do?"

"What do you mean?"

"The bloody house is on fire."

She glanced across the field at the plume of acrid smoke, the sagging roof, the flames leaping from the windows and doors. "Yes," she agreed. "It is, isn't it?"

"Erica, what the fu—"

"To be fair, it was like that when I found it."

"You can't j—"

"God, this is typical of you lot, isn't it? You blame me for bloody everything." She tugged on Annie, forcing me back into step. "Next you'll be telling me it's my fault your DCI's dead."

I dropped Annie's feet, my own cry drowning out both hers and the wail of approaching sirens. "Jenny's dead? Where?"

Erica stopped again. "No, I just wanted to see if you'd be sad about it."

"You fucking arsehole. Where is she?"

"In the back of that van over there, the one on top of your car."

I looked over to the van, and my car, and the queue of ambulances and armed response cars forming behind it. "You didn't let her out?"

"Nope."

I glared at her incredulously, despite knowing that in Erica's shoes, I probably would have done the same thing.

"I was busy," she said flatly.

"Ali, this really hurts."

"We'll talk about this later," I said, and picked up Annie's legs, and together we carried her to where a trio of paramedics were clambering through the undergrowth amid a horde of armed officers.

We laid her out in the grass, and I knelt beside her, and squeezed her hand, and put my lips to her ear, and said, "You never met that man before today."

There wasn't a lot else to say. Kevin was unconscious by the time the medics got to him, but get to him they did. He wasn't going to be at work for a while, but he'd be back eventually, and with a badass-looking scar to show off about.

In the meantime, once I'd personally brought Kerry Farrow's body home from Emily's Wood, I'd have six women's funerals to attend, six new stories to learn—of hard times, or hard choices, or just plain hard luck. I'd write them down and file them away. Others would write them down and, if they thought them interesting or salacious enough, or their subjects worthy of remembrance, they might print them for the morbid and the curious to enjoy over cozy breakfasts in cozy homes untouched by violence or tragedy.

For me, though, the trivia of those stories would remain just that, the details an irrelevant distraction. They were six different women, with six different names, and with dreams and fears and loved ones and lives, and all of it stripped from them at the whim of a man who never once questioned his right to do so.

Well, fuck that man. Reed, or Faulkner, or whatever other bullshit name I had written down in this infernal book of mine. He was finished, and if anyone bothered to find him before the animals did, then I'd be washing my hair when they laid him to rest.

"I'll drink to that," Erica said. "Annie definitely would. She'll drink to anything."

I looked down at my hands, my shirt, my jeans, my shoes, all of them dyed shades of red. I imagined my face was the same. Annie had made a hell of a mess, in more ways than one. "I wish I was drunk right now," I said.

Erica smiled. "The night's still young."

I smiled back at her as we sat in front of the house, letting the flames bake the blood into our skin. It would be hours before they moved the wreckage from the driveway. There'd be nothing more than a smoldering shell by the time the fire brigade got to it.

"What are you going to do now?"

I shrugged. My mind was pleasantly blank. "Go home and have a bath," I said. "Then I'm going to go see your lawyer, who probably can't be my girlfriend now, and figure out how we're going to get you out of this big old mess."

She looked back to where Jenny was being fussed over by medics, having finally been released from captivity. "What are you going to tell her?"

"Well, not that you set fire to the house, Captain Chaos, that's for damn sure."

Her face was a picture of practiced innocence. "I told you, I didn't go anywhere near the house."

"You wrapped Kevin in a curtain."

"No, you're remembering it wrong." She smirked, shot me a wink. "And anyway, what if I did? I've been so careful lately, but accidents are accidents. We all have them."

"You *are* an accident."

"That's what my mum always says. I don't think she likes me much."

I laughed. "Your mum was ready to go to jail for you, and don't you forget it."

"Fair point," she sighed, and looked over her shoulder again, and said, "Shit."

I followed her gaze. Jenny was looking our way, breaking off a conversation, waving away a clingy paramedic.

"We'd better get our stories straight," she said, "or else you're going to be in a shitload of trouble."

"Me?!"

"Just saying. Think fast."

I glanced back; Jenny was heading our way. I sighed, and looked up at the sky. It really was a beautiful shade of blue, somewhere, behind the billowing cloud of thick black smoke. I hoped that, of all things, it would stick in my mind.

I pulled the notebook from my pocket. Flipped to the most recent page and said, "Emily's Wood."

Erica looked at me, puzzled. "Emily's Wood?"

I nodded. "Remind me later," I said. "And help me up."

Erica stood and held out a hand for me. I grasped it and groaned to my feet. Took half a dozen steps closer to the house. Took careful aim at the kitchen window. Tossed the notebook into the fire.

"Let me do the talking," I said.

Erica looked me up and down, wide-eyed. "You think that's a good idea? What are you going to do?"

"Dunno," I said. "Just make up any old shit. I won't know if it isn't true, will I?"

Erica gasped, as though the answer hadn't occurred to her before it was even a question.

I smiled. "Between you and me," I said, "I can't remember a goddamned thing."

★★★★★

ACKNOWLEDGMENTS

Writing a novel is a long and stressful task at the best of times. When that novel is more successful than you could have hoped or imagined, figuring out how to follow it up can be quite nerve-racking. So, firstly, to everyone who read and supported *Normal*, thank you for making my life simultaneously so much easier and so much more difficult!

If it takes a village to raise a child, it takes a whole city to produce a book, and *Dead Girls* would not be here if it weren't for the amazing group of people I've been fortunate enough to have around me. I owe heartfelt thanks to:

My long-suffering editor, Sally Williamson, whose patience may never regain its former elasticity.

My improbably dogged and supportive agent, Amy Moore-Benson, who's never yet left me to die in battle.

Tim Cooper, for turning Champagne into gold.

Emily Ohanjanians and Erika Imranyi at Harlequin, for having faith. Sophie Calder, Alison Lindsay, Cara Thompson, Joe Thomas and the rest of the team at HQ HQ.

Derek Burke, for being the thorn in my side. James Spicer,

for being a great friend and bossing being a boss. The team of orange superheroes at Snetterton for keeping me earthed and mostly not on fire: Andrew Davey, Darrin Chalu, Dave Ovens, David Wick, Dennis Jackman, Gerald Pearce, James Ledford, Jamie Thompson, Lee Pearce, Marcus Bowyer, Mark Thompson, Martin Bowley, Neil Howes, Phil Keen, Richard Rogers, Sam Cross, Simon Thomas, Stan Burton, Tim Cook and the eighth natural wonder of the world, Tom Scheving.

Domenica De Rosa, for allowing worlds to intersect and for numerous other indulgences.

Elizabeth Haynes, for half-remembered information on computer systems, which I then half remembered. Any mistakes in that regard are probably someone else's.

Dan Rayner of Thetford CID, for being the kind of copper Kevin wants to be when he grows up.

Leila Solomons, whose cameo appearance earned her a generous charitable donation, or vice versa.

The amazing community of bloggers, book groups and superfans, many of them authors and industry professionals in their own right, whose tireless enthusiasm has an immeasurable impact on readership and keeps the rest of us in a job—including such luminaries as Liz Barnsley, Tracy Fenton, Anne Cater, Rebecca Bradley, Margaret Madden, Sumaira Wilson, Timea Cassera, Alex Golding, Ayo Onatade and many, many more.

Lee Child, Jamie Mason, Michael Robotham, Fiona Cummins and the several dozen members of the British crime writing community I'm contractually forbidden from mentioning but who know who they are.

Chris Rushby and the very much above-average Annie at Jarrold's.

The collective staff of Jack Daniel's distillery and the Norwich North branch of Domino's, for the all-nighters.

Everyone who took the time to share their thoughts about *Normal*—some of which had a profound effect on me and on the direction of my writing. That's what this game is all about.

Mum and Andrew, for all the questions. Dad, for all the listening.

My children, Oscar, Lewis, Sophie and Eve, for lighting up my life, and thereby illuminating all the extra gray hairs they've given me.

My wonderful partner, Claire, to whom at least one character owes their survival, for her unwavering support and for ten pages worth of other things I couldn't have managed without.

Helen Cadbury, whose generosity and encouragement I'll never be able to repay, and to whose memory this book is dedicated.

And of course, perhaps more than anyone: you, for still being here. Thank you, and please come again.

If you enjoyed DEAD GIRLS,
be sure to pick up Graeme Cameron's
internationally bestselling first novel,
NORMAL.

He lives on your street,
in a nice house with a tidy garden.

He shops at your local supermarket.
He drives beside you on the highway,
waving to let you into the lane ahead of him.

He also has an elaborate cage in a
secret basement under his garage.

The food he's carefully shopping for is to feed a young woman
he's holding there against her will—one in a string of many,
unaware of the fate that awaits her.

This is how it's been for a long time.
It's normal...and it works.
Perfectly.

But this time it's different...

Turn the page for a thrilling taste of
NORMAL...

CHAPTER ONE

I'd learned some interesting things about Sarah. She was eighteen years old and had finished school back in July with grade-A passes in biology, chemistry, physics and English. Her certificate stood in a plain silver frame on a corner table in the living room, alongside her acceptance letter from Oxford University. She was expected to attend St. John's College in the coming September to commence her degree in experimental psychology. She was currently taking a year out, doing voluntary work for the Dogs Trust.

In her spare time, Sarah enjoyed drawing celebrity caricatures, playing with the Wensum volleyball team and collecting teddy bears. She was also an avid reader of fantasy novels and was currently bookmarking chapter two, part eight of Clive Barker's *Weaveworld*. She'd been seeing a boy named Paul, though she considered him a giant wanker. He refused to separate from "almighty slut" Hannah, who was evidently endowed with a well-developed bosom and a high gag threshold. This caused Sarah considerable consternation, but she could not confide in her mother because "she wouldn't understand" and would "just freak out again like last time." She instead turned to her friend Erica, who was a year or two older and thus possessed of worldliness and abundant wisdom. Erica's advice, apparently in line with her general problem-solving ethos, was to "cut off his dick and feed it to him." Sarah didn't talk to her mother about Erica, either.

All four walls of Sarah's bedroom were painted a delicate shade of lilac, through which traces of old, patterned wallpaper were still visible. She had a single bed with a plain, white, buttoned cotton cover. She also had a habit of leaving clothes and wet towels on the floor. Her stuffed animals commanded every available inch of shelf and dresser space. The collection consisted of plush bears manufactured in the traditional method, and all had tags intact. It was too vast to waste time counting. But there were sixty-seven.

That morning, Sarah had spent just under half an hour in the bath and just over five minutes cleaning her teeth. She had no fillings or cavities, but the enamel on her upper front teeth was wearing thin from overbrushing. She also applied toothpaste to the index and middle finger of her left hand in a vain attempt at stain removal. There were no ashtrays in the house, and her cigarettes and lighter were hidden inside a balled-up pair of tights in the middle drawer of her dresser.

The following day was Sarah's birthday. Many cards had already arrived and stood in a uniform row on the living room mantelpiece. Someone had tidied in there early in the morning, but there was already an empty mug and a *heat* magazine on the coffee table. Sarah had a habit of leaving the TV on, whether she was watching it or not.

I'd discovered, too, that she plucked her bikini line. Most of her clothes were green. She dreamed of visiting Australia. She had a license but no car. The last DVD she watched was *Buffy the Vampire Slayer*—the feature film, not the more popular television series—and coincidentally, or rather perhaps not, Buffy was also the name of her cat.

Oh, and I knew three more things. I knew that her last hot meal was lasagna, her cause of death was a ruptured aorta and her tongue tasted of sugar and spice.

Fortunately, the kitchen floor was laid with terra-cotta tiles, and I easily located the cleaning cupboard, which held a mop and bucket, bleach, cloths, a roll of black bin liners and numerous antibacterial sprays. I hadn't planned on doing this here, since I had a thousand and one other things to do and not enough time to do them, so my accidental severing of the artery was inconvenient, to say the least. Happily, I'd reacted quickly to deflect most of the blood and keep it off the walls.

I'd used a fourteen-inch hacksaw to remove the limbs, halving each one for portability. The arms and lower legs fitted easily inside a bin bag with the head and the hair lost in the struggle to escape. Using a separate bag for the buttocks and thighs, I'd placed these parts by the back door, away from the puddle of blood. The torso was unusually heavy despite Sarah's small frame, and required a heavy-duty rubble sack to prevent tearing and seepage. Thoughtfully, I'd brought one with me.

The cleaning operation was relatively easy. My clothes went into a carrier bag, and I washed my face over the sink. Warm water followed by Dettol spray was adequate for removing the spatter from the cupboard doors and for disinfecting the worktops and the dining table once I'd swiped most of the blood onto the floor. Mopping the floor took three buckets of diluted bleach, which went down the drain in the backyard. The waste disposal in the sink dealt with stray slivers of flesh; the basin was stainless steel and simply needed a cursory wipe afterward.

The only concern was a couple of small nicks in the breakfast table, courtesy of my clumsiness with the carving knife. One or two spots of blood had worked their way into the wood, but these were barely visible, and since the table was far from new, it was unlikely they'd be noticed by chance. Altogether, you'd never have known I was there.

In fact, the only thing out of place, once I'd moved the bin bags to the yard and returned each of Mum's implements to its rightful home, was me. Fortunately, Sarah's father was about my size, and I'd already dug out a pair of fawn slacks and an old olive fleece from the back of his wardrobe. The fleece was frayed at the elbows and smelled a little musty, but more importantly it was dry and unstained.

Satisfied, I slipped into my jacket and shoes, stepped outside and closed the door gently behind me.

In keeping with modern town-planning philosophy, the Abbotts' house was separated from those to either side by the width of the garden path. In a token effort at providing some privacy from the neighbors, each garden had been bordered on both sides with high, oppressive panel fencing, secured at the bottom of the plot to a common brick wall. This wall was a good six inches taller than I was and, mindful of the difficulty in bundling Sarah over unseen, I elected to fetch the van and come back for her.

I took a lengthy run-up and hauled myself over, dropping down onto a carpet of twigs and soft brown leaves. The tree line was a matter of feet from the edge of the plot, at the foot of a steep incline. It was from here that I'd seen the upstairs window mist over and heard the bath running, watched Sarah in silhouette pulling off her clothes, waited until she closed the door and her ears were full of the roar of running water before I let myself in.

It was an altogether different scene now as I picked my way back between the rows of pines toward the road. All that had made the dawn so perfect was gone—the dusting of snow on the rooftops, the faint crackling of twigs under muntjac hooves, the rustling of leaves disturbed by inquisitive foxes. In their place, the clatter of diesel engines and the grating thrum of cement mixers, the white noise of breakfast radio and the tap-tap-tap of trowel on brick. It had started soon after my arrival and, while the development would be blissfully quiet and neighborly once complete, for now the inescapable din of suburban sprawl rendered it a living hell. Although, on the other hand, it had at least allowed me the luxury of not having to tiptoe.

Thinking about it, there was something else missing, too—something I couldn't quite put my finger on. Some weighty comfort I was accustomed to feeling against my leg as I walked, and which just wasn't there anymore.

It wasn't until I reached the van that I realized I'd locked the bastard keys in it.

I was loath to break a window, but the Transit was fitted with reinforced double deadlocks, and I specified the optional full-perimeter alarm system when ordering. Consequently, just as anyone else would have trouble breaking in, so did I. Having weighed up this option, considering my various time constraints against that of taking a cab home for the spare key, it didn't take me long to find a brick. I was back in business, albeit at the mercy of the heater.

I'd left Sarah just behind the side gate, and I backed right up onto the two-car driveway to minimize my exposure. I took a moment to double-check the small toilet window at the back of the house; I'd chipped some of the paint away, and there were obvious indentations in the wood, but it was shut, and the glass was intact. Judging by the number of boxes and blankets piled up inside, and the concentration of long-abandoned cobwebs, the damage wouldn't be discovered this side of summer. Good.

I was happy to find that Sarah hadn't leaked out of any of the bags, and it took seconds to load the lighter ones into the van. But as I turned to collect the rubble sack, I happened to glance toward the doorstep, and my heart dropped. The face staring inquisitively back at me was a familiar one; I'd studied it briefly, in a tiny photograph from one of those instant booths you find in malls, fallen from Sarah's diary as I lay on her bed. But it was unmistakable.

Erica's hesitation was such that I could almost hear the whirring of her brain as she stood there, finger poised over the doorbell, eyebrows cocked, mouth agape. I knew all too well where her train of thought was carrying her, and so diverted it with a smile and a friendly wave.

"Hello, there," I called. "Don't panic, I'm not a burglar."

Her expression turned instantly to one of apology. "Oh, no, no, I wasn't thinking that," she laughed, letting a few ringlets fall down to hide her eyes.

"Age Concern," I explained. "Just collecting some old bags." Ha ha. "I mean bags of old clothes. Are you looking for the young lady?"

She was walking toward me now. Dark curls bouncing, woolen scarf swaying to the rhythm of her hips. Breasts struggling to work the top button of her jacket loose with each confident stride. The blood began to race through my veins, the noise of the mechanical diggers and pneumatic drills fading to a low hum. "Yeah, do you know where she is? She's not answering the door." Close enough now that I could hear the rub of the denim between her thighs. I could take this one of two ways, probably avoid a scene by way of swift, decisive action, but as so often happens in the face of outstanding natural beauty, my honesty beat me to the punch.

"Yes," I said. "She's in the garden."

Available wherever books are sold.